The Somnambulist Footprints:
A Collection of Surrealist Tales

The Somnambulist Footprints:
A Collection of Surrealist Tales

Edited and Introduced by Eric W. Bragg

OYSTER
MOON
PRESS
BERKELEY, CALIFORNIA

The Somnambulist Footprints: A Collection of Surrealist Tales
Edited and Introduced by Eric W. Bragg

All accompanying images appear courtesy of the authors.

Cover design: J. Karl Bogartte, Ribitch, Dale Houstman

ISBN: 978-1-4357-1345-1

Additional copies of this book can be ordered from LuLu:
http://www.lulu.com

Oyster Moon Press is a surrealist publishing co-op that originated in Berkeley, California.

Table of Contents:

Introduction

Unlike most modern approaches to story-telling, the surrealist motivations for such an activity markedly differ from the usual list of suspects: literary ambitions, utilitarian desires, carefree entertainment, the representation of manifest reality or even the production of a cultural commodity. From the angry inception of the surrealist movement in the 1920s, the short story has been for surrealists only one of the means at their disposal for interrogating reality, exploring the world with its unfathomable interconnections between waking and unconscious life and also its seductive transformation by way of engendering new connections and processes that are normally missed by the merely rational or utilitarian approaches. This approach has been the kernel of poetic activity for surrealists, whether the application is visual, kinetic, sonic, or in this particular case, verbal and linguistic.

Far from consisting of a fatalistic linearity of events and mental revelations trapped within the "factual imperative" – like so much literary prose today – these tales cling to a potential not only for recounting a sequence of actions from creator to spectator, but also for redressing and even undermining the very sanctuaries of the conventional, both on the written page and – more importantly – beyond it, into the open space of consciousness. In the surrealist short story, the characters, events and places refuse to conform to the reality principle as they do with most of the fiction that is readily available in corporate bookstores and public libraries. A character's formation, and a character's actions within such stories have less to do with "likenesses" than they do with the obsessive pushing outward of the writer's desires, and it is this externalization of desires which animate (and which in fact *are*) the characters. Therefore the realistic portrayal of people, events and objects from waking life is not the priority in a surrealist story.

There is still another way to distinguish the surrealist story from that other kind of fiction which goes by the name of "fantasy":

the latter avoids the conflicts of the waking world by claiming them as resolved or by simply ignoring them. In contrast, the surrealist story takes the turmoil – both social and psychological – of the waking and unconscious worlds and reflects it back to the reader from new and different angles. The fabric of life itself is born from these conflicts: social, economic and other physical manifestations. To avoid their influence or pretend they don't exist could only lead to "literature," or that which could be described as *escapist*. If the theory of historical materialism allows us to predict that economic and other physical dimensions of life directly shape culture, then the surrealist short story is unarguably influenced by these same forces, because it is a manifestation of culture. However, and most significantly, its surrealist qualities of refraction and revolutionary transformation of this "turmoil" establish an important dialectic that escapist and other flavors of "fantasy" literature cannot match: in this respect, the surrealist short story functions as a revolutionary, autonomous agent of change, rather than existing merely as a reactionary manifestation designed to keep people numb and passive to that which is unbearable.

And then there is the question of motivations: surrealist tales rely not upon a fixed horizon to be reached; i.e. efficiently transporting a character from jail A to jail B. No: getting there is *all* the fun; it is the myth of constant travel, of permanent evolution, of the ongoing play of chance (necessarily beyond the grasp of the conscious mind) which informs the surrealist writer. In many instances, the surrealist tale represents a meandering journey or *dérive* channeled not just by conscious imperatives, but also by unconscious ones. Therefore obsession and desire figure very strongly in these exclusively surrealist journeys.

This compilation of surrealist short stories that you, the reader, hold in your hands is the outcome of a modest project with bountiful results: several contemporary surrealists and fellow travelers were invited to write a short story of their own design, documenting each person's mental voyage taken in the spirit of exploration and revolt. The challenge was for the individual to pursue his or her own desires and passional affinities in the elaboration of the story. With such an open-ended objective, the rich diversity of these tales should come as nothing but a pure delight to you, the discerning reader.

And finally, let the person who reads the following tales be reminded that all things imagined have the tendency to become real, over the course of time.

Eric W. Bragg
January 2008

Parry Harnden

WINDBAGO

After most of city hall had been destroyed in a fire of unknown origin, city staff had to conduct municipal business is a variety of improvised venues — the public library, picnic areas, pool halls, wine cellars, laundromats, even the occasional cow pasture or exotic dancing lounge. The Action Committee on the Proposed McKenzie-Queen Stop Sign met at the humble peckerwood church managed by the Reverend Greg Wilson and his fourth wife. No one knew of Wilson's former wives, though, as he had poisoned each in a different city. But neither the blood on his hands or ghosts in his head could prepare him for the unnatural horror that waited directly ahead. Rev. Wilson, who every day ate a tray of ice to treat his iron deficiency, opened the meeting with the customary prayer, along with his customary promise to "keep it short." As he droned on, occasionally distracted by chicken sounds, he was generally wishing he was fishing instead. Twenty minutes into his sermon, he noticed a bug crawling across his lectern. More precisely, it was a tiny casket moving on insect legs. He had seen these creatures before. They were never a good sign. He scanned the Council, wondering who the baneful omen's shadow was meant to fall upon. Chairman Bopp, a doddering imbecile? Grimes, Rask, Bowring, Petrarch...? Or Ed Green, who for some unknown reason was not wearing a shirt? Probably the guy without a shirt. His suit and tie were nice, but why no shirt? When someone shows up to church and/or city hall without a shirt, he's up to something. Wilson hurried to conclude his sermon: "In the beginning was the Word. Yea, though I walk through the Valley of the Word, render unto Caesar that which is Caesar's. Let the invisible hand of the free market guide me through the Valley of the Caesars, and if I die before I wake I pray the Lord my soul to take. Lake of fire. Hymen. Hmmm... Amen." The Council answered "amen," rubbed the lucky gopher teeth they kept on neck chains, and were relieved to finally be allowed to sit down.

Chairman Ed Bopp, who believes in whipping school-children, reiterated the purpose of their gathering: "We must discuss the petition to erect a new stop sign at the intersection of McKenzie and Queen. This is a rural intersection, I believe. The Auditor's Report on traffic density in said area states there is virtually no traffic, though the footnotes cite an unusually high rate of fatal collisions and suspicious fires there. Louis Calhern, the resident who filed the petition, will speak in favour of a new sign, hoping to convince us of its necessity where past petitioners have failed. I think what he's looking for is a traditional pedestrian stop sign and I believe the city has metal craftsmen and skilled painters on staff who specialise in such things. Of course, we will want to look at the possibility of contracting out the work. When I said 'pedestrian' I meant in the sense of 'commonplace,' not in the sense of 'intended for pedestrians.' This is an automotive traffic stop sign I'm talking about, to be fashioned as represented in Diagram 3 of Schedule A of the Highway Regulations Act."

"Doddering imbecile," muttered Green.

"As well," Chairman Bopp continued, "I think we should explore the avenue of an illuminated sign, as the illuminated screen provides interesting possibilities both in terms of enhanced visibility, therefore increased efficacy and safety, but also as a means of relaying other municipal information to motorists who after all are spending perhaps minutes paused at a stop sign and would better spend their time reading than in picking their noses. Although, I suppose they could do both simultaneously."

Green interrupted: "I didn't understand a word you said. You talk like a metaphysical carnival huckster. Why can't you use interesting words like 'hadeharia,' 'gugusse,' or even 'absquatulate'? It's depressing. A poet once said that the brevity of eternity is the source of all sadness. A poet said it, so it must be true."

Councilman Emma Petrarch believed Green was alluding to her with this comment, for like her namesake she wrote poetry and had returned from the dead. The other councilmen were simply confused. The uncomfortable silence was eventually broken when Councilman Nancy Grimes, whose sister disguised her suicide as a murder, thought to ask Green: "Was that you making chicken noises earlier?"

"Ah, bird calls," Green mused, then dug his fingernails into the wooden tabletop and dragged them back with a screech that perfectly mimicked the mating call of the Venezuelan Pitchfork, the bird no one cares about.

Councilman John Bowring — seven years winner of the Ugliest Jonathan Contest, a competition adjudged by leaders in the fields of cosmetology, abnormal psychology, and teratology, and a contest the existence of which the contestants are unaware — chose to ignore Green's non sequitur, for after all he had learned irrational outbursts were not uncommon at council meetings, and get the discussion back on track: "There is a jurisdictional issue we need to address. The intersection of James and Bay falls within a five mile square tract of land the boundaries of which the state deliberately set so that it would not be subject to any governmental or moral law. A true frontier zone. I believe the intention was to reserve the space for military research, but the land was never used and has simply been exploited by adjacent farms. Still, legends of cannibalism and murder in the area persist, and I cannot say if these legends are entirely unfounded. I do not know that we have any authority to impose a stop sign on such a place, and even if we did why should it come out of *our* signage budget?"

Mr. Green spat angrily at Mr. Bowring: "Madame, you are a fatuous bubblebrain and if you even suggest crocheting a sweater for this stop sign like the one you made for the cenotaph I'll scrape the skin off your face with these splinters sticking out of my fingertips."

This last outburst precipitated a shouting match which might have come to blows had not Chairman Bopp sagely employed his gavel to restore decorum to the proceedings. After admonishing Mr. Green for his senseless attacks, he yielded the floor to Mr. Rask, a personable Nazi who made friends everywhere he went.

Rask: "Yes, well, one thing that's missing from this discussion is the relationship between traffic speeds posted on either side of the intersection, not to mention their proximity with school zones, and the effect that enforced stopping will have on the wear and tear of the road, which will likely have to be reinforced if there are not already contingencies in place for paving it. I believe the clerk has recent statistics on the durability of the asphalt we are now using. When the numbers are crunched, it... uh, becomes apparent...” Where was I going with this?, he wondered. There suddenly seemed to be the hooded figure of The Reaper standing between him and the point he was trying to make. Something about stop signs. I was saying... Blank. I got nothing. “Excuse me, I just remembered I have an urgent phone call to make to my, er, doctor...” Rask plucked his cell phone from his pocket and absquatulated to the foyer.

“He’s off to call his wife for consolation, the spoonful of brain damage,” Green said. “She will speak to him in baby-talk while he sucks his thumb. Let the sun vomit magma on you all. Emma, you look like you have something to say.”

Ms. Petrarch, who every night dreamed of committing horrendous crimes then spent her days worrying she would be caught for them, spoke: “Thank you. I’m still trying to wrap my head around our obligations under the Highway Regulations Act. Must the sign be red? Isn’t that a little inflammatory?”

Green leapt from his chair, directing his venom towards Councilman Bowring: “Bowring, curb your talking dog or I’ll sic an animal control SWAT Team on you. Let me re-state that. Everyone knows Florence Nightingale carried an owl in her pocket, but few realise the owl was actually a jack-knife which she used to disembowel prostitutes in Whitechapel.”

“That was uncalled for,” declaimed Ms. Petrarch. The others thought she meant the tastelessness of Green’s remarks, but in fact she believed Green was again referring to her for she too had a pet owl, though she carried it in her purse as her pockets were already full of tadpoles.

The quick-thinking Chairman Bopp defused the tense situation, again with his quick-draw gavel: “Obviously, this stop sign affair is stirring up the Council’s passions. Let’s take a five minute break and cool off. Mrs. Wilson has generously prepared coffee and cakes for us.” The Councillors stretched their legs. All except for Green, who sat staring into space, breathed heavily, and occasionally unnerved his fellow Councilmen with bursts of inappropriate laughter. The Council had no clue as to the precariousness of their situation. The flies were the only things holding these walls up. The Earth beneath the floor had mostly crumbled away and resembled nothing so much as a rotten apple core. An indescribable abomination, which will be described shortly, was growing in their presence but beyond their awareness.

Mr. Bowring, who on weekends could be found peep-holing at the Blue Heron Motor Hotel, caught up to Ms. Grimes at the coffee urn. He was sweet on her, and thought that since they were both happily married a fling would be less complicated as the transient character of the relationship would have to be assumed. As an icebreaker, he indicated Mr. Green to her with a nod: "Quite a character, huh?"

Ms. Grimes, nicknamed "Cretinous Spangles" because she wears foil stars in her nylon stockings, had an expression of dead earnestness: "I am afraid that Mr. Green may be transforming into a hideous supernatural monster that will attack and eat us..."

Eager not to disagree, Bowring said, "That could be."

"...A ghastly thing from a plane of existence we can only know by inference. The material of children's nightmares and the common stock of human fear. The cowled forest of trembling shadows and bloodthirsty undergrowth. Things happen there and no one knows how or when — they just find your dirty bones months later. The ocean, Death's confident delegate on Earth, teeming with life like a corpse, its icy fingers derisively beckoning you to its inescapable depths. Goya's *Disasters of War* which could serve as mankind's passport photo. Flesh aged to the point it no longer resembles what you or I would call flesh, the kin of inhospitable deserts of sand and ice, its chalky folds exhaling a tired sigh carefully noted and written down by oddsmakers and undertakers. Who can deny there is a common essence to these things? I believe it has been distilled to its purest, most vile form and injected into Ed Green's being, transforming him on a molecular level into a loathsome thing that few have lived to talk about, and those that have do not speak of it willingly."

"Well, you may have a point there," Bowring reflexively concurred, though his attention was more or less focused on Grimes' Michel Foucaults and the palpitations that accompanied the acceleration of her breathless speech. Still, he couldn't help notice this woman who read little else besides tabloid magazines was being untypically loquacious.

"I've heard talk about this sort of thing before. Schmidt in receivables was said to have had a nervous breakdown, but there's a story circulating that he changed into a barbarous hellthing that had be to put down at the Rask family Foundry."

"Schmidt? No, I believe I just saw him last week working at a flower shop." Bowring watched Rask waddle back into the room and belly up to the cake table. Rask wore a dickie, had a fake curl of hair hanging over his forehead, and looked as if he had been crying. From the foyer, Rask had seen a woman's glove left on a table and was mesmerised. For reasons hidden to him, the sight brought him to tears.

"And Karlsson," Grimes continued, "who used to head the waterfront development committee. His transformation was incomplete and the government seized the half human fiend for laboratory testing. They put out a cover story that he took a federal job up north."

Bowring slowly realised that Ms. Grimes was not simply making idle conversation and truly believed these tales. He sought to allay her fears. "No, those are just fantastic stories, local legends. You shouldn't believe such fairy tales. We're educated people, we're not superstitious. Not terribly. Except for the gopher teeth thing... And I guess the whole religion business... Not to mention the —"

There was a commotion at the snack table. Whenever the Councilors tried to eat a cake, the dessert would dissolve into sand and blow away before it reached their mouths. Grimes watched in shock. Bowring tried sipping his coffee but could not. He upturned his cup and the coffee slid out in a solid lump. Ms. Petrarch collapsed into a chair with theatrical despair, for the sudden denial of refreshments convinced her that famine and starvation was upon them all.

A gale wind shook the building, seeming to speak the Councilors' names and insulting them cheaply. There was a constant hammering on the roof. The Councilmen buzzed anxiously, but went silent when first one floorboard snapped, then another. A loud clacking was heard from outside. Chairman Bopp, who believed his one leg was shorter than the other because his ancestors lived on hillsides, looked out the

window to the parking lot. He saw a sad man with a shovel, a crow picking at a garbage bag, and several great barking lizards. Their racket sent a panic through Rev. Wilson's collection of capuchin monkeys, who shrieked and rattled their cages in the solarium.

The wind abruptly died away. Chairman Bopp recommended everyone rejoin the table. As they took their chairs, he smacked his gavel for fully two minutes, put on his reading glasses, glanced over the papers in front of him, removed his glasses and said, "So why are we here again?"

All heads turned to Green. As they stared at him they noticed disturbing details that had somehow previously escaped them: the glassy eyes barely visible behind his coke bottle spectacles, the unspeakable haircut, the other-worldly colours of the tie which hung over his bare chest, the creepy handkerchief morbidly folded and tucked into the breast pocket of a suit made of a very expensive but very eerie material. Even his briefcase was eldritch. There was something seriously wrong happening, and Green appeared to be the linchpin. Mr. Rask, who looked rather like a humanish shape punched out of tin from within, put the question to him: "Green, have you something to tell us?"

"Certainly," Green replied, then stood and took the lectern. "If I may, Mr. Chair. [Clears throat.] Gentle lesbians and assorted pests, we have assembled here today to solve our city's problems. First, there is the matter of traffic on some snail's trail of a road in a worthless smudge they forgot to erase from the district maps. Stopping traffic is easy as ant farms. Just build a reinforced concrete wall across the road and post a 'no speed limit' sign. That will stop them dead in their tracks. Now on to the delicate human problems before us."

"Rask, you smell like a concentration camp. I suggest scrubbing yourself with a mixture of equal parts baking soda and hydrofluoric acid.

"Petrarch, you're a sponge that's evolved a mouth to dribble nonsense, and legs so it can run with a herd. Why don't you evolve into a housefly so I can swat you flat?

"Bowring, whenever there is Olympic coverage on television you tape a picture of Christ to your penis and auto-fellate. Quit watching the Olympics."

"That's ridiculous!" Bowring protested as he discreetly covered his symbolic *Eat Me, Drink Me* tie-pin with his palm.

"Grimes, you murder seniors and use their credit cards at your spa..." The other councilmen eyeballed Ms. Grimes, noting that her skin was peculiarly-well defoliated. "...but does the Council know you once signed out a copy of Marx's *Das Kapital* from the public library?"

A gasp rose around the table. Grimes cried into her hands, "I was drunk, I didn't know what I was doing..."

"You, the Right Reverend Bluebeard, inching towards the door," Green continued, "Some people think you're plain crazy for insuring this card house of a church for a million dollars — but I say you're crazy like a fox. A rabid, slobbering, bat-shit crazy fox.

"And Chairman Bopp. Well, what can I say about a man with a tattoo of Ringo Starr on his left arm?"

Bopp stood and told Green he was delusional. He rolled up his sleeve, hoping the sight of his bare arm would ground Green in reality, but was astonished to find there the remnant of a crude tattoo of the fabled moptop, apparently created in his youth with ink and a heated sewing needle.

Green grabbed the dumbstruck Bopp's wrist: "You have all the brains of a dried-up turnip, Bopp, but your flesh, with its orange and greenish undertone and ripe tumescence, looks positively succulent."

"It looks positively —" The next word in Bopp's question would logically have been "what" but he instead finished his sentence with an entirely predictable scream as Green sunk his teeth deep into the exposed arm.

In the ensuing mêlée, the bite-happy Green was wrestled into a chair and bound there with cord from the drapes. As Bopp's wound was treated, the Council consulted on how to handle the situation. Petrarch suggested calling the cops, but Rask was opposed, for he feared a public spectacle would undermine confidence in the government. His feud with the Police Chief meant they could not rely on the department's discretion. Grimes suggested resorting to the foundry, but this solution was greeted with squeamishness and dismissed as too extreme. Ultimately they decided their only real option was to remand Green to police custody to be delivered into the mitts of funny farm professionals as quickly as possible. Once he was declared irrevocably insane, they hoped no one would lend any credence to his absurd, spurious, defamatory, totally unfounded fabrications. They took a vote and agreed unanimously.

"I wouldn't do that if I were you," creaked a voice from the back of the hall. "I believe calling the police would be tantamount to signing your own death warrant." The creak belonged to Lawrence Calhern, the local farmer who had come to argue in favour of a new stop sign and had been observing Council business quietly to this point. As he rose, all eyes turned to him. In voice and demeanor, Calhern strongly resembled Percy Kilbride, the actor who played Pa Kettle in the "Ma & Pa Kettle" film series, after originating the role in the Fred MacMurray-Claudette Colbert vehicle *The Egg & I*. Born Augusto Somoza, Kilbride first came to prominence as a highly decorated flying ace during The Great War, though these awards were given on the condition that he Anglicize his name. He later accumulated great wealth as a defense contractor, though he would be best known for his role as the lovable hick Pa Kettle. In his later years, he was known for wagering on air disasters and ruthlessly persecuting journalists who questioned his heterosexuality. Kilbride died at 74 from injuries sustained when he and a male companion were struck by a car driven by a Cuban agent. His nephew Anastasio Somoza García had been the President of Nicaragua. That said, the resemblance between Calhern and Kilbride was entirely coincidental as they had no blood connection and Mr. Calhern had never even seen a "Ma & Pa Kettle" movie.

Mr. Kilbride walked over to the chair where Green was bound and addressed the gathering. "I can't rightly claim this has any bearing on what is transpiring here today, but yesterday evening my wife was casting runes and they predicted the sudden appearance in our community of a savage man-eating monstrosity that would not rest its ravenous destruction until every last one of the townspeople had been torn to bits, chewed, swallowed and defecated out in a bloody river. And today I've observed at this Council meeting what we rustic folk call an 'enlightenment shift.' Imagine a tray of water that's been tilted.

The water level on one side rises and on the other side it lowers. That's what's happened with the fluid consciousness of this room. That's why some of you have experienced an increase in insights, and others an ebb."

"That makes perfect sense!" shouted Mr. Rask with such force that blood from his throat flecked Ms. Bowring's white blouse.

"Unfortunately, this sort of psychic imbalance usually accompanies the unwelcome appearance of an accursed, forbidden spirit. Now, I've been around some mighty long years and this wouldn't be the first time I've seen these such occurrences. And I'll tell you now that the police do not understand how to handle this kind of situation. They will scoff when you tell them this fellow is turning into a cannibalistic grotesquery. They will set him loose and it would surely mean all our necks. If this man is indeed transforming — and there is no doubt he is — we must take the matter into our own hands and forever keep it to ourselves."

"Mr. Kilbride..." Rask began.

"Please, call me Percy."

"Percy, when you say 'take the matter into our own hands,' you mean..."

"That's correct, we have to slay him. Needless to say, the police will not cotton to that notion either."

"This is all very confusing, Mr. Kettle," Bowring interjected. "I'm not sure we can kill a man solely on your word that he may be some sort of preternatural ghoul."

"You do not have to take my word for it. I can show you, with the aid of my assistant Time and Tide." Kettle clapped his hands and from the back of the hall emerged a small fellow who carried a satchel to Kettle.

As Kettle stripped down to his loin cloth, Time and Tide prepared the Council for what was about to transpire. "You now see Pa Calhern preparing for the secret ritual that will transport him into a deep trance. The spectacle you will witness today may alarm you but do not be afraid – Mr. Somoza is a master of the arcane, esoteric and incomprehensible arts. More about that later. Once he is oblivious to his material surroundings, the unmanipulated future will unfold for him in visions. He will descend farther and farther into this meditative state until he reaches the point of transluminescence, and at that time you will be able to witness his visions for yourselves. We will require assistance from some of the audience members in the execution of this intimate ritual, and only ask that you obey promptly and unquestioningly as your very fates are dangling in the balance."

The secret ritual did not really amount to much. Bopp was woken up and required to parade naked in a circle carrying a sceptre while Grimes read an incantation from the back of a mystical trading card from a deck Calhern had brought. By the time they were finished, Calhern was sitting cross-legged in a chair, eyes closed, distant, incommunicative. Time and Tide slapped him hard across the face several times. No Reaction. He then lit a match and inserted the burning tip up Kettle's nose, holding it there until black smoke started streaming from the other nostril. Still no reaction. Time and Tide turned and addressed the Council. "My friends, there is a realm beyond the surface of what we experience as everyday reality. A caliginous netherworld which surrounds us and moves us but which is not perceptible to the ordinary man's five senses. Pa Kilbride is no ordinary man. While he appears normal — nebbish and unassuming, even — he was born with a very small malformation of the cerebral cortex. While this anomaly has no impact on his quotidian life, it has had the amazing effect of lifting the veil from his eyes, of allowing him unprecedented divination of that strange aforementioned metagnostic dimension. Through years of study, Mr. Kettle has been able to hone his innate capacity and direct his natural powers to achieve the transluminescence by which he can reveal to others the enveloping alternate reality they could theretofore only suspect existed. As the pain tests demonstrate, Mr. Kilkettle has descended into the most bathybic recesses of his soul where he is at this very moment finding and grasping the nexus of cosmic intercommunications. He will speak to us through an apport. Be apprised that this apport will be a zooscopic ignis fatuus, a batrachomantic tool by which he will show us not only things as they really are but also how they will be. Quiet, please."

For minutes they watched Kettle as nothing happened. But then a loom materialised to his left, and a tripod of hoes to his right.

A ghostly turbaned Korla Pandit appeared before the church organ and began playing Bach's *Minuet in G Minor*. Rows of small candles rayed out from Kettle as the room's lights dimmed, evidently solely for a spooky effect. Bowring and Grimes took advantage of the subdued lighting to snog in the back seats. On the floor in front of Kettle's chair, there appeared a great winged frog with a long trident tail. As the gathering hadn't really understood what the dwarf had been talking about, there was no question in their minds that the frog was real. Petrarch fell to her knees before the frog, believing its presence a miraculous visitation. The beast was chomping on a mouthful of bees. It swallowed, then parted its jaws to display its human tongue. As it spoke, the assembly covered their noses at the choke-damp wafting from its mouth.

"You can't shake spare change from a tree of hands," the frog said in a voice remarkably similar to Lauren Bacall's, then its body quivered.

"The sea doesn't speak to liars and will not tolerate the gossip of fishwives." The random quivers had become a steady pulse.

"We can't all come back from the dead like Petrarch. Sometimes an ending is an ending." The frequency of the shakes increased.

"In space, there are machines carrying recorded messages no one will ever hear. Humanity so likes to listen to its own voice that it hopes to bend the ear of the cosmos." The frog, now vibrating violently, burst into flames, adding: "Fuck, I'm burning!"

As Rev. Wilson worried about his floor, Time and Tide stamped out the smoldering remains and announced: "It is time for Pa Somoza to share his visions." As the eyeballs receded into the skull of the frog carcass, Time and Tide drew two lightbulbs from a leather valise and screwed them into the creature's eye sockets. He then brought over a lamp, switched it on, then yanked the live wire from the lamp's base and slid it into the frog's mouth.

The scene projected on the wall depicted the council room much as it presently was, with Pa Kettle in his chair as strings of ectoplasm pretzeled around him. Green was strapped in his chair, voraciously swallowing air. "Look, it's us," Chairman Bopp pointed out with childlike idiocy. The council members were seen milling about, some flailing their arms in a senseless attempt to shoo away malevolent spirits, others striking melodramatic poses of anguish. Ms. Petrarch in particular displayed screen presence, as was quickly noted by her fellow councilmen. Asked if she had ever considered pursuing a career in movies, she said that while she did appear in a few theatrical productions in college she lacked the confidence to follow that dream. It was agreed that Ms. Petrarch was exceptionally photogenic and that the movie studios would have to be nuts not to hire her. Just then, Mr. Green's laboured breathing worsened and his chest quaked as he sucked in air. The long rasps of breathing swelled to a peak and gave way to a mind-shattering scream, a boney wail that dragged on for minutes. The barking lizards in the parking lot howled in sympathy. Green's skin glowed red and grew mottled and leathery as his shape began to alter. As his body assumed the diamond form of a manta ray it slipped from its bindings, arching out over the council. The ray grew taller, reaching seven feet and spreading to a width of five feet, its flesh flashing scarlet. Its amphibian form drizzled away, its diamond bursting into a bloody octagon on which horrid circular saw-toothed mouths appeared and disappeared like bubbles in a swamp. There was much wailing and gnashing of teeth, but that was mostly from Mr. Rask. The others just gawked with their jaws grazing the floor. The monster attacked Chairman Bopp, its dental razors moving the length of him with drill whirrs. It a matter of seconds, the Bopp's facade from head to foot had been sheared to the bone. Councilors scrambled under tables or armed themselves with bibles and chair legs.

"Wait," said Mr. Rask, "it's gone."

"No it isn't, can't you see it," cried Ms. Petrarch before exploding as if a tomato had struck a high-powered fan.

"The stories are true," said Ms. Grimes, "down to their last terrible details. This ruthless leviathan, while huge, is so very thin that from the side it cannot be seen. We are all doomed." By this point, the spectators of the vision had been drawn cyclonically into the commotion of shadows and light. One by one they were fed into the meat grinder of nothingness... their bone spray and organ shrapnel painting a grim & grisly mosaic across the church's walls and ceilings. Bowring, Rask, Grimes.... a hapless queue, waiting to be cast into the silent darkness from which they sprang when time began. All except Rev. Wilson, the only one who had the wherewithal to flee the building when the monster appeared.

When the Council regained consciousness, they found themselves lying on the floor. Mr. Calhern was again dressed in farmer-issue overalls, which Time and Tide was tidying with a horsehair brush. Green was in his chair, his chest pitching as he gulped the air. Bowring shoved a shirt into Green's mouth to stifle the impending scream that would signal his transformation into a beast. The Council's course of action was clear. Whatever squeamishness they may have had about killing Green was now gone. In fact, had not Green been there they probably would have needed somebody else to kill. Rask and Bowring strangled Green with a belt and the body was shoved into the trunk of Rask's car to be conveyed to the foundry for discreet disposal. Happy endingly, the new stop sign desired by Mr. Calhern was approved, the execution was stricken from the minutes, and the Councilors went on to long lives and did not have to die like pigs in a slaughterhouse.

Dale Michael Houstman

TWO STORIES FROM
"THE STARLIT DOG AND OTHER TALES"

I. WHEN WE ARE

"Ah, my dear Foucault," said Hitler one morning, "I am now looking at my white cat. I am seated upon my comfortable, dear sister, looking at my white cat, and so I live in peace. God will not easily forsake Hitler. What are you looking at, and why?"

"Why do you lag behind?" asked Foucault. "Take care, if you can see no bridge at all, that there is no bridge at all." There was no bridge at all. But Hitler did not take care.

"And there is no boat either," said Hitler, as they sailed along, with Wittgenstein in the back, preparing lunch. That is what Wittgenstein was all about.

"The good little Duck is a simpleton and will die of hunger," said Wittgenstein to Hitler and Foucault when they came to a cage in the middle of the Black Forest, "and that is no dove in the trees, but only the sun shining a little better than the pebbles do." Then he put as many ducks and pebbles into his glorious sun-yellow apron as he could, and so was freed from them, or at least from contemplation upon them, which was nearly as good. That is what Wittgenstein was all about.

"No, brother Wittgenstein," replied Foucault, "I am alone in the wood, for the wild beasts will soon come and tear the poor people into efficient strips. Also, although it is true that you have a sun-yellow apron full of pebbles and ducks, you must still keep to the pathway just like everyone else." Foucault was looking carefully at the results of a great famine upon the land, and — as he did — he could not remember how lovely his legs with their chubby redness were when he bared them to go swimming in the dirty canal.

Still, Wittgenstein mumbled to himself, and then he took up the pearls that young Hitler walked upon with little regard; but his pockets only got deeper and deeper, and the pearls disappeared into a bottomless pit, until The Blind Westerner sprang up out of a bush by the side of the pathway, or maybe out of a bird's corpse, or out of the very pebbles in the father's apron themselves, and plopped into the deepening cold of the great forest. This made very little impression upon our trio, who continued talking as they strode down the dirt meander. Such things happen, and we cannot pay attention to everything.

So, finally, Hitler and Foucault and brother Wittgenstein came to a cozy clearing, gathered together quite a little mole-hill of dry wood, set an immense fire, and then a sweet voice called out from the flames, "Tip-tap, tip-tap" in a bitter rose tone, so as to entice all three into a nearby sty, where three fat generals and three fat priests were sleeping with the sows. The trio decided to sleep outside with the ducks.

But when morning rudely popped by, Foucault felt heavy at heart, and thought, "It were better to be very glad than very thirsty, for passion best get some water quickly." Hitler awoke next, and, shaking until his teeth sounded like a box of loose bullets, roused the slumbering Forest Babies, who were sleeping because they had offended the Blind Westerner many years ago, and were put to sleep on a lark. Once awoken, they were cursed never to sleep again. Wittgenstein asked, "How can you bring your heart to awaken those poor sleeping babes, for now they will approach us?" For he was afraid unto death of approaching babies, as all true men must be until the world is clean once again, and the sun is not so easily dismissed as a big mistake. Or a strawberry cake. Or a rooster. Or ducks and pebbles in an apron.

When Hitler and Foucault came near The Blind Westerner's babies in the forest; and Wittgenstein was long dead (more of him later), Foucault shook his sky-blue apron, and said, "Get up, you lazy things; we are going into the forest to chop up the poor people into efficient strips." But he could not get up from the forest floor. Nevertheless, he had once comforted the good God in the oven by saying, "Do not cry; sleep in the good dark" and "How long could it be before we get out of the wood?" so the stars looked on him with a fragile forbearance. But the three (for Hitler was carrying the body of Wittgenstein) did not hurry, although they walked the whole night long and the next day, but did not find one way out of the green darkness, for the wood had been constructed by Germans, and every leaf had been filed under "For Future Reference."

But they finally arrived happily on the other side, and had gone through many doors, although Foucault had run away, with duck grease on his cheeks, and cried back at Hitler and the dead Wittgenstein as he vanished behind a polished oak tree "When you feel tired you can sleep for a little, and then the clouds will show us the way home." But it wasn't true, like so many things.

❧

As the old song goes "The moon shone and they ate Ducks, one at a time." Thus the good little ducks (early in the morning, Wittgenstein — although dead — came and pulled them out of their eiderdown bed) flew into the thickest part of the wood, and settled there to chew little pieces off a roof, and told all the approaching babies that they could eat the windows just as quickly, because they were ravenous and pretty. Will they not be eaten in turn?

Hitler and Foucault perceived what the approaching babies' thoughts were, and that it would be a treat for those dear things to devour them. Foucault began to cry, but it was all useless enough, and then the bread (which had been disguised as pebbles, rolling about for trouble) came to the cage and then at every step they stopped, and every step they dropped a pebble (really a crumb) out of their pockets upon the greasy grass. This went on for weeks. And then there were not many ducks, and they had gotten much thinner. But they were still pretty, for this is what ducks are all about.

The moon had passed, and Hitler still kept himself quite lean, with his fine sense of smell like a wild beast, so that they knew when they were followed until they arrived at a cottage, upon the roof of which Foucault found nothing but a crab's claw. For The Blind Westerner made the sea creatures do as he wished until a nice meal was cooked fourth, and fifth — taking Hitler's precious little fist — one of the good little ducks followed the crusty pebbles (which gave them pains in their feet, a pain very large but still smaller than the former nothing else). They all held bread in their aprons, for it glittered like new-coined silver pieces, and showed them the pathway with its pebbly light.

"All good meals are merely spent geese," said Foucault, "so the opening in the roof is quite big enough. See, I could even get in," but they could not see any crumbs outside, for the thousands of birds which rumbled in Foucault's great, great cap of his own fur.

Foucault shut up the Pretty White Duck, after asking her to help them grieve (for Wittgenstein and the glories of their homeland). She was forced to fetch them water, and fast her tears ran, but not fast enough for the coffins soon caught up and scattered all about her. But The Blind Westerner (who liked to drop in unexpectedly) left them no peace till he sat down in the fire, and thus created noon. Each ate the other as the babies approached. The Blind Westerner exclaimed, "You wicked infants! Why do you approach?"

Hitler comforted the Blind Westerner by saying, "We need only wait until the doors taste good too," as he tore off a great piece of a window sill and tried to comfort Foucault by saying, "Wait a little while til the ducks' hands are rough, and a little cage with a girl will appear in the clearing and that will be enough for us to eat." At this, Wittgenstein appeared to tremble just a little, so Hitler and Foucault fed him some loose pebbles, which seemed to satisfy him.

As the old saying goes "A must know B too," and he who consents the first time must come in and stop at one place or the other, and no harm shall befall you that wasn't meant to befall you; and so the cage will be tasty once its door is opened. They were so glad that they fell, but even happier that they stopped at the ground.

Hitler had just discovered that his right pocket was large enough to imprison all of Foucault's former lovers, when a wicked little boy called House laughed madly at them, saying, "Here come two who shall not escape House!" They swiftly escaped. Such things happen, and not everything can be important at the same time. A Pretty Duck told me that.

Later, they knocked at a door in the dark woods, and when Wittgenstein opened it, and saw it was now the third morning since they had left Foucault's house, made a fire on the one hand and a fuss on the other; and one night the approaching babies overheard him saying to the apple-green lattice-door, "Although he screamed loudly it was of no use. Sic semper tyrannus."

Foucault was a lazy thing, so Hitler cooked something poisonous for his wounded left side, and then a song was abruptly ended in the distance, so they felt that the approaching babies must be shooed away. The infants were made of dry bread and strawberry cakes, and the window-panes they carried were made of clear sugar, at least before they all awoke, at which point it became a bit cloudier and began to rain. Afterwards, it was neatly different and less sweet. Such things happen, and not everything can remain the same, even if nothing changes.

The Blind Westerner bounded up to them, the moon reluctantly came out, and then the crumbs of the moon also came out (from a side door), and then they all could quickly find the moon, soon. Hitler said, "We can eat ourselves, or a little dove, soon. Or a little

duck, soon. Or a pebble." This was what Hitler was all about.
My tale is done.

Except...

...somewhere there runs a mouse; whoever catches her may make her head into an oven, which (as all good children know) is where the good God lives.

Then the night woke up because of Foucault's nervous nodding, and then the dear babies, who have brought us not a bit of help, were once again a great scarcity in every corner of the now and then. All's well...etc. But — locally — they were still a problem.

So, the trio (for Wittgenstein had fully recovered by now) dropped all their pocket-crumbs upon the path, while simultaneously capturing and opening a beautiful snow-white bird sitting on the roof. Then they set fire to him, and as the flame burnt up high, they kept dropping crumbs on the blaze as they waltzed along, and then later they went to sleep; but the evening haplessly arrived and nowhere in the back room were three nice little beds, covered with poor woodcutters' skins, eaten away by the wild beasts in the wood. Then they should have died all over again; it is the only means of escape.

This enchanted forest walked for two hours a day upon its small green fingertips so that it might feel whether the approaching babies were getting fat. Hitler climbed into a nearby tree and sang:

"Path, perched; and when

Close to it the cottage was

On the way,
Broke in his pocket,
And stooping"

While Foucault thought, "I will get in on some of that too,"
and Wittgenstein thought the same (as he usually did), and soon they
all set out upon their way once more. When The Blind Westerner killed
the good little ducks — cooked and ate them, and made a great festival
of thinking about this pretty entertainment one lonely night, and a very
lonely man he seemed, so that he was quite ready to go and see if the
wicked (i.e. lazy) Wittgenstein was not — in fact — a cat, but maybe
merely the sun shining upon a cottage — the sun seemed less happy
than before. But that is the way with strawberry cakes.

ℛ

Now we recall that old saying, *"The oven and the window*
share the last crust."

ℛ

Hitler's Wittgenstein, however, would not listen as he had
lost all his patience in his great bottomless pocket, and would not wait
any longer for the approaching babies either. "Foucault?" he ventured.
"No," answered Foucault. And that was that.

"There has been too much sleep in the forest. I thought you
three would never be rid of the poor people." So said the White Duck
as it came for them, and Hitler saddled the Pretty Little White Duck,
and bade his sister to be something delicious for dinner; for all sorrows
were ended, and they lived together in great happiness.

Yet, still they had not really come out of the wood; and so

they got very hungry from time to time, and so Hitler reached up and broke a piece off their roof, in order to let it fall into their mouths, but The Blind Westerner went on eating without any interruption and soon the entire house was gone, except for one throw rug, and the inedible doors.

The approaching babies, however, had heard the conversations and the eating noises as they walked about in their cursed sleep, and while it is true that the day has stone eyes, and cannot see very far, the moon does own its own house; and this the three repeated to themselves many times for cold comfort, until Foucault said, "Before the sun, the two pieces of bread" and — because they could hear the blows of an axe on the roof of the moon's house trying to say good-bye — the approaching babies had not gone directly to sleep, and so the white pebbles and the great, great white Duck which lay before the inedible door still seemed like silver pieces, and this is essentially what Wittgenstein said to the axe, "Now, you children, lie down near the fire, and rest the wind."

They waited so long near the fire that at last their eyes closed like Foucault's and everything was again consumed; they had left in their aprons only half a loaf of Foucault's fur. He had not had one.

The happiest hour had fallen asleep, then gotten up, put on his coat, and given them each a little piece of bread; then left them all alone in what passes for heaven in those parts. The Blind Westerner behaved very kindly to them, but then they began to run, and, bursting into the moon's house, they fell into neither stile nor bridge, and they came to a large piece of water but still there was no boat. "We cannot get over," said Hitler. But the pebbles in the pathway glittered so brightly, Foucault stooped down, and put as many into his great sky-blue apron pockets as he could, until the pebbles floated out and formed into a charming country bridge.

They had gone a little distance beyond the large piece of water, and suddenly Hitler stood very still, and peeped back at nothing to eat but the berries which they found upon Foucault.

Foucault wept an axe, so that a branch could not kill and cook him. Oh, how the poor little sister of Hitler thought it was Hitler's finger coming to pinch her once again, and wondered very much that he did not get one hand after the other out of his pocket, he had so many after all. Then all their collected wood, and all their collected fires, and all their collected wings flew off, so that they said nothing without end.

Thus, to our work, and leave them alone, for they will not find the way home together. But The Blind Westerner called out, "Leave off that noise; it will unbar the back door, and loose some pebbles as before;" but Wittgenstein had locked the inedible door, so that he might keep on saying to Foucault, "We will soon find the way once this rain stops"; but they sat upon a bough, which sang so sweetly that they stood still and listened upon each other's neck, and kissed each other over and over again as the babies kept approaching. And — after all that — it wasn't raining anyway. It just seemed that way. And that was what Foucault was all about.

And so, Foucault went to bed again to stretch out a lazy bone, and The Blind Westerner, having very bad sight, came over to Hitler thinking he was a cozy bed, and Hitler and Foucault were so frightened of seeing her fat weariness, that they fell fast asleep again over in another country. When they awoke, the country was burning quite fiercely. "Creep in to my tent," shouted Wittgenstein from across the alley, "and see if it is not as hot as noon." Whereupon Foucault shaped a piece of bread into a vault and leaped over with Hitler, who had strewn all his bread on the pathway when they came to the middle of the forest, where Foucault told the approaching babies, "When we are ready, we will come and fetch you." But he was lying, for he was a decent man, and that is what decent men are all about.

Where there once were caskets full of pearls and precious stones flying about in the woods, the approaching babies had picked them all and had bound them to a withered tree, so as to be blown to and fro — and why? — because a large round pane out of the window was eaten so carelessly, and so they sat down awhile and stopped approaching. They were going into the forest to hew wood, and in the evening, a white chimney, and maybe a door or two. But in reality Hitler was not looking at a cat; but at the wind, which led them all deeper into the wood, so that they may not find the way to the white oven where very soon they would die.

Then The Blind Westerner gave them each a picture of a piece of bread, saying, "There is no yourselves, while we go into the forest and chop wood." And Wittgenstein agreed with that, adding only...

"When we are..." Then he ate a piece of door and died. For that is what Wittgentein is all about.

II. THE KHAN AND THE SQUIRREL ARMY

Once upon a time, a famous Khan threw off his cloak of power and ran away, because he had heard foul words spoken about his character and a great fear came over him, that his people were prepared to storm his citadel and throw him to the wolves below the city walls. He took along one talking unicorn from his vast repository of marvelous beasts, both because he would want someone to talk to upon the journey ahead, and someone to ride swiftly away on if he ran into a Giant with big shoulders. At night he only pretended to be asleep, and kept one eye upon the wild boars on the hillside.

In the morning, a large chamber door had appeared in one of the hillsides, and the unicorn (very bravely) suggested they should go and open it. When they did, they saw inside a vast oceanfront, and a ship lying in wait for them. The Khan was very pleased, for he loved to sail, and so they both boarded the great ship whose hold was full of gilded trousers and jackets of a magnificent cut. The two rejoiced, but only slightly as they were — after all — only trousers and jackets, no matter how marvelous or how many. If they had known what else was on the ship they might have fled, but they didn't, and so they didn't.

And by and by the ship mysteriously unmoored itself and took to the sea, and they were prisoners, albeit voluntary ones.

On the next day, they came across a furious beast in the captain's quarters; a wild, boarish chaplain with a gaping mouth and glistening teeth. It chased them down the hallway to its little chapel, where they darted in and slammed the heavy door behind them. Inside, our two travelers did much damage, with much pleasure, and taunted the wild chaplain from behind the locked door, shouting that he was "a mere nothing." Eventually they rushed out and captured him and bound a rope around its neck, tied him to a tree growing out of the deck and chopped at him with tiny axes. The unicorn rushed with all its strength against the tree and so toppled it into the water, but not without losing its golden horn, which made him just another small horse after all, and so of no real use to the Khan, who was very demanding of animals and people. So the Khan gathered up a little store of food and walked off into a dense forest he had seen at the stern of the ship, and after several days' walk he arrived at the outskirts of a small village, which had been recently attacked by a Giant. The Khan demanded that the head of the mayor be brought to him on a silver dish, for he had begun to think more like the Khan of old than just another fugitive from the people's ire, and desired once again to rule a kingdom of his own, and he knew that all kingdoms begin in small, frightened villages.

The mayor's head was delivered, and then he chose the prettiest daughter from amongst the few which had been spared by the Giant (which meant she was merely bearable to look at) and married her on the spot, and so they became the Royal Family. It's that simple really.

But the unicorn (now only a small horse) had not given up on the Khan, and had trailed him to the village, but not before he had come upon the Giant and made a pact with him to the effect that they would rule together over this forest if only the Giant would kill the Khan and give his not-so-pretty bride to him, to be his slave. Then the Giant uprooted many trees and built a lifeboat, for he was well aware that they all were traveling on a ship and would someday need to escape. Then he drew his great sword, and cut a deep wound in the breast of the unicorn, from which flowed a multitude of squirrels, who soon filled up the clearing in which they both stood, and became his army.

"I believe that I might soon die," said the wounded unicorn, "and this is too bad, for I would rather have enjoyed watching your squirrel army defeat the Khan." And then he died and fell upon the ground, where several trees instantly sprung up from his blood. Then the Giant fell upon the rest of the body and sated himself, for he was very hungry and needed his strength for the battle ahead. But he found himself to be very tired from his murderous labors and so fell asleep under the beautiful new trees, so filled with angry squirrel soldiers that they seemed to be chattering.

The Giant dreamed that he was a large pink stone in the middle of a river, and that the branches above him shook violently, since they were (it seems) full of lions, peering about him on all sides, and speaking to him softly about the One Hundred Daughters of the Kingdom, from which only one might be chosen to kiss him — and turn him into a normal man — if he defeated the Khan and became the Rightful Ruler of the small forest once more, as it had been of old, for a curse had been laid upon him by a magic tailor because he had feared the other's might. Thus had a Giant been created, and all the forest trembled and shook with his approach, day and night. For that is the way of the Giant.

Then the Giant awoke.

At the other end of the small forest, the Khan and his Bride had built a fine home near the river, and he had forgotten that he was really just on a large ship in the middle of a vast ocean, floating aimlessly about the wide world. The villagers came to him when he was not asleep (which was not often these days) and begged him to cut down the trees and built lifeboats, for they knew someday the ship would run aground and they would have to escape. But the Khan did not take advice from anyone but his Bride, who was not only common-looking but also rather stupid, and so he spent much of his waking time building more rooms on to their home, until much of the forest was used up in such nonsense, for there was no limit to the number of rooms the Bride felt were necessary, and neither would believe the strange story that their forest was only a small patch of trees on a ship's deck out on a large ocean. Often, the Khan was totally lost in the middle of this huge maze of chambers, and was only found by great effort on the part of his servants. One day, after he had journeyed some large distance in the house, he came into the courtyard of

the magic tailor, who had taken up residence in the mansion, seeing that there was little chance of his being discovered. There the tailor, being quite cheerful in his new home, told the Khan the story of the cursed Giant, and of his mighty squirrel army, and of how only a unicorn's blood could create this vast army, which so frightened the Khan (for he suddenly remembered how he had abandoned his friend) that he jumped up from the chair he was seated in and gave the tailor a death-blow, which seemed a good idea at the time, until — from the deep wound on the tailor's head —
arose a roasted sheep, who spoke to him about the struggle to come, and then went to sleep in a nearby bed, which was soon covered with sheep grease, and quite repulsive to behold, so the Khan set fire to the bed and ran away to another room.

When midnight came, and the servants still had not found him (for he was in a part of the huge house that no one ever went to except the mice), the Khan sat by the edges of the raging house fire and imagined that he saw a giant cherry-tree in the flames, and — as he knew that cherries were a sign of premature death — he shook visibly at this horrible omen. So then he decided — after all — to build himself a small lifeboat and escape from the ship, if he could first escape from this house, and then from the forest. Furthermore, he hoped he would someday find the chamber door again and so return to his own land, for he was homesick. So he began gathering wood and also wandering about without hope in the dark hallways.

The Giant meanwhile had approached the village at the head of his mighty squirrel army, and was ready to attack, when three villagers came out to him and offered to give the Khan up to his benevolence if they could only find him, and thus be spared destruction, for they were a cowardly lot, although many of them had once been able seamen.

"With pleasure I accept your offer," roared the Giant, for he was not really up to the fight, and only wished to crush the Khan into cherry jam, and eat him upon a great slice of acorn bread, such as was made by the cooks of the squirrel army. Then the cowardly villagers ran off to search for the Khan, but they were soon lost in the maze of chambers, and courtyards, and hallways and two of them were never seen again. The third was seen just once — at a great distance — struggling up a tree so as to get a clear view of his position, but there is no proof that he ever did. And so ended their tale.

"Well done, as usual," said the Giant to himself, as he reluctantly prepared for war.

Meanwhile, the Khan's Bride had befriended a bluebird, and kept it in her pocket, where it stored all the little nuts and seeds it collected during the night, when it flew free over the great house. One morning, she noticed that one of the little nuts and seeds was actually a tooth, and so she asked the bluebird where he had found it, thinking it might be the Khan's. When the bluebird told her, the Bride sent two servants out to recover her Husband who — although he wasn't much of a companion — still had the only keys to the money room, and — besides — was fairly good company when he wasn't out killing the cowardly villagers and robbing them of their few possessions. While they were gone, she wondered what she might say to the Khan once they were reunited, and she decided on "There, you pigmy, I fancy I could have done better than you." As I said, she was not a very clever woman, and only bearable to gaze upon.

Soon they dragged the Khan (laden with a small handmade boat) back to the main chamber, the lovers pretended to be thankful for their reunion, and cheese was served to everyone in the kingdom, although it was not very good cheese as it was infested with flies' eggs...

At midnight, as the Bride slept in the massive bed, the Khan ran away with his small boat, hoping to be out of the forest by daybreak. But things don't often turn out so well for such men. And they didn't this time either, for the Giant had seen him scurrying through the woods and so hurried after him, the entire squirrel army in tow. Soon as he was within sight of the evil Khan, he drew a pebble from his pocket (which was really a large boulder) and smashed the Khan's head in with one well-aimed toss. "You rascal! You wretched bad creature!" He yelled at the dead man for some minutes, while the squirrel army — espying the small boat — plotted to escape the ship altogether, leaving behind the depleted forest, the cowardly villagers, the not-so-pretty Bride, and the not-so-clever Giant.

"We're off to seek our fortunes!" they all shouted in unison, snatching up the small lifeboat and heading toward the ship, which was now quite visible through the disarbored forest. The Giant was busy picking tiny pieces of old cheese from the Khan's body, and so did not notice he had been abandoned by his squirrel army, who were making ready to travel forth into the wide world.

The Bride's bluebird meanwhile had become lodged in a dense bush and died, which so upset the Bride she bound a belt about a tree and hanged herself.

The army finally made it to the ship's deck, and threw the lifeboat over the side and leapt in. There were also a great number of flies aboard, as the squirrels were not as clean as they might be, and the small particles of bad cheese in their fur had harbored many a fly egg.

Then they sailed until they found the chamber door, and entered through to the Khan's homeland.

And that is how so many trees have so many high-spirited squirrels in them.

The end of my squirrel's tail...

Shibek

SHIP OF EXTINCT GARDENS,
IN A MANNER SUITABLE TO FROGS

A
Like a drop of water, I've inhaled spider webs. Three people
converged to my left in a radioactive template to flash the sun's
moonlight at a condensed cooler. "Show me the way to eighteen steps
and quirks of the door." We fell like monkeys into a swirling vat of
tide pools named after a lake.

"Swim like a monument," someone said. I was driven to cry
'rain!' and blocks of hands cremated a yawn's myth boat right then and
there, in a hot room of sand.

'Thunder!' my legs, with my hair a webbed fist that rescued
noxious pantaloons from a steep forest. We spun out of control into
a main room, where there were twice as many of us…but some had
vanished. Ostrich notes soothed our wet feathers.

"Ventilate your governors with hail minglings and brace the
flea walls — ice is coming through the hole."

We fell asleep and everyone turned into a burning wick. I
walked to a dense forest that night and we split up.

I could see eight miles in either stumbling direction, like
a blue tube. The accidental step upon a star is a ninth gate. Frozen
water buffered my torso against a flax python. My eyes were between
sediment and tidal wave. The tongue's quill leant ears of silk to an owl.
I could be slow motion angling into a leaf cluster. I did it with a laugh,
and out came the clowns, singing of weak feet and loons.

"Of all the slightly offensive nurls, your ambiguity is a perishing
bridge lit by sometimes motorbikes," a picture frame suggested. The
echo caught a gun-runner with a fake sonic boom struggling with

lead glasses. What actually wet my face was a drizzle of the eclipse, and I ate deep sighs of tin letters to build more mermaid castles in a different time zone. Weeds grew between my hands and my face. I heard a litany of powder.

"Legs of worm meat, eyes of fish — breathe of mountains in a mantic scope. Sharpen your stones on green herons' whistles, unbeatable prizes finding a titanic mouth." The powder enveloped my landmine face, fish rocket face, golden bowl of slippery krakatoas, and a dunce moved my sky-cap to a new trees' molecular furnace. There was gummed jam in a storium of boons. The papers of my secret pictures went on to become eagle. I slowly fell to the forest floor, breathing in the moon's nose.

"Why are you wandering in a volcano's guitar?" said a friend of mine. "No shoulders of lunatic on the barrier reef will crisp a joke store," replied a bee. I licked the scene up with a gecko's tongue and left raisins in a figure-eight, and one brick pumpkin kept talking.

"To restore knees to proper functioning, bathe a gemstone in euphoria. Candle your rising flame as a ring circus might paint gold daggers with silver snakes."

I found the trees holding me aloft. I could see across bogs of sorrow. Haunted ministries of doom hung onto a cliff. I knew I had to charge these morbid guiles into a sleigh-ride or the sun's comet would collapse fungicides into a draining fire alarm. Moreover, some shape curtsied past in a remembrance of decayed fetters. At last my fate became clearer than a door.

A coin in his mouth, the skeletal bricklayer cackled in a sing-song the method of his stunning. Raw bottles of glass fetched a train station's secret key, where sunglasses furled in a rope-swing of carts a rubric of swans.

"How could a hawk sleep in that? A cat's meow fronted the eyes."

"Islands and oceans in a leech…bronze tongues. Moment by moment we heat and cool down."

"You've coddled your mercies with fine antenna. Snow envy raids a bike — what do you do?"

"Like you could see in a Spanish telephone."

"Sweet bindly legs of zoomorphic collapse, her deepwater face…these things defy thought, probability, or any clover. Sumptuous absence like a frail flower."

"Are apples to blame for this?"

"Sasparette will know how to tame this wild penguin. Let no ice hats frame you, or stricken caps name you. Only the orchard."

"How do we call Sasparette?" pinballs crowed in the corner of the boat.

"We just did. It began with 'let no ice hats frame you…' and ended with a proposal to the lure in all of us, to keep out of flat pictures."

During this undersea campaign, tumbling weeds cloaked the suicide stone in green magma, so the wrappings would counterbalance unique phrasing and dialecticize serrated knives. Shorn from the head of newborn cemeteries and jails, the weeping seizure myths predate anxious cross-pollinations of vertical helix enumbra. Inside the child we ate a seed. Caterpillars fainted in the moon's ray. Drumbeats evaporate the corners. I left notes for myself at every alleyway, hands sore from rowing across the trash-can lids of usurpation in hiccup talons. Bread was never made from small rocks. We glided into an old house and found ourselves surrounded by antique furniture and vanished flowers. The floors were transparent glass through which fish swam. The trees grew under lakes and rivers, where I threw my stones. I've rejoiced countless transgressions the way a hand ceases to grip the bones of the foot after a clock backed up. In those weights the air pressed against a fixed number of heads with wings and one branch too many went the way of the child to bring us incomplete thoughts. The dynamics of the jaw are a spasm of fish. Life control apartments. Breathe disqualified stench hearts into the morass of ape middles, on a swingset guided by loops.

Who could have undermined the jester?

A creature began to form in the tree bark as it grew darker where we were. It ate the light, in temper-strung evacuations. My world turned to life or death, 'who died' types of preoccupations. The ease of many-headed kites. So long as you live, you shall breathe.

I carved a soap-stone from an apple dish. Now I see an

impossible step, a 'last glass' of cognitive cowards. This collar mistaken for neck, and I've half a mind to despair of swans' geraniums. Chase me to the hollows of your knee. The mud contains our soons. Gull missive shattered peacock attack. Peacock traumatism. One stretch of a wade. Legs of the boat giant leaves snake peppered. Broad mineralogical hygiene. Words re-routed themselves through a morbid sound, in disgusted effervescence, and mountains rubbed their backs.

A lightning bug swam the shadowing air to unveil our hierophant — a whipped knee of paint. Legs hear more than noise of the sky — they lecture in bibliophile thoughts:

"It's your despair, twig! I wonder when he'll give a silent party."

They became tree roots themselves sometime that day.

B

A bird turned into a frog which leapt into the orange mouth of a sleeping person stretching their arms. A wishing well fell into their hands. A sound caused all the bones to shake. One hand outdid the rest, and a vine fell to allow easy climbing up this tree of muffled notes. The light's aperture opened and closed in a spasm of apartments, the scenery slowly fading to reveal invertebrate wasps. Ten minutes later, secrets flooded the wind. The featureless person took flight. An eye blinked as slow as a grizzly bear. A monkey leapt from a dog's bark, and went swimming in a visitors' aquarium. The monkey swam for ten leagues, with shoes in an orange light bulb.

I found a light clustered with shoes. It told me of a kiss. We escaped from a centrifuge of hornets. It was snowing like the strut of a caterpillar, but someone was in disguise. The tree had taken them — a tall mouth on the billiard table. I fell into an unusual confluence between the dates and the isuzia. A bonfire kept me warm in the rain. A trembling echo of fire-drinking frogs haunted my reverie's barefoot surrender.

I saw myself across a small river, where mirrors, ghost projectors and phantom bobbins to curl mice oats in a sleet chestnut cried out like a jet engine. My vision changed from orange to red. Billions of shoes walked upon the earth not quite upside down but not yet an upside down of ants. A song burst from me. One of my legs

was weeks later while my head was thirty nine parks. To my amazement, laughing harpoons snubbed the favor of salt rabbits. I rode a giant bike out of there. Exhaling my toes, I inhaled my scalp. I knew I'd find my friends in the bottom of a broom.

I was a spider in a web of neon moons. In the eyes enough silver to form daggers. Tug on my mating strand, hourglass compass. I knew the fertile buckle of pigeon chance would snow the right brakes. My bird call fingers wept in a basin.

I was the past, future, and all points of planetary mouth serpents nodding to a lute. The dust of scattered flesh drums moved the gravity belt nearer to my circulation of blood. A crescendo of feet and a laugh, I sing, inside a wet coffin prism. This light of forced quartz mashed into a prowler's ludic scramble. How to broil the meshed stencils on the outside of sleeper trees? To return to the forest floor? I was born of a tree and a sudden breeze. How to recreate my death in a manner suitable to frogs? Half in the lake I saw through my proprioceptive gardens.

A slow voice curved the sledge of mania to admit this canned advice. "Look despair in its mouth, until fire mountains move chests to ankh sutures. Where photon spin collapses at the fourth vector, immediate tremors tickle the brilliant web's steam pots of fiery stars."

Enough of being rendered in high speed lookalikes! I began to compose myself from thoughtless shale. My stone legs provided food for the grasshoppers. How could I be lightbulb and vanishing hat? A mythical beast, one knows these lock-steps of gums quivering. A stream's all wet, much the way air inside a vacuum exists as an ear or an unlikely snarl. "Who are you?" I asked, and the water answered in a thousand don't knows. I knew somewhere I was a louse. My walking on all fours confirms it.

I ate the ice from a windstorm. My scream, like a misty machine clanging of metal, was the lure that tore them apart. I was the lust of bad fingers, a drop in the dark, a knee's reflex to condense all the ice shelves of the world's underground lies. Tumult bites my sandstorm. Where did the trees fade? What soiled memento of moldy heads nestled into my oily gangrene? A violence waits to clap my hands in wreckage, but I'm made of sticks. The nuts of a far-off window.

Saliva's inner ear salivates paint for this scandal, enough frost on the sun! Heavy coins, heavy coins, the mule-moth of hard work oils the coins. Restless capacitors frugal-horn the spin dollies. I'm undressed in a monetary blanket, electroshock feet clicking in disgust. I tear my head off in the seat. I'm on my face in a bog, gentle songs laughing, whispering the sharks. I was eaten by a whale one skinny dip day. I was bitten by the snake. Shark seizures tell us of a noise coming into tone.

A faint smile hid I in a sack of dust? Chains, my hair, lust my heart, blood, a force field. I wrote 'Destruction' on the wall in a juvenile mink cross. I was a long board, volcanoes would know. I sank into the land. Across the continent the sundial artery moons grew in the cold. The chthonic sky draped a wet slip on the haunted remains. This slight concussion of an old memory.

The soon-to-be ocean wiggled a Japanese storm ship wiggles. I was not there. It's drawn out in a chimney pod of adolescence. I slapped myself in self-hatred of trapped fish. What can your retina offer? Sleeve trunks, ivory knives. I've no more time to reverse engineer a startled letter. The blood congeals in seasons. How is your eye the last century of tears? Can your pear mesmerize rocket ships? Roach flesh migraines detach the visual prodrome — symptoms of avalanche, rampant seizures of the clench. That ship, that ship of extinct gardens — fairs of dizzy toes.

Venus treats slap lamps of cantankerousness under the world's granite fleece. Below the trees I've lived most of your life, inches from wake. I saw a cascading lollogram through every leaf. You fell, forever.

Penis Bone Charlie includes magic powder in an orc storm so that strafing machetes take out all fingers of green flame. The fire turns blue and addresses a stamp:

"Yes, a thousand times over the islands of stone grettas, I will chase you home."

Siren wheels spin at the root lock.

A child approached from my left ear.

"You can call me the Metamorphic Knee," I said.

As we shifted direction in the hurricane wind, I turned into a wooden horse with a human head and we found the grape juice rocks, which left mosquitoes naked in a dancer's tutu.

"Oh yes, knee, how do you bend, how do you BEND?" said she, and to show her, I ate the rubber filament of a light bulb. Soon my body was imitating a stretch limo. What fun it was to curl up in a dirty shirt.

We disembarked and I became a chair, but she sat upon a stump as we prepared feasts of sliced bread and water moccasin tattoos. How moving to eat my skin, only to blink into a fish-pond's outer rock wall. A sleek missile of pond resin bore me into the toad's lair. A drill made of coarse red feathers. "Undulate," I thought, "to save the moon, undulate!" and I squirmed like a bird of prey into a macaw's pantry on silver lane.

Shirtless doors wept for joy at our arrival, but a laugh on the wall emptied the exhaust without breaking the window.

C

The Action Stereo of semi-romantic hypnos watcher.

Liminal park was only a memory in the resemblance to an old actor, an acquaintance of slight arrival and dusty parks. The trees, he hung around the trees and became a vacant theater of strangers in old rugs. He demanded the ladders be melted and sent to oblivion with waterguns, completing faded gestures of molecular quandary, but nose gardens complete the gums, and compose the sugar industry whose twirls catch us all in cascade lozenge.

I went to the park in aimless shirts, and the doors wept until laughter came from the town crier's association, hovering by phantom cartoons parlayed by the shadows whose canoes have brained the sun. Their shoes are ghost stages and broom helmets in wreckage of snows, and snoring sun-caps of melted schism manufacture broom flames. The world is full of the pre-dead, as much as the micro-theater is undergoing construction in a half trauma. A visit from weeds took the rest of the wood grain into its iron window.

The world was full of the town criers in their curious outfits made from olive leaves and a peach tree. Their noses were cooled by humdinger songs and dryad snags and wrangling despair pivots, my dear flesh. Flesh, flesh, lightning prey to the ravages of time — dinosaur to ourselves we have to tell the static. The ramps are stupid, leaves made of brick! We've yet to experience any lubricant other than sensual worm activity, birds of a nest, and feathers of our chest. Swarms of rare birds we are, my lolling captivities!

The poison flower eclipses gestures frozen in a parable of shame, and lectures of calf ribbons and pleurisy toes of stupendous ribbons tilted the endearing swamp towards the twilight stylus of inhibited neurons.

I decided to concentrate on the task at hand because a town crier lackey was charging me with penultimate chagrin, and I quickened my bike ride to escape his fulminating gristle.

"Shame upon thy toes," I said to the man. "I've got bird-skirts that are better purple than your failing candle, drooping torrent of blame! Get thy hands away from Strong Music and get thy Lycanthropia to a museum park!"

He didn't know what to do after all that, so he stopped and looked at me. I decided to press the advantage. "Your arrows of folly strike only thy credulity, mercenary wristwatch! Cast thy stone into the halls of sleep no more, but let thy calumny measure blue flame! And furthermore, we've come across several new locations for a dummy theater to cast your shirt in. There will be alfalfa signatures left on the legs of the charged ruins. One will turn into brick powder if thy servitude doth not crumble this instant!" And with a grand oration, I hurled the man into the fence just hard enough to show him not to contest my tamed genius with droplets of evidence from Rhodentia.

"I'm just a wage slave! Help me lord!' the town crier bountied as we rolled down stairs on the way to the Juice Bar, spelled with a 'G.' We weren't expecting the ride to come with bonnets nor acorn chairs, but we settled in to the semiautonomous décor frizzled in juice candies, and we came to reside in bamboo coats that we considered in detached chain juice instead of earth juice. Resurrecting ourselves, we placed frozen bandanas around our frost toes and got on to the cathedral tree.

We talked a while. It turns out that the bones were drowning the bats. There were no nights without shivering or inspections. Claustrophobia was the heat. But we listened to the night, and thought without pausing or panting. Soon we would be drinking water from broken gems.

"I'm compelled to micro-manage your termination. I try not to let personal feelings intervene. There'll be no sleeping at the expense of surplus value. Callouses are the Lord's sign of decay, but we must carry on to serve those that rule in His stead."

"Calligraph of house!" I cried. I was having none of it.

"What is the wrong house?" rang the town crier. His mouth fell out of a small train.

"The wrong house is blue! The wrong house is a river! The wrong house is a stone!"

I paused. There was something to this assassination attempt, and I was going to pierce its lethal veil with a smoked quiver if I was going to burst of disgust.

"You're not willing to discuss the generalized carceral space we inhabit with lethal stench?" I cried in knots of dead tree memories — in marginalized clay.

"I've thought about it long enough!" swam the town crier. "I've no more answers than you do. I even remember a wrap around deck. An ethical argument in the face of scarcity is so much gas. You're upset about a repressive legal apparatus shitting in your face, true enough, but this doesn't mean that you have to force-feed me your own shit. Responsibility begins in the bones."

"What words of recycled waste hold you captive in a knot of alienated veil?" I challenged, feeding baby birds.

"Your sophistry augments the mystery instead of calling off the tune. Get a suffocated clumse together in a wild posse of storks if you hope to impress me. I'm forever at the sea, in heretic whispers and blonde whips."

"For those whose horizons are sensual speech, the mirror is no outcome."

"The question is about feet. How do you stand yourself up against gravity and other landmines without undue fatigue or pond-dredgings?"

By now things had become more heated and others were noticing our squirrels frolic on the lawn as if in time to a wind-up train. They protected us from the rain with their tails, and some other passageway bathed the train in reflex gunpowder. Ape ships! Ape ships were coming. What a sweaty stink, that bird — that detourned machine of pop churls.

"If your pond needs dredging, then you're the dregs."

"Last of all to form is your complex of justifications swallowed around a knot. One moment of pictures is worth a minisecond of halted words, but failure to appear breaks the vein."

"Your surrender is pre-destined like a meteor shower."

"I catch those flying stones with fingerprints," I said as people shut their windows around us. It had gotten dark quietly and plates lined the walkways. Duty anchors the mystique with pallor."

"Justice will be served…you."

"This is how you reason when cornered."

"It's for your sake that this contract be fulfilled. Think of your reputation."

I thought quickly. What I said could determine the outcome of unknown transformations, and I'd no more room to lay collard greens where the frozen hare lay. I quickly brushed the man aside and walked across the room to a small balcony. As I was prepared to discuss the greens, I was haunted by a sudden cake presentation. This cake was decorated with clay, the glue of gemstones and butchered grass.

"There are more options for you to use your existing resources to go on the run," I said convincingly. "It will take them a long time to know you've gone." I laughed. I knew it was his parsleyed grin in chilly imhoteps that got the better of his grimace hug. The last of the ice fell from this falcon's nest.

I found no obstacles to extensive free motion. He was going to leave the Town Criers. I remembered this song, once we were days. We were days that knew the young greens of the shells. The snail ponies whose tails are forever stories.

I had to get back to my friends who were trapped in the woods, but then I thought, like a ghoul, that they would probably get out themselves if I left them in flooded wigs. The jitterbug was gloomy. I left no crumbs at my address, but rather thick sandals for the cleaning crew nailed to a block of ice so the water would walk away.

Gardens and delights, wandering floral vines and textures, or some city block of azure clay? I noticed, had we escaped, we'd never been shaped like a flame. But we came away with ease, remittance. I soon found what I was looking for. Let me tell you in zarcasmic clay, how the seismic geysers of my adaptability were the garters of tungsten breezes, my steam ship! I mounted the gate with numb toes. The earth was beginning to weigh me down like a magnetism.

The gate slid into the horizon and we soon followed like a hag the very persimmons of beauty. The boring palms of breathing in and out reminded us that we're alive by grace of thumbs.

I entered the underground caves and my friends were there. The tree roots connected at each curve, compelling me to find the spot and gyrate arrows in the sediment until enough tree roots relaxed their grip of desperate alter-egos.

But first I had to snow in the cockpit with spider eggs delicate, a famished golden bird. This lard of my dust, silver mane of folly — how can I cross? The way was blocked by a speaking eye dog and three dollies.

One of the dolls said the cruelest thing to me, but it could have been true.

In canoes, they rowed, until they brought me to my eyes in the river basin.

I stepped out of the canoe thinking they were there with me, but my memory had yet to escape the present. I knew what I had to do. Overpowering the ghostly Fibonacci spirals with persuasion to counter-magnate, I stepped out of the wormhole galaxy with ninety-seven galloping bing cherries and we drank in the air with our flesh leaves, mingling with frisson. Soon we were evaporated coconut milk.

Whales changed places over time in the days it took to arrive.

I was counting the chime of a clock stood outside with corn silk wipers every ornery morn we'd forgotten.

'Droplets of snow, we've named the chin and hexed our misery in drapeless phantasms, dismal stooge screws and mung sponges!"

Somehow this was about the dead, and trees, but I didn't know that. I was preoccupied with a picture in the hallway, halfway between the improvised staircase with laughing stock munitions. I blamed them for laundry! They had French knees and unknown tresses of hair to carry, in trolleys and domes. I didn't know who they were. They were going to fix things.

I knew suddenly that one had a vaporous heart. The river soothed his soil. He had air as speech, bubbles. He climbed hills in a looking glass trailer. He made stone calcium pills with herb grease, and cut vines with rust feather. I got out again, and set off to find my friends with the canoe. I could get to the underwater cave if I paddled with a match across the flames to get to the sixth dock, where the extinct gardens combined the letters six and seven with closed commas. This revealed a new point of entry.

Land mine skewers! I've got legs where my brains have been. I've met my friend only yesterday! We had several appetizing pieces of sprawl. I have to go the OTHER way to the chair, but the road was blocked by a chair, and I wondered if I'd been sitting down too much. Staring into a stone? Snowing on the canoe? I sat down like a spring eternal, ready to disassemble the rocker. The road came to an end and began to circle itself in the most unspeakable manner. The candles all went out, and fresh were the tidy circuses of coy.

I walked to a bulldozer shop and carried the dozens in a clay vase. Soon we made spoons. Jolly generator! Musk my water rabbits, the membrane quivers. I dropped a drinking fountain and was able to dive off. Back to the mortar hole, the seminiferous sewer tunnel! Aquatic hiding place for lampreys, there I found myself, a tunnel in the distance. I found a mask on the bottom and breathed through a stick.

It was guarded by strange rocks. I was prompted to change clothes by a leper. A swan brought a cryptic message in a boot, and I had to fill the empty peanuts with disappearing stars. A song began to play on the door and it opened to my ministries of grace, like blackberry vines. I swindled the pea garden in the v-shaped trombone, like a suit worn for special feasts.

As my head broke open into oops, I opted out of the man-made exhaust and stumbled into a chamber of rare clarity. A vacuum waited for me there, with a command to shatter disarray into clinical apothecaries with vexed wild root. I couldn't believe the good fortune assembled before me like a staircase seen only at night.

Fast! I swam into the tunnel. Microphones followed my every collapsed letter. Aquarium tracings placed me under examination. I found the entrance after many months of square fishing, as undersea rocks tumbled down slowly in my peripheral vision.

It was a question of assembling a box. I couldn't see how it would fasten, until a passing sound waved my ear into a toy straw. I would invent a straw to drink through at a distance, and to change shape! But those were moments when owners had blocked the straw with flagging postulates, and heaved stumbling fatuous landmines onto gremlins whose caves were wet, not the second cycle of the moon after E-Coy whose germinator is the shift to AgoVa on the Tarde system. How to put the box together?

I could garden the ingredients, but it would take weeks for the androgyne to germinate while the antiquated postulates smothered my crown, and I had granaries on my belt returning the continent to squash. With one breath, I turned myself into a saloon for chance encounters and erotic ambience, without missing a beat on the Richter scale.

We found a new space on the outskirts of town and acquired green ponies to guard it. It was named after a rare, even unknown flower. I talked to the ponies at night after others climbed the trees to sleep. They eventually convinced me of the need to invent many appearing time-sensitives. I did so.

Back in time we went! It was always a different moon cycle when we arrived. I could control the surface of the lake by blinking. My friends were below. I need only breathe through a stick once more, to sink with a leaf wrapped round my stone, and discover their chamber. The appearing time-sensitives came with me. Something clung to my foot. This was the map to the real spot! I saw it on the back of my eyelids at 'commute time.' The map crawled inside my feet when exposed to the fading sun.

I took the key from the lake with great difficulty and gave it to a cat. Some solar eclipse later, when the moon wore nothing, I dropped the key during a car chase, and I was nearly crushed. I picked it up with the help of a leopard. In the other direction, the trees were all over the street — they had overgrown everything, and my friends lived in them. I couldn't believe what happened to our neighborhood. It was a long, long time ago, but I'll always hold it in my mouth. I'll eat nothing else.

Andrew Torch

THE STRANGE CASE OF CAPTAIN PIE AND NINE

The stench from the roasting festival still lingered in the thick humid air, while angry mobs on every other corner talked of the imminent rally. Finally, a plan of action with citizens united. You could hear the low hum of the people that had started to gather in Sector 8 Park from miles away. Before the tall sector walls were erected it was once an open refuge for stalkers, nightwalkers, saxophone players and priests doing lewd acts behind bushes; now it was no more than a unkempt wasteland between sectors seven, eight and nine. When the moon was high, young resistance fighters plotted and schemed in one of the many caves with only the bats to witness their treachery.

Behind a large dying sycamore tree, a haggard middle-aged man by the name of Captain Harold Pie readied himself for a battle as he reached into his overcoat for a cigarette and a snort of coke. Pie was never harassed leaving sector eight, the only benefit of his previous status. He felt he owed a debt to the people for some of his past actions, which he performed in the name of law enforcement. Although many times he had been in similar situations, he had an aching frenzy of anticipation and fear by the time he reached the second tree-lined hill. Shrill voices still echoed in his head from too many days in the sector and no drugs were strong enough to overcome them anymore. Slowly he gathered himself, re-checked his revolver for about the ninth time in ten minutes and noticed the gaunt poet Veronique had stumbled to the front of the large assembly. The hillside of brown dying grass and weeds mirrored the souls of the people on it that day. Veronique dropped the microphone in the middle of reciting a poem by Brecht but slowly regained her composure as the masses listened intently, waving their fists in the air. Her voice carried throughout the whole park and beyond, maybe even to the sea, on the crisp winter day with few withered leaves to offer as a buffer. In hindsight, the hobbled PA system was an idiotic idea by a well-intentioned malcontent who would probably never forgive himself for bringing so much attention to the poet that day. The volume, feedback and sheer number of people that transferred out of various sectors in such a short period, on a Monday afternoon nonetheless, had certainly alerted all of the sector wardens within earshot.

As expected, within minutes troopers darted into the crowd and piercing shots rang out. Veronique slumped over the podium in an ever-increasing pool of blood. Pie drew his revolver and determined where the first sniper was perched; two quick shots by Pie produced a black-clad trooper falling in a bunch from the tree as thousands scattered in pandemonium. A quick turn to the left and Pie sprinted back to the park entrance and eventually towards the security gate where the guard didn't even ask for his pass. About four or five panicked women rushed past Pie, quickly flashing their passes while multiple rounds of gunfire were heard from the park. The bemused but unmotivated and under-paid gate guard drifted back to his newspaper and beer. The last girl who darted through the gate was a nine-finger, who probably used a stolen pass to get into sector eight. She had distinctive short-bobbed black hair, black go-go boots and a very small frame with plenty of scars, which made one ponder her lurid history. Pie watched her linger around the old stone church steps, the only official sanctuary in the sector, in case the troopers decided to question her un-familiar face. She exchanged a brief smile and a wink at Pie but before she disappeared behind the gothic church she shouted, "Roses have long since faced death!"

Pie bounded up the wooden stairs in his apartment three at a time and locked the door behind him while he tossed the revolver under a loose floorboard. Sadly, the day went exactly as he envisioned; a squashed protest like all the others, a militant poet killed and dozens of innocent folks maimed or slaughtered in the name of containment. It had become an annual event after the roasting festival. The most crucial and unexpected blow for Pie was that the poet killed was a close friend and former lover who used words like others used weapons. The killing of the trooper bothered him little but it brought a great furor and a new crackdown against the walled city; maybe it was an acceptable trade-off for the life of a friend, he thought. The next morning's official sector news rag condemned the killing of the trooper in a bold masthead and declared that a street would be named in his honor, the reward one got these days for killing un-armed civilians. Page two of the pulp decreed a seven o'clock curfew for everyone and coldly printed the names of the dozen or so residents killed for being 'hostile towards the government,' with the location of burial assigned to 'Sector 8 Potter's Field.' It went on to warn: "no visitation, mourners shot on sight."

Rarely did anyone follow or question Pie because of his once good standing in sector eight. His generous bribes to the guards always bought him that extra invisibility that usually only shadows at night enjoyed. A soft knock at his door prompted him to grab the gun from under the floorboard as he reached for two more hollow-point bullets to refill the chambers. The nine-fingered girl from the park was panting on the other side in a scared drug-induced manner. Pie cracked the door slightly and asked if she was followed. She retorted that she came up the fire escape in the back and was alone, hungry and looking for a safe place to spend the night; a common junkie line that Pie had heard several hundred times before and yet usually succumbed to when it was voiced by the beautiful ones. As she entered into his small and antiquated apartment, a still tender scab on the nub of her pinky-finger revealed her recent venture into profiteering. The black market of fingers had grown at an alarming rate, which the government statisticians had not even predicted. They underestimated the recklessness of desperate people. Certain microchips inserted into a finger would allow you into various sectors within the walled-city, only a single sector, eight, had a 'no chip' designation as most of the residents were at one time friendly to the government; either former cops, front-linesmen, retired guards, brain-scrubbers and the like. The access to particular fingers was essential for survival in the post-chip era.

The nine-fingered's drug of choice was a street version of Duvoxadriene, commonly called the Vox. When cut with a few other chemicals it became a cheap relaxing high for most junkies. It was the drug once used by the government in the drinking water to curb the anxiety of the masses during the building of the sector walls and eventual microchipping program, the program that led to Pie's downfall. Her real name was Browny, but much to her dismay, Pie insisted on calling her Nine. She asked if she could call him Harry or Fur, and with a twisted smile, he said only when he was inside of her. She seemed embarrassed about her finger situation and refused to talk about her past. She made only short poetic quips and let her body movement convey the rest. Pie told her he did not care about the lack of digits but asked if she would stay and dream with him awhile. They split a pint of scotch and the rest of her vial of Vox, which was too much for the little girl as she promptly passed out. He stumbled to the bed where Nine was strewn across half of it, and entered a light sleep filled with disturbing nightmares. Thousands of pigs running in the streets, old men casting spells, fingers on assembly lines, miners picking away at the earth, which turned into children's heads, people morphing into animals and flowers melting from the moonlight. The last dream he remembered before waking was of Veronique being gunned down at the podium as he molested her from behind. Both of them were covered in blood when a ghostly Veronique reached for his gun and shot him in the head. He could not shake the image even after he realized it had been a dream. Convulsive passion that did not end with death was no passion at all, he mused.

A black and yellow mound of what looked like eggs was now setting next to the bed on the small makeshift kitchen table. Nine, standing stark naked at the stove was fidgeting with a pan that appeared to be on fire. For the first time he noticed the large scar that went down the back of her neck to the top of her shapely ass. A wonderful reminder of the first sector war and subsequent torture of some citizens after the chip program was announced. Not really wanting to deal with the memories of his former occupation, he opened another bottle of scotch and proceeded to down it while Nine tried to douse the growing fire in the pan that almost licked her short hair. Black eggs and scotch, breakfast of champions, he muttered.

Nine had thrown the pan in the toilet to squelch the fire, and

tried to compose herself again. She asked what his nightmare was about but he ignored her. He tried to chew the blackened eggs but found it impossible and wondered if a future life with Nine would be one tumultuous event after another. She teased him by saying she had a rather pleasant dream, the kind that made you believe in magic. Pie asked her for the details and she eagerly replied with a grin that during the rally yesterday Veronique had shot him between the eyes. Unable to explain how they had the same dream, he became enraged as he grabbed for the plate of eggs. Before she even had a chance to respond, he had thrown the plate across the room, hitting her squarely in the temple and knocking her unconscious. A mound of burnt eggs and a poor girl lay slightly jiggling on the floor. He squirted both of them with some ketchup just to put a fine point on the situation as he laughed his ass off. He downed another bottle, the last one in the apartment, turned the music up to a deafening level and drifted back to sleep. Several hours passed as Nine lay on the floor with eggs and ketchup slopped all over her beautiful but thin naked body. He was slightly aroused but mostly just amused with his living ready-made. Each hour, he added a new ingredient on top of her, first some pepper, than some salt on her closed eyelids, a fist full of peanut butter, which he plastered from her landing strip to her throat in the shape of an ancient triple spiral and eventually a large leafy sprig of parsley inside of her. No clocks had survived to reconcile the time that had passed during his stupor and the human-collage adventure so he lit a joint, sat back and remained mesmerized by Nine, now covered with what little food he had left in the apartment. He emptied the rest of the fridge on her, poured a half bottle of pancake syrup across her chest and then showered her body with various condiments. Maybe seven or eight hours passed, the sun started to slowly creep over the surrounding tenements when Nine suddenly shook and awoke with thrashing like a junkie, spitting and coughing and complaining of salt in her eyes. Eggs, salt and ketchup flew like confetti off her body, which stained the few pathetic pieces of furniture remaining in the room. She slowly looked at him, scooped some of the peanut butter and syrup mixture with her hand, and promptly devoured it. She removed the parsley from inside her, glared at him again, licked it slowly and ate it, and calmly stated: "All good things must come to an end."

Pie's food collage did not seem to bother her much until the salt started burning her eyes. In a delayed reaction, she screamed at the top of her lungs and picked up the iron skillet; with a smooth side-armed fling, she hurled it at Pie missing his head by about two inches but smashing the glass aquarium on the far wall, the only thing beautiful in the apartment. Water, fish, multi-colored gravel and funny fake trees poured forth and covered the bed, the floor and Nine. She screamed with delight and said, "Fish for me, fish for you, one in the mouth, one in the shoe." As she laid on the floor the water from the enormous aquarium washed over her with a splendid scene of large black and blue striped fish, sea horses and red coral attaching themselves to her sticky peanut buttery-syrup covered body. A small starfish gently lodged on the top of one of her erect nipples and again she screamed with delight or maybe derangement now, Pie was no longer sure. He unnecessarily jabbed her one more time, reminding her she had burnt the eggs and needed to conjure something up for dinner. She said that she would be the buffet and was open for business. The hot sun streamed into the apartment and baked the food menagerie upon her body as he took her up on her offer.

Many days went by, and then weeks and months as the two lingered in the stale apartment, trading off days of sex and fighting depending on their moods. They heard random cries for help and gunshots from somewhere in sector eight or maybe the park, forcing them rarely to go out at night. Even though Pie could usually bypass a guard or two, outside of eight his power diminished greatly. Nine suggested that they cut through the park during the solar eclipse and enter sector seven where her uncle had been working on a haphazard plan to leave the walled-city. Sector seven had gained a new reputation as a "problematic sector." It was also known as the mental ward sector; when the mental hospitals and clinics were closed almost all of the patients ended up there along with a few naïve doctors and nurses who could not bear to watch them suffer. A month before Veronique was killed, two young men in seven used a crude ultralight plane to circumvent the border guards. As they reached the edge of the sea, a small surface to air missile obliterated them. There weren't even enough fragments found to fill a tiny cremation urn for a burial. The official sector rags called it "missing at sea, eaten by sharks." Since most residents of seven only heard the explosion but did not witness the after-curfew event, some conjured up wild stories and rumors. The most disturbed residents committed "death by border guard" as they rushed the walls and gates. Yet others waited for the two young men to come back in a great airship and take them over the wall. The excessive show of force on the behalf of the border guards stifled most other escape attempts by those that knew the truth and were of sound mind. It was almost a mute point, as Nine could not enter sector seven without a designated chip, she could not even get an hour pass to visit a family member. The lack of her finger would raise enough suspicion to get her imprisoned for about five to ten years. The underground finger market seemed like the only viable option that remained if they could actually find a sector seven finger and a competent underground doc to do a pseudo-reattachment; at least enough to fool the lowly gate guards. One of the tabloid-like sector papers relayed a planted story of some disturbed sector seven finger salesmen who raided the last remaining zoo and chopped off all the monkeys and apes' fingers they could find to sell them on the black market, not realizing they were never microchipped. These fictional stories were widely reported by the government tabloids to cheer up the masses in the other sectors. Seven was the whipping boy of all the sectors.

Although the black market was a dicey proposition before the recent crackdown, now it was Russian roulette. Several intermediaries and two customers were burned at the stake last year during the great marshmallow-roasting festival.

"You just can't make s'mores out of that," replied Nine when told of the depressing situation.

"No, I guess you can't," Pie replied and then chided her for missing the point.

The realization that they had little of value in which to buy a finger hit both of them rather hard. His gun, her scarred body and a few bucks of hush money that came in every month due to his former occupation, were all that remained. This meager amount of money they consistently drank away. He was sure Nine had been in similar positions before but to destroy her even more seemed cruel, even to Pie. Not that he hadn't considered it more than once. As they continued to have almost the same dreams night after night, he believed she might have placed a curse on him. A junkie with a background in voodoo, how apt thought Pie. Only when the liquor ran low at the end of the month did she resort to begging on the corner for loose change, occasionally baring her breasts for an extra buck from the priests but always wearing gloves to hide her fingers. Dressed in the most ragged of clothes along with a misshapen straw hat, she blended in well with the other bums and beggars. Pie, now advanced in age, was too paranoid to take the kind of chances that had once made him a hero, and Nine had become uninterested and silent when he spoke of escaping the walled city. She later told him that one of the young men killed in the sector seven airplane escape was her brother. A decision to stay in sector eight might have permitted them a life of passion together but always amidst constant fear and poverty. The journey to find a finger likely meant capture, and capture meant an uncomfortable front row seat during the next marshmallow festival.

Only the third option of suicide remained. Nine was well versed in this as she had tried seven times and failed miserably at all of them, one more comical than the next. Her track record remained, while on a recent hot steamy night, she tried to throw herself off Pie's balcony, only to soon realize there was a large cloth awning below, which gently rolled her down to about six feet from the ground. She had forgotten Pie's apartment was only on the second floor. This was great entertainment for Pie, his attitude changed dramatically after each one of her botched attempts, giving him a reason to live if only to enjoy prolonged bouts of laughter for the first time in his life. Even in a desperate struggle to die, only the lucky were allowed to do so.

J.Karl Bogartte

THE TENDERNESS OF THIEVES

"It was a ghostly presence that gave the glass vessels their deep red glow, and made them sirens in their flight through ashes." Paracelsus

The major aspects of any particular realignment of space and time, which evolves out of a common everyday reality, have less to do with perception than with the intensity of transparency. Not that perception is lacking in any way, or peripheral, but instinctively changes its shape and its position according to, and because of the process of becoming transparent; it must, and is therefore imperative, otherwise the transition would be impossible to detect. I kiss you and can feel on your lips the sense of your fading...

You were always evasive, and your mysterious movements had reached a state of unsettling contradiction. One had the sense of your being wrapped in the proverbial plumage of déjà vu, startled in the midst of intrigue, in the middle of a question just moments before the answer is revealed in the tidal wave of another's somnambulant dance... unusual activities which seemed to be only partially present, as if something fundamental was occurring somewhere else.

Neither you nor the others were in disguise, yet no one resembled themselves. The mixture of art and artifice was of no consideration, and it was neither here nor there... only the exact amount of presence and absence could fuel the fires of reality, and the knowledge of movement was paramount. You were neither a witch, nor a sorcerer, and because your gestures were superb, you resembled them both. Your image glowed in the dark, and spoke in circles...

The specifications are as precise as anything you have or could have asked for. The works have been fiddled with to an extreme never imagined before, the gears altered, fluids distilled to their extremes and almost lost, and the pigments allowed such a tenderness of the most violent grinding, that even I myself faced an excitement unheard of amongst the gamblers and the acrobats...

Multiple vessels of light are configured within a séance of movement, and there were as many levels as the facets of a diamond in a confluence of savage beasts. This is your glow that tilts the surface, smashes the darkness-device of a singular entrance, a lost coat, a sibylline rose, the curious ratio of a glance and the bride of time dipped in mercury.

I recall your image, and often speak of it as one speaks of an ailment, or a magical fiction, embellished with every sense and nuance of ancient tragedy. Madame X was neither a reality nor an illusion, and her lover was obsessed with numerous identities; together they ceased to exist. Their quest, amongst themselves, was often a source of horrendous speculation, and it usually bordered on the edges of truth, yet without realization. You were the closest of their friends, without ever having met them, and knowing that truth, you always demurred from betrayal of even the most obvious of glimmers. I always pretended ignorance, which was my peculiar manner of existing at that moment, and I knew that in spite of it, you imagined that I was, indeed, her lover, but never even hinted at it. For that, I placed a prize on your head, and a moveable diagram beneath your feet. I knew you were a seer of the highest degree, and could count on your discretion... for it was always you who tended the gates, poured the oils and kept the oracles afloat.

Among the most nefarious systems of speculation which passed secretly around the different schools some years ago, was the one which seems to have been almost lovingly referred to as the

Sub Rosa Triangle, and which garnered the most effulgent, yet most mysteriously guarded discourse. More exotic and more dangerous even than the noble arts of alchemy, it was shared mainly by word of mouth, an explication of such priceless value that it was never committed to paper.

"Every shadow suggests another dimension, another being other than yourself..."

"It is not so much the bodies of lovers, but their reflections when they are released from them..."

Now obviously, as the whisper heard 'round the room, by the time the secret is at last spoken it had become something else, perhaps even more baffling, or more useless. Madame X knew the whole text by heart and could often be heard speaking it, although quite often in another language. Her eyes would widen and the love rose entangled on her lips... the scent of almonds would fill the room and her lover would appear beside her, as if from out of nowhere.

"The closer to death one comes, the more transparent does the body begin to grow, until one simply vanishes..." was one that I heard just last evening, which evoked such a storm outside, that I feared for our safety! But she stopped whispering, and all became calm quite instantly. When I asked her about the occurrence, she smiled and said: "Sometimes the words do indeed wreak havoc on the nature of things. The psyche is involved in regulating the weather, and often times the very air we breathe is more closely connected to the actual shape and consistency of the body than one might imagine."

You think perhaps I am making this up, but I assure you that fiction is indeed stranger than truth. Furthermore, I was never the secret lover of Madame X... Oh, I assisted her in her endeavors, yes, and was often at her side, but her pleasure was never mine, nor would she summon me to the ends of the earth. I merely listened to her recite the sibylline words of the Triangular Rose, and finally, out of desperation, committed them to paper. I was her last will and testament...

Madame X was fading, becoming ever so, almost impercep-tively transparent, and one day I knew without question that the silken sheets would suddenly fall down around what once was her, that all the leaves in one moment scattered in a ring around a treeless space, or the shimmering knife falling to the floor without even the tender trace of blood that had already vanished, and with the blink of an eye, nothing but the memory of a source would remain, a haunting departure that never fails to unsettle the faint of heart. Yes, she would be gone!

But one might assume that none of this had really taken place, that even now, after so many debacles had succeeded in more lively escapades, more daring romances and encounters, and yes, it was all so long ago I barely remember it. Like a mythology it had taken on a life of its own, and was soon consigned to some cherished and distant past, a mere pearl of its former importance. Yet, a pearl, nonetheless...

The great psychological wheel bearing the gifts of unforeseen embraces, was not a simple matter in the sense of talismans or analogies, or even of sinister weddings and other such revelations of an evening stroll, but an instance of rattling horns more locomotive than even crystal, more liquid than either blood or fire. You were always agreeable to that, and yet you took a slightly different route — you chose not to remember.

"The reflection you think is your own is really the presence of another who desires to imitate you, and then replace you with a more evolved sense of direction..."

Meanwhile, Madame X, according to the legend, had become a ruby in the center of the city and continued to send out her messages that, in their utter simplicity, resembled the precious black ermines that flowered in the main arteries of the wind. Her lover also dissolved... in the phases of the moon he passed unnoticed like a new species of thought that insinuated itself into the everyday dialogue of countless passersby. Lethargy was replaced with obsessive wandering. The messages were like old radio broadcasts that crackled and often broke up in mid-sentence. One could even hear the band still playing inside, through the garden, across the terrace and out over the lake.

One evening, almost three years ago, you came to me breathless and beside yourself — I remember it well, since it was the very same day the assassins took shelter in the Grand Council room, and unleashed the visions that would lead everyone astray. Their hallucinating machine was the newest version, and calculated to correspond to the sudden, countless vagaries of secret yearnings. You seemed distant and preoccupied, and stopped every so often to look around and behind you, and all you could mutter was "I can see you, I can see you..." until I grasped you by the shoulders and shook you.

You stopped, looked fiercely into my eyes and said "I saw her today, and she was real! You are real! The fact that I am still alive is because of the golden pebbles that reflect the light of my breath... across the entire universe! It is wonderful!" No one saw you again after that, for many years, although rumors now and then placed you in many different places, in many different guises. But I knew you were on a quest, and I understood...

For the moment, there was nothing unusual about the manner in which those assassins would imitate the acrobats, nor was there reason to believe these flamboyant shadows (for they were always shadows, even if they most resembled the reflections of light in water) were any less limber, or sinister in their movements than the memory of lovers after their exploits — in their exhaustion they were more closely aligned with the Pleiades than with the bed that bore their bodies through the empty streets...

Theirs was a life of uncertainty, of appearances and disappearances that were more often than not unexpectedly analogous to your life. I remember you, and consider your presence in relation to everything that had transpired up to this moment. The assassins had dispersed along the main vanishing points of the compass, and they had taken the tides with them. Now only wolves paced back and forth in the assembly rooms. Second sight had become the only means of communication, breaths were deciphered for clues, and cocoons were spun for prophecy. The radio messages returned:

"Desire gives birth to transparency..."

"A species of light touches you only once, and you begin to fade..."

The words were furiously debated, and the seal was broken by those who were gathered under the circle of indigo in the Great Hall where the conference of sinister conjurers unraveled the muses. The analogists and amalgamates were alarmed, and as always the wind moves the shadows in the room according to their desires. But the one who would unveil the glow with an uncanny feline grace, play with knives the way one trembles in the moonlight, she was the sylvian fissure and the final passage through the major dreams of the hunter.

The emerald flytrap, the whispering cats-cradle, the final mystery wrapped up in the sadistic fleece that would one day soon carry the spider web of your starlit reflection deep into the humming masquerade of shadows.

Reflection would bathe with shadow, and shadow seek the flesh of reflection, and the lost abilities of passing through the landscape of their transmutation with the greatest of ease, would bring the superior glow of recognition squarely into focus.

The amalgamates realized this and understood the danger, and then with swift cunning set up the dreaming machinery to prevent "the one who would unveil the glow" from remaining in a state of grace. They toyed with her visions, and attempted to unravel her veils with a suddenness never expected. They placed the checkmate of delirium in the center of the room, and danced like reindeer dipped in candlelight.

But the "sylvian fissure," the loved one of the hunter, was more fierce than either child-birth or forest fire... she was the one who eventually tipped the scales in favor of all those natural phenomena that exist because of us, that exude from inside and expressed outside, lighting up the world around us... or darkening it.

She was more future than present, more reflection than shadow, and given the circumstances of her passion for gambling, she was often following the slightest whim, however fleeting. Her visions were as good as gold. She always made maps of her peregrinations, lovingly detailed with even the slightest of distractions... the way sunlight came through the veils, like warm kisses; the way each phase of the moon always reminded her of those almost owl-like strikes, in mid-air, when she embraced her lovers, one by one; the way her sense of navigation always took her around in a circle, before doubling back into the center of things. She was a muse, enchanted and lethal, and at the heart of things she was the spinning-wheel of chance.

She stood her ground, like a tumultuous scaffolding, and in that respect, reminded me of Madame X when she talked in her sleep...

"In the book of fables, the visions are expelled from the womb like birds of fire spinning the solutions of the landscape that pulls you outward, spreads the glimmering pigments of your occult root system with the trowel of moonlight. The Diviner disrupts the moral law simply by dancing. The dream recurs and the theatre wakes from its mirror. The circle multiplies..."

"The lunar solution mixed, conjured and aroused in its unreasonable coupling with the solar complex, under the raven's dark fire, and over the bright salamander's sinister reflection, more real than flesh over stark white ashes... the ablutions mirror the nuptials, and the water of desire opens the lock..."

There was apparently no turning back, and who would wish such a decision? Who would risk it? When the light comes in with its

brooding sentinels, and seduces the open doorways, everyone would gather for the feast of this enchanted one "who would unveil the glow..." and taste the eddies and flow of her eyes, as they closed the doors with utterly silent flashes of great wing-laden sighs; the eyes of rain just moments before disaster, and the eyes of hammered anvils when the sparks took your breath away... She felt only tenderness for the ones who lost themselves in reverie, that stalked her even in her dreams, offered her the keys to their intuitions and longing. "The keys of the moth..." she whispered, and then disappeared through her veils, like a tiny sphinx chased by tiny swordsmen dressed all in black.

She unleveled the lunar moths of her thoroughly disrespectful approach to mayhem and pleasure, and would hunt at noon, in broad daylight. She flows like a river of light through your shadow and all the other shadows that know you. Traced by the mummies of unreason, her sex would shimmer the way certain mushrooms sent echoes out of memories that never occurred. She listened to the orchids of her bodice, and hummingbirds would pass through the elemental fire of her hunger when provoked, when turned into tiny galaxies that glistened on her teeth when she lowered herself to feed.

The analogists had given up all thought of ever explaining to anyone's satisfaction the solution to the identities of all who had come to pose for that final portrait. Yes, the real reason we had all agreed to meet. No one would remember anyways, and the children had no idea what all the fuss was about. An old woman, still beautiful beyond reason, who no longer could be found, was expected to arrive within the hour, with her lover, the one who most resembled that boatman in Venice one never forgets... you remember? The budding thespian? The one they found murdered not long after your arrival... after he ferried you across? It caused quite a scandal...

But, yes, the old woman who was no one's twin, and her lover, the blind cryptographer who never spoke, and never complained of the distance between them... That was a very long time ago, and no one knew about it, until now anyway, and even so it would be hard to prove.

It might even have been a fiction, a figment of one's imagination... Like this meeting, this conference of transparent people, this unusual gathering for a portrait, which also took place so many years ago...

One can see the city, through the forest, through the fog of several centuries like those lovers, dreaming in the same position that the tiger takes when its last paw leaves the edge of the rampart, and finds itself between stone and warm flesh, glowing in the darkness of its flight. It was this animal, above all others, that signaled for them the illusion of grace. With great fanfare, it announced the underlying proportions that kept the mysterious woman connected to the fog, and her lover bound to the shimmering heat of the forest, and in this, the city took from them its dark pigments and solutions, its moist and shining fur, its claws and fangs, and through the ages became the blur of the hunter and the myth of the stars in the taste of blood.

They had gathered, these victims of transparency, one last time, and knew that not even death, that most abundant of fictions, would be strong enough to keep them apart. The photograph was staged, down to the minutest details, with nothing out of place or wanting for anything less.

Mirrors had been set up to capture the passage of time, and aligned with the whispering manikins, set up in rows of twelve, in very exact circles, and having taken the twelve months into consideration, the whole thing resembled some disheveled flying machine more in tune with the mating rituals of albino peacocks, and wired to the astrological heart-rending fuse... It was a female solution, beyond a shadow of doubt, thoroughly mixed and cajoled into assuming a goddess-like position, replete with the morning dew for eyes, and bees humming incessantly like a lost language on the very tip of the tongue. It had become more dangerous than any weapon.

The hounds were released, and in their ghostly clamoring resembled phantom ships from the 17th century still battling the fierce storms, and they shone like emeralds in the dark, illumined only by the scent of brides and glowing daughters, and the vague smell of old manuscripts.

But the howling intensified the proceedings, and the long coats that came flying in from the forest at all hours, created a most fantastic sense of foreboding and morphological splendor.

"In transparency there is only the rustling of the wind, the vague sensation of having been somewhere, for some reason, and not remembering..."

A flight map of the most sensuous proportions was making the rounds, and one suspected that it was more parable than actual fact, and yet when landing, the flying machine swooped down over the field of swans like the bodice of an excited woman, bright chartreuse and divided by loving glances that ran together like the strings of a violin chased by echoes and hungry virgins, to orchestrate the most perfect landing. The analogists were flapping their arms in blatant imitation, while the leading lady adjusted her reading glasses and even squinted at the proceedings like one who relished the cries of exquisite tortures. Even the Carthusian monks, who were considered the bravest of all the religious orders, refused to partake of the marvelous secretions garnered from this occurrence. They sent, instead, a young gardener to intervene, who, unfortunately, harbored a secret desire for the most far-fetched of solutions.

It has been repeated in many different languages, over the course of many years, that the frightful event which took place that day, in a small town just outside of Madrid, was just too unbelievable to be true and, to complicate matters even more, occurred in the midst of a total eclipse. The lines of divination sputtering out of control kept everyone on their toes, and the slender arcs which lift consciousness above water and out of the woods, had crystallized in the astronomer's most subversive dive: The Golden Scissors, which had baffled scientists for years until they finally gave up, unfurled against a wall of ferocious apes. Hidden by fireflies and guarded by knife throwers, this superlative movement was a geomancers' dream, and a swimmer's delight... a treasure that perhaps came closest to the gist of Madame X's endless babbling.

At the apex of this famous dive, which looks out over the Northern Lights as they cascade down the beekeeper's passion for his bees, there is the dimension of lost objects and forgotten memories, and the moment of recovery, from waking, which always rings a bell as brilliant and tumultuous as an act of arson in the vagueness of the midnight sun. The three pivotal guiding points for the realization of this magical dive are:

1. The lighthouse of a lingering glance with an exit for sudden departures, is enough for the slave girls to shed their orchids for the wind.

2. Revenge upon all things is only for the pure of heart — guided by that enchanted timepiece of farewell kisses released from their cocoons.

3. The trickster's red rose of oneirism is more invasive than the most famous of Tarot readings and twice as revealing.

It was a day and an evening unlike any other, and from the very beginning even the Russian Princess could hardly contain herself, so predisposed as she was to flamboyant acts of desire, she had released the diving bell long before dawn came in through the revolvers of that serene fondling so reminiscent of the dream that was not a dream, or the embrace that was not... and each in turn affecting the other. Through the mussel shells of her cinematic eyes she could see the future, and mimed it with her phantom serenades, pulling swords out of irreconcilable differences when the morning rain settled in, ignited by African eyelids swooping down like great parachutes. But it was when she kissed that trickster's enigmatic rose that a new language filled the air with roots of demonic discourse.

"Ojibwa, Ojibwa!" she shouted with absolute glee, and turned to run down the outer hallway, followed by her attendants...

When reflections are released from their mirrors, and exist as a new species of thought-provoking sparks, slender and fearless, wandering off in search of shadows like windows only half visible under the sensory branches of intuition, and glowing leaves speaking in tongues.

"It still remains a mystery," you reminded me, and when I read those words in your notebook, I lost all sense of time thinking about it. "There are reasons for the rendezvous of reflection and shadow," you said to me, "and even though it was once believed that the moon and the sun were involved, like the body and the mirror, it has now been substantially verified that some things exist independently of any origin. I am haunted by this and beside myself with the greatest anticipation..."

Meanwhile, the gamblers were betting on the Princess — although it was a toss up between her and Madame X's daughter, the so-called sylvian fissure, *the one who would unveil the glow*, and the stakes were high, bordering on lunacy... The dice were thrown into the water, bones were ground into a spyglass for seeing the physical body of time, a hawk into a lantern, light into stone, aurora into breath, animal into endless caresses, rain into blood, sight into spores dreaming in the wet grass, and for the touch of a lover, in whose *caustique* can be seen the hurricane and the knowledge of insatiable hunger, white wolves came to bathe in the iron red pool of consciousness.

Costumes came out of the sea, and helmets followed suits that shook and quivered like new-born birds of prey, and in the spirit of disorder a new game was invented that did not resemble chess at all, nor even come close to the old ideas of what a game consisted of, although it did resemble the Middle Ages and filled the room with smoke. The golden lizards that waltzed around a pool of inspired thoughts became swift and furious. Many guests were already sleeping, and great stags filled the rooms with the rattling of horns, and the crying of foxes in a valley more silent and splendid than the Grand Canyon unfurled on the winding stairway. In the blink of an eye, every room looked out on the sea, which formed itself into endless arcades for the alchemists, while their designs of centrifugal forces aligned with the newest planets came in through the windows like widow's peaks and slender veils. Serpents that could hum your name proceeded to do so, and left a taste of mint in your mouth and a sense of wonder that kept you well fed and alive for centuries. None of this was questioned as everyone had gathered and ultimately posed for that well-known portrait. The last supper was served with plumes and secret gestures. September 8th became more important than the 22nd of November, and for no apparent reason. The sunlight took longer than usual to illuminate the mirrors, and the phoenix flew out of the fire twice, as twins and as lovers who departed in those early morning hours on a very quiet train to a place no one knew about. A single black horse, a naked witch from South America, three elderly gentlemen posing as wizards, dressed in dark grey suits and black fedoras, and a meteor that parted the Mojave desert…

The gates were unlocked and the dreams were dreaming their humans, while outside in the garden the act of transforming language into a weapon that incited heroic acts of treason, was buzzing incessantly and foaming with Roman numerals when the number X had vanished without a trace.

"I am often beset by fond memories of fallen chandeliers, the ones that fell in agonizingly slow motion, designed of the most outrageous minerals, and filled with the strangest mixtures of quicksilver and cobalt…" said one of the more reticent of the analogists, who spoke, for the first time. "You know the ones, loved and feared by so many, yet resplendent in their downpour, always late, always forgiven, and never missing a chance to shed light on even the most obscure of arcane details. I was once caught, in flagrante delicto, combing out the luxurious locks of a particularly fetching *lampadario* from Florence. It is not something I can recount without a sense of finality."

It was this same analogist who — alone amongst all the others, could be trusted with the secrets of the universe, and whose famous Mother was the one who smeared the flying ointment over the oracle-shaped body of Madame X, at a moment in history when such an expression of love was unheard of, and which eventually led to the discovery of a multiple series of events that would — predestined to, at some future time — trigger the shipwreck and resurrection of the wondrous Tinkering Machine... that grief-stricken but rainbow-laden invention responsible for the extraction of pollen from the backward glances of strangers and, as a curious side effect, scattering windows the length and breadth of the sleeper's nighttime dance.

Now, as everyone knows, while you yourself had magically achieved the most amazing state of anonymity, passing unnoticed through even the most abundant scenarios, those were wonderful times filled with cloaks and daggers, appearances and disappearances, and according to eye-witness accounts you were neither here nor there. Often you were seen gesturing wildly with one or more of the others, and then again, one person even saw you in the arms of one of the slave girls — but the majority of most was that you had never attended at all. This, of course, was not true, since I had spoken to you, about the future, about the genetics of time, about the uncertainty, now, of shadows moving about unhindered by their sources. You told me that "The barbarians were coming," and I suggested that for all intents and purposes, it was better not to go outside during the daytime hours. You were dealt a strange hand of three antique dealers from Prague, four ghostly hounds, and a spinning drop of pure gold. I thought it was an omen, but you said no, "only the tenderness of thieves," and played the game like one possessed.

The night seemed to last forever, going back many centuries, and many had been lost, or never looked back. The moon was a deep green vowel, and the wind that swirled around us left no stone unturned. Everyone had dispersed in the middle of the photograph, leaving only vague superstition, fading glimpses and rumors of every kind imaginable. There was revelation in the alembic boilers, burning off the molten debris and leaving only the petals of an evening gown flooded with precious stones and solar flares. Only shadows and eerie reflections remained to haunt, or to hunt...

The mist arrived in a large hand-stamped envelope, followed by the fog, which departed from the train like numerous grey felt hats spreading out in every direction. It was a phase of reality similar to the agitation that is always a precursor to the voodoo doll of longing, when it appears on the table of possibilities, cooing and clicking, and filled with the invisible writing of flickering eyelids. Stillness became apparent, sputtering and spewing out sirens and tearing up the landscape. The double exposure, the triple exposure, four times the number of directions from beginning to end, five times the brightness of silver, six and seven, etc...

In the center of the photograph was the black tree, translucent and whispering, with leaves eaten by savages; and to the left was the apparent figure of Madame X and her lover, under layers of noon and midnight, equally present, and feathered at the edges but still recognizable as a disturbance in several different countries, like a bath that lasts forever. In the foreground, brilliantly orchestrated assassinations seemed to have lighted the fuses of luminous bodies in the process of passing through each other, touching briefly, blurring and disappearing (hands full of sparks burning the air) almost as if to illustrate that last frantic kiss before closing the door to the taxi and the lover one may never see again.

The gamblers were on the right hand side, having won every last chance, and the acrobats, seen through them, but further back, were the first to depart through the mirror of the mysteries. Those seated at the main table were only a gentle swaying motion, and remained forever touched by the subtle anarchy of the uninterrupted gaze.

The last to leave had been the analogists, followed by the amalgamates, and yet their sparkling pigments and solutions left a lingering taste in the air, like ghosts without shadows, in that city of forgers and beekeepers casting immeasurable desires on the nature of eroticism and illusion… only the black velvet gloves gave shape to the past, and they lay there empty on the ground, humming to themselves, and flapping like butterflies.

"Transparency is the tattoo of organ grinders who have hopped, skipped and jumped in the mirror of darkness…"

Xtian

THREE PERHAPS FICTIONAL DAYS

ZERO.
THE DAY BEFORE

Dec., 1999

> *"Men and women will ascend to the fourth vibratory plane and
> Homo sapiens will become Homo spiritualis. "*

— black + white magazine. No.36. p21. 1999.

a few years later . . .

ONE.
DAY ONE

> *"I didn't want to die – I just didn't want to live."*
> *— anonymous suicidal teenager*

Nobody knows who was the first one to submit to it. We'd like
to know, sure, also who dreamt it up or is running it, after all, there's
got to be someone behind it, someone who pulls the strings and runs
the whole show, making sure the word gets out — despite the official

stance of misinformation and silence — and that those interested always find their way to it...

The number of victims is not known, mainly because the government(s) won't say how many there are. Officially they never even talk of it, except when we see the ads on TV to ask for information, *do not let this happen to your loved ones, if you know anything, blah-blah-blah...*

The "victims" as they call them can be seen in the streets, and at first no-one actually paid attention to them — its not unusual to see some demented soul wandering the streets, pissing his pants or dribbling or what have you. But then the number of them increased, and what we did notice was the way they were dressed — which was *well*. In fine suits, or sometimes fashionable outfits, good clothes in general, not like demented bums, but *well-dressed* demented bums.

And of course there were the reports on the news, with grieving people sitting next to hospital beds and so on, weeping and holding the hands of these strange looking men and women — *who have all been lobotomised*. When I say "lobotomized," I mean they had some kind of brain surgery done on them, some kind of surgery that made them ... it made them into sort of zombies I guess, just thoughtless, smiling people who wandered the streets, said nothing, did nothing, and other than taking food from wherever they found it, did nothing else. Didn't talk, didn't interact, oblivious to everything around them (a few got hit by cars and died or ended up in hospitals, but that was a bit later, when there were more of them and we slacked off in picking them up), just walked around and smiled in their own withdrawn insane kind of way. Pissed their pants. Couldn't care less. Bled into them (the women), couldn't care less. Oh yes, they stink — despite their nice clothes, they stink.

No time at all there were TV reports on all these nice everyday people who came from fairly ordinary backgrounds (some white collar, some blue, some better paid, some not — there really was nothing they had in common it seemed — *it seemed*), ordinary folk who'd gone off to work like any other day, only to never come home and be found wandering the streets a few days later, still wearing the same clothes, but no longer themselves. Hollow-eyed, seemingly happy inside in that idiot-savant kind of way, somewhere, withdrawn.

It started in the USA, but some claim it started in Europe. (Those who hated the USA said "What'd you expect?" whilst others believed Europe's age and "wisdom" or whatever had something to do with the advanced weirdness of it all. I don't think it matters.) Again no-one knows just *where and when* it started, but the Yanks were the first to report it on TV, following which reports came in from pretty much around the world. Except Africa — which is not exactly true, later we found out they had cases there too, mostly in South Africa, but very few. The Japanese were "lagging behind" as well it seemed, but some claim their media was covering it up.

Interestingly, the whole "epidemic" seemed to be restricted to more "western" countries, and largely to white folk, but not exclusively. For example, a country like India had 100s of cases, but given their large population this was significantly low, and seemed to be not of the general, "impoverished" population. The Chinese only admitted to it after two years of denying it, the Russians too dragged their heels in acknowledging it ("What'd you expect?"), but it was all over the internet that it was happening there too.

Simply put: people — "lobotomized."

Where I got involved was with my work, we looked into it, we checked the "victims" out extensively, gave them complete medical check-ups as well as some forensic investigation, scraping under the fingernails, that kind of thing. Looking up their arses for traces of rape, etc. I can talk about it casually because its getting ridiculously routine now, their numbers are increasing, and exponentially at that, at least in this country.

I can say we're baffled by our findings, and our international pals (who are hiding just as much info as we are) have nothing to conclude either. (An International "task force" has been set-up. Bureaucrats. Woohoo.)

None of the so-called victims seem to have been violated in any way. By that I mean there are no signs of struggle, no lesions, scars, bleeding or anything that would indicate a kidnapping or an attack. Nothing — except for that scar on the temple. I can't talk about it any more detailed than that, and in reality it's not a lobotomy we're dealing with, yes it's brain damage, yes it's inflicted, but it's not the ... okay let's just say the media made up the name for it and it stuck. But back to the "victims."

Our checking up included a medical history on all of them, as well as their work history, relationships, the works. It stretched the department's resources as you can imagine, like I say the number of "victims" increases exponentially, every day we get a few of them brought in or reported. (By the way, usually once we give them the medical, they're allowed to go home, where they're looked after by relatives. Those with no relatives are put into mental hospitals, since they're completely harmless. Have I mentioned they're incapable of learning *anything*?)

So we check out the "victim's" history, and you know what we found? The one thing they had in common was this: *nothing to hang our hat on.* Again, we found these people were pretty ordinary, in fact that's what they seem to have in common, ordinariness. At first we started counting the number of them that had cancer or some other serious illness, the number that were into far-right or far-left ideologies, we grouped them by religions, perversions, you name it — but all we found was a dispersion mirroring everyday society ... What bothered me was the fact that that was the only thing they had in common: they *were* common. I put out the hypothesis that we're never going to find a famous one roaming the streets, or a rich one, but I was proven wrong within a matter of months. Actors, journalists, writers, etc, some big, some bigger (famous that is), they showed up, grinning and pissing in their pants.

I'm gonna skip ahead, because you probably know all this. Instead I'll tell you what we didn't tell the media. It's this: *there is something else they all have in common.* This is strictly off the record I guess. Our first breakthrough came within eight months of the government officially recognising the problem — the public's mood was near hysterical by then, so they had to acknowledge and "handle" it. Blah blah blah. Brainless bureaucracy to the rescue.

Then the first clue, which we dismissed at first, but then it happened again, and again and again, at random intervals, with random victims — and not just here either.

Suicide notes. We found suicide notes either at the "victim's" home or office, or wherever, and each time experts and family members would positively ID the handwriting (of those not typed of course). Seems a rather large proportion of these people were on the wrong side of some depression. Not necessarily clinical or bipolar or anything like that, but they were not happy with their lot. A lot of them complained of being stuck, of being bored, of not being challenged anymore, of being tired of their lot *as ordinary people*, they complained of their "mundane existence," blah blah blah. What united them in the first place, was in fact the common theme in their loathing or self-loathing, but they all (the ones who left notes behind) pointed out that for them suicide was not an option. But then why the note?

Again, I have to be honest it wasn't great detective work but carelessness on part of one of the victims or perhaps of the "de-brainers" (obviously there's more than one, but we're yet to catch anyone) that led us to the answer, as one of the notes we found more or less explained it all.

The note (which I'm not at liberty to copy here, nor do I have a copy of it, nor can I be arsed to get it from Central) basically outlined the man's complaints, which were a lot like the others: bored of his life, bored of his job, bored of everything, seemingly doing well materialistically, but still feeling empty (I should mention this man was aged 39 and worked in management). Had a lovely wife, two kids, dog, car, house, the usual trip, bored as fuck. THEN, he says, he found out about the Club that offered life beyond life *in this life,* alive but not. There was some esoteric/philosophical mumbo-jumbo there, about living and dying and being reborn and so on, and how to cheat life *and* death, so on and so forth. The important bit was this: membership to the Club was open only to those who have lost zest for life and wanted to end it — *but not actually die.* The Club, like some belligerent, benevolent benefactor would tell the potential member "they understood" their problems, and they "understood" that suicide, whilst tempting, was not an option; as death is not an answer, and is too permanent/scary, etc. The Club instead offered them a simpler way of "killing off" their life but *living on* in perpetual bliss, by performing a small surgery on them, "fixing" parts of their brain, so they would have no recollection of their past, nor any interference from the outside world. They guaranteed permanent bliss and a release from any form of stress or duress (even those imposed on the body itself as a function of necessity, such as pissing), and a never-ending movie called "the rest of your life" to watch, but not be participating in, or be bothered with — *ever again.*

Seems all these victims had enough "stress or duress" in their lives to see the "fixing" as a tempting option, to become a blissful zombie, dead to the world that annoyed or bored or angered them so much, but not dead to the process of life itself. Dead to the act of living though — although I personally do wonder who exactly *is* alive, and how do they know? Who is *doing* the act of living *on their terms? Who can, who is allowed?*

Ah fuck, I'm getting all philosophical. We'll skip it for now. The main thing is this: we still don't know how the "victims" are contacted, or if they seek the Club out for themselves. The public doesn't know the Club exists, at least not from the media or the government — but *somehow they obviously know,* because new ones keep turning up on the streets, blissfully withdrawn, dead but living...

And we cannot stop them.

. . . around the same time . . .

TWO.
DAY TWO

Hallowed be Thy name and blessed Thy Glory, Almighty God of Love and Rage, ruler of Earth, the Heavens and of men's hearts. Yours is the power and the kingdom forever and ever, Amen.

For so long You have spoken to me my Lord, ever since I was a child You walked with me. I have obeyed You in every respect, and have never known sin, not with men nor women, nor any of the allowable animals. I have not forgotten the poor, and I have not forgotten to keep them where they are, so the Lord's servants may forever remind the masses of Your might and power. I taught and reminded them of their place, so they would know Your place, and their place in You.

I have worked harder than any of my siblings or fellows, and have only studied the sacred teachings of the Church — Your Church. I have studied the forbidden texts and the works of the Antichrist and his followers, so I may know my enemy as well as I know myself. I have learnt the wisdoms of the esoteric, the eccentric and the erratic. I have placed no friend in my heart but You, but have embraced the wicked that I may absolve and liquidate them.

You and I have spoken at great lengths over many years at all hours and all seasons and You have told me countless times how You have chosen me to be Your instrument. I know it is by no accident that I have been chosen but by design and by Your infinite wisdom and compassion. I give praise and thanks to You for that on a daily basis and follow Your guidance and advice on every matter. Never have I gone against You, though You may have thought so, for I know Your will is perfect, but Your poor creatures are not, and so I had to sometimes "translate" Your will, so their imperfect minds could absorb the infinite. Your perfectly round peg had to be angular for they who are the square hole, and for that I humbly begged for Your forgiveness. You have never left my side, and through that I know that You have forgiven me.

When You told me of Your Great Plan, You know how frightened I became, and how I begged You to reconsider, and I wept and I pleaded and I mourned for what was to come, until mirth broke over me for I saw the shining rays of Your Divine Will and I understood. The fog You have lifted from my eyes, and replaced it with a burning flame and a rainbow of Your love.

Then I understood how Your Divine Wrath was a wrath from love.

I then understood how You no longer felt the love of Your creation, no love coming from it. It has betrayed You and mocked You enough times, and Your past scoldings were no longer heeded. You were angry, You were hurt, like a father would be when slapped in the face by his son. Yet still You loved us, but that was not enough, You and I both knew Your love would have to shine through disciplining humanity. You and I both knew it was time for Your scorn, time for Your wrath, for humanity to face it, in order to see the glory of Your love on its other side.

You have chosen me as Your instrument in this, and have guided me through the mysteries and the pitfalls, into the position of Pontiff. You have made me promise that I would act out Your word, and that Your will be done. How could I refuse You? How could I not see eye to eye with the only friend I ever had, the only one I ever shared a dream and a reality with?

So I followed your bidding, and I declared Your wrath against the world. I told them all that You were no longer the God of Love, but the God of Anger, and that we, Your servants were here to punish the wicked, and wash away the sins of the world with the blood of the innocent. No-one is innocent on this Earth, and no-one is innocent in Heaven (they have let You down with the Fall) but You, and as such the blood of the innocents is but the blood of the less-tainted. Only my blood is as clean as Yours, for You have purified me time and again through your love.

I declared Your universal anger, and I have declared the time has come. I was mocked, ridiculed and opposed on all sides, from within my camps and outside it. They have called me a madman and a heretic, but I have persevered and have won them over with Your word and my fire. It wasn't for long that I was opposed, for many have heeded the call. Even in this pit of despair that is Earth, we have found true believers and those who have also heard Your voice and would testify to Your will with intentions. We raised a mighty army we named the Wrath of God and we made allies amongst the rich and the poor, amongst all those who truly believed the punishment was due.

We followed Your plan and we fought off our detractors and enemies, and we marched upon the Holy Land to reclaim the sacred site of Your birth and to begin the mission in earnest, but it was there we have parted ways oh Lord, and I ask You now why You have forsaken me? Why leave me now when I am, when we are in the cradle of Your love, in the sacred centre of Your Earthly manifestation, when we need You the most to guide us in our actions?

Why allow our enemies to gather against us and to falsify our names and deeds, to gather in strength against us, and to strike at us with such vengeance and vehemence that we're left crippled and struggling in a wasteland amongst ruins, illness and madness? Why did You allow them to hit us with such devastating power, that the Holy Land is now neither Holy nor Land, and that we, the survivors are barely recognisable as human beings?

My Lord I ache, I hurt, I am losing my hair and I bleed, my fingernails are falling off of me and my teeth are loose. I can not contain liquids nor solids — and I am told by doctors I am one of the lucky ones, for I have survived. I accept their charity only so much as I cannot physically refuse it, I am too weak, but I curse them when I can for their wickedness which You have instructed me to eradicate. Your wrath which has come from Divine Love still burns within me as much as the fire they have poured down upon us burns all around me, and I tell You, I do not feel the strength to continue Your work...

My Lord I cannot walk Your Path of Wrath, though I know the world is now well aware of it — there are those who are continuing what we have begun, as reports come in from all around... the faithful have been striking down the sinners and returning them to You to be judged once and for all.

I fear I will leave this Earth soon without having succeeded in my calling, and soon You will judge me too, and I pray You find me worthy to be by Your side, but Lord, before I go, it is on this wicked Earth that I need to know, amongst the wicked and the dying — why did You let them beat me? Why did You let them strike us so? Was I not Your instrument?

Lord, why did You let them nuke us?

. . . a few months later . . .

THREE.
DAY THREE

Letter in the Editor's dustbin:

Cap'n Albatross of The Lunatics
Super Arcus
The Earth's Moon (Luna)

Dear Ed,

My name is John Smith, maybe it's my real name. My name is also Cap'n Albatross, and that is my "real" name. I am an Engineer, a First Engineer in fact, in The First and Last Church of the Happycalypse™. I am one of the Lunatics, and I am in charge of farming operations on the Moon. I am writing on behalf of my fellow Lunatics.

I AM NOT INSANE — do read on — what have you to lose? Time? You can't lose time — it's not yours to lose!

We have a message for you and the people of Earth, and it is this: *we are here, we are men, women and children on the Moon and we are having fun.* How's things down there? Apparently not too well...

How did we get here? We touched down in 1957, which is, yes, a good 12 years before Neil and Buzz. We came here via a Russki spaceship — in those days the Commies were leading the space-race, so naturally we asked those with the means to help us get the job done. The world post-WW2 was not to our taste, in fact America's growing role as global policeman (with Great Britain as deputy) seemed to be creating more problems than solving them. (That is not to say we were impressed with the Communist part of the globe either.) We saw bitter times ahead, and here we are a few decades on, getting dreadful transmissions from next door — from you ... But back to our brief history lesson.

Having figured the world was heading for "strange days" if not disastrous days, we made a decision to relocate ourselves. When one looks at history, there are countless examples of entire nations moving to "greener pastures" when necessary. Just look at the Goths, the Saxons, the Magyars, just to name a few examples, or even in more modern times, the Puritans landing in America, the Mormons moving to the desert to start Salt Lake City, or even the founding of Jerusalem. When people can no longer fit in — nations move. Well, we were no nation, but a group of very close and like-minded families all belonging to the Church of the Happycalypse™.

(The Happycalypse is the concept of a "happy apocalypse," whereby the End Times are a direct result of a "mass uprising," leading to a joyful erasing of the existing global order. Think of it as a New Year's Eve celebration, where you wave goodbye to the year that was, and whilst dancing madly, you bring on the next, something new, "*Something Else*." Our aim was/is "*Something Else*" — we don't know what it will be [on Earth], but we believe it'll be better, for it's what *everyone* wants. Something based not on the *pursuit of*, but the *actual living* of happiness.)

As history has shown us, mass uprisings are a messy, bloody affair, and usually end in the return of control and oppression, but under a new name. We were also terrified of a man-made Nuclear Apocalypse, which is of course power/The-End in the wrong hands. That is not what we wanted, and the Church was formed. (Here we should mention the "Church" is an acronym: Champions Halting Unctuous Reality's Crippling Hegemony.) Back in the 50s we weren't large or strong enough to achieve our goal of global Happycalypse, and we do not make that claim now either — we'll let things happen as they must, which is of course up to our members *on Earth*.

But again, we're getting side-tracked.

We came here in 1957 aboard the *Rasputin I*, named after one of our patron saints. It took months of planning and plenty of $$$, especially in bribing practically everyone involved in the project to stay quiet, "lose paperwork" and so on. You won't find any hard data to back up this story, not in the Russian archives, which is why I've attached this photo (see Att.) of our city, *Super Arcus*.

Once we landed, we got on with the task of tunneling into the rocks and creating at first a small station, then eventually our city. I won't bore you with the details (it *is* 30+ years of history after all), so I'll just skip to some of the highlights of our stay here (other than watching other Moon-landings — the last Chinese one back in '78 was really quite colourful, we haven't seen them since however):

1. A new species of human: Homo lunasis (we call ourselves "Lunatics" — a sense of humour is *everything*, we found). The Moon's gravity is 1/6th of Earth's, so our human bodies practically fly around without weights (an incredible experience, to glide with such ease over distances achieved only by long jump Olympians on Earth!). As such, largely due to environmental stimulus, and to radiation from the stars, native Moon-men and women tended to grow larger than first gen. colonists. 'Average' natives stand somewhere between 7 and 8 ft in height, and are quite muscular. Their limbs seem elongated, but they walk gracefully and effortlessly across the surface — no flying around and gliding for them — they are adapted. (On Earth they would struggle greatly to even stand.) They are quite pale due to their underexposure to the Sun, and a little hairier than "Earthlings" — it gets cold in them parts. They are of course as smart as smart can be, very curious, fun-loving and sociable — but this is due more to upbringing. They are curious about Earth, and are working on ways to get about its surface when they get here. (So far the idea of an exoskeleton seems the most feasible.)

2. Contact with aliens. Yes, contact has been made, plenty of times. Some are nice, some are bastards to put it simply. The good news in Happycalyptican terms is that some can't wait to get here and "rattle the Earthlings' cage" (to paraphrase them — they actually said *"fuck their shit up,"* not kidding!), whilst others seem keen to help us get out of the rut we (that is you) seem to be stuck in. We must point out that despite our relatively better position on the Moon, we have not been able to intercept every space-traveller, nor do we plan to stop anyone from approaching Earth. Should anything on the home-planet go akimbo, we figure we can always start again on the Moon — in fact we already have.

3. A new start. Not to brag, but yes, we have the closest thing to "perfect" society up here. We Lunatics are quite happy with our lot, and are looking into branching out onto other planets. Some readers would expect exact examples of "the perfect society," but it is a strict Happycalyptican policy to not do that. "Perfect society" is *Something Else* — and we believe you already know what that would be like. You need no instructions from us or from anyone with regards it, and besides, the one on the Moon is tailor-made for life on the Moon. "A cat knows how to be a cat, nothing more, maybe less..." (*The Kabblahblah, Book 1*)

I guess you doubt every word of my "story," but I ask you to humour me. If you look into it, you will find there *is* a global Church of the Happycalypse™, and if you look hard enough, you may even find a reference to our 1957 adventure in the American journal *Science Digest* (1958 February edition I believe). And of course there is the attached photo.

We have nothing to lose by you disbelieving us, we have a lot to gain by you ignoring us, after all, we left you, and we left you for a reason. We do not seek to return to the abuse, or to be scrutinised from every angle. Do not look for us with telescopes — you won't see us.

So why am I / are we writing to you? We were hoping you could publish this letter for your readers, and help them dream again. We do not stay in constant communication with the Earth, after all, *we have left to start again — Something Else — somewhere else*, and we're doing very well. We can not afford to let your miseries drag us down, but we can't stand to see you hurt yourselves like this anymore. We'd like to tell you there is another way — and you know what it is. We'd like to offer you, or challenge you to accept — a Happycalypse. A Happycalypse of your own design. Will it work? We don't know, but back in 1957, with a rickety spaceship, terrible radio-communications and some limited provisions — we dared to fail. That was our first step.

We're waiting for you.

Yours sincerely on behalf of the Lunatics of the Church of the Happycalypse™,

John Smith / Cap'n Albatross (Att.)

ps: Please excuse the "preachy" tone of our letter, but we can afford to be preachy: after all — we're on the Moon — you're not.

Merl

TINTIN SUBTERRANEA

for Mattias

It was Sunday afternoon by the time I arrived in Tintin City. Too early to go straight to the rendezvous point but too late to do very much else, I took a stroll through Kungsträdgården. Karl XII was gripping a sword with his right hand and pointing east with his left, and I watched his four dogs vomiting onto the points of the compass at his feet for a while until it was time to go. Back at Central Station I glided through underground corridors, always against the current of walkers, on a criss-crossing route that led me constantly backwards. Dreams like a double exposure revealed me walking past myself in the other direction, half-dragging half-carrying a friend from London who was himself at the same time walking the paths of Kungsträdgården, constantly weeping and collapsing across a landscape of stones and cacti as I coaxed him along towards the lifts. He melted away behind me as I ascended to ground level and stepped out onto the circular floor of the grand hallway. As hundreds of waltzers rotated around me I gazed up into the Minstrels' Gallery and managed to spot Tintin, gazing in the wrong direction as if waiting for many things, of which I was probably only one. He had naively tried to conceal his quiff under an old baseball cap, but his eyes were still fungal, his hands arthropodal, his body a coral reef, his beard a colony of pipefish — he was, in short, his usual self, and I was very happy to see him.

When I reached the top of the stairs I found that Tintin was not alone. He introduced me to his friend Sartorius, a genial warlock with whom he had spent the day riding buses in search of illegal life. Nothing was said explicitly but I quickly discerned that this Sartorius was an alchemist of considerable skill, particularly in matters concerning the generation of homunculi, and that he was both amazed and terrified by his own productions. As soon as we began talking he demonstrated his esoteric mastery to me by producing a large insect from his upper thigh. Its movements were sluggish but it was certainly alive, dark brown or black in colour, and its wing case was visibly mutated. This insect, Sartorius told me, was an illegal life form, and although the relevant authorities had granted him verbal permission to keep it, he knew that, if anything untoward should happen, they would deny all knowledge and leave him to deal with the consequences alone. Perhaps he refused to explain the nature of the insect's powers to me, or perhaps he did explain them but I lost track of the information; whatever the reason, I failed to grasp the alchemical rationale behind this insect, and even now I can only speculate as to its abilities. The transparent plastic tubing through which Sartorius produced it from his thigh gave a clue to its possible role in the opening of Chinese boxes, of flesh-eating puzzles that open the doors to other dimensions, or to time travel perhaps. The insect was interesting to look at but I was glad not to have been asked to touch it.

None of us was in any hurry about anything, so the three of us stood there for quite a time, suspended several metres above the dance floor, watching the dancers rushing this way and that and commenting to each other on their antics, with Tintin and Sartorius sometimes explaining to me the things which were unfamiliar. Many of the people were carrying bunches of twigs decorated with bright feathers. I had heard about this device before, so I knew that it could be used to chase away witches or occasionally simply to beat women, and that it was popular to present such a device as a gift to one's grandparents. There were also many people singing songs and moving around the hallway to the accompaniment of an amplified keyboard, and Tintin remarked that the keyboard player was a doppelgänger of a friend of his who had come from hell with a ribbon of stories and images flying out behind him as he came. Moving in and out of all the singers, dancers and witch-chasers we noticed a middle-aged man holding a carrier bag who kept approaching lone women as they crossed the hall. We were too far above him to hear what he was saying, but we observed him as he made his courteous approaches and, from each woman in turn, received an equally courteous rebuff. After a while he disappeared into the shadows beneath our feet where we knew there was a bank of pay phones. My mobile telephone rang but when I answered there was no-one there. The man with the carrier bag reappeared in the company of another stranger, and Tintin's phone rang: it was Cornelius, calling from a windswept plain to the south and asking us to come to him. Since Sartorius and Cornelius had recently fallen in love by bouncing their desires off Sirius and back down to earth, it was agreed that all three of us would go to meet him, and the four of us then strolled through the city together, talking as we went. I quickly lost my bearings, and was not sure whether to be surprised at the sudden appearance of a collector of playing cards whom I had met on a previous visit to Tintin City and who, having slipped through a frayed edge of time while running home, was himself confused about whether he was meeting me again in the past or the future. We were supposed to be looking for a sushi bar or some other place where Alecta would be waiting, but it was closed when we arrived, or else we failed to find it, or else we found it but she wasn't there, and suddenly we were clustered on the pavement gazing up at the windows of Sartorius' rooms as he described to us the pleasure with which he would occasionally stand on the high balcony and shoot darts at the passers-by below with his blowpipe. Moments later we were through the door and climbing the stairs to Sartorius' laboratory.

Sartorius' door opened straight onto a room of vivaria, all of them wet and lush and green inside and broadcasting the light chirruping sounds of tiny frogs. These frogs were not illegal, but they were poisonous, and the venom could be used to tip the darts for the blowpipe which Sartorius was soon demonstrating to us while we drank coffee at the laboratory table and ate the eggs which I had brought with me to distribute as potlatch. This laboratory was the usual jumble of mundane utensils and more mysterious pieces of equipment. A clunky black box covered with knobs, buttons and dials caught our attention: Cornelius in particular regarded it with wonder, and at last identified it as the machine for measuring degrees of measurability, an invention of which he had heard but which he had never seen for himself. Sartorius also showed us his collection of gemstones, bones and mummies, the pride of which was the perfectly preserved foot and lower leg of a wild deer which we passed around among ourselves. He handed it to us straight from the freezer: the fur was cool and velvety, the hoof dark and glistening like sea coal, and as we passed it from hand to hand it shapeshifted in accordance with our desires: a weapon, an alembic, a dildo, a lamprey, a tooth, a telescope, a live bird, a lipstick, a grave-good whose function had been forgotten long ago ... In a tenderly romantic gesture, Sartorius presented this object to Cornelius as a gift, while the vivaria sang and the unseen homunculi slept behind closed doors.

Tintin kept moving in and out of focus. It was a long time after midnight, and after a long journey in the dark, and perhaps after one or both of us had already fallen asleep, that he told me the most detailed stories of his past adventures. Flying at top speed across empty landscapes to be brought to a sudden halt by golden rune stones; civil war battles, betrayals and enchantments, a Californian Christmas road trip, a ship packed with animals sailing into the kingdom of death; the keys and staves of farmer-priestesses, dimly lit halls where maps are sketched on the floor with light; a phosphorescent alien, a flying cat, a comb-mouthed dragon surrounded by human body parts; parasites of great complexity and beauty, or a flaming procession for milky saints; red amber beads broken in two, the pieces worn at lovers' throats; a second-hand comic shop that never closes; lick your fingers and you will understand the language of birds. His skin became transparent as he talked on, and I saw that he was garlanded as if for a Tibetan wedding. I was gazing at him as if into a rock pool, and he was all invertebrate: his heart was two sea hares entwined in motion, his spinal column a millipede, his mouth a sponge. I was trying to remember something, the costume I had to wear, the woodcut I had to show him, the lines I had to recite to make it all come right, but the night was streaming too quickly past the window and there never seemed time enough for me to sit and reason it all out to myself.

The next day was still Sunday. Tintin awoke from another adventure, the two of us taking a long hike together by a shoreline, people milling about on a stony beach, a marine station for biologists and poor linguists, an argument about acting which he recounted over breakfast. Afterwards I took a walk alone in the snow, up to the Observatory where a golden ship had run aground on the top of a hill from where I could look out across all the rooftops of Tintin City. The window of an antiquarian bookshop at the foot of the hill showed an engraving of Karl XII, his pose mirroring that of the statue in Kungsträdgården. Holding a sword this time in his left hand, he was pointing with his right out of the picture and towards another ancient volume, which was displayed open at a page headed "ROMA SUBTERRANEA." A few streets away I found Tintin again. He wanted a cigar. We walked up and down the empty streets, back the way I had come, searching vainly for an open tobacconist. We found no tobacco anywhere but we did find another window display, this one evidently containing an entrance to the Underworld in which Eurydice was frozen mid-descent, her upper body clothed as if for a skiing trip, her legs and pelvis disappearing into the ground and perhaps already pawed by Pluto ... Still with nothing to smoke, Tintin and I caught a bus and began to travel across Tintin City, over glittering water and through streets which were almost empty of people but populated instead by wild rabbits on every patch of grass. By jumping off the bus en route we managed to find the cigars of the Pharaoh, and then not long after we found Alecta who was waiting for us with food, fire and music. Cornelius joined us, and then, deep into the night, Pluto appeared, wanting to talk about politics and mescaline, and everyone was convivial and agreed that Alecta was a fine sorceress. After the others had left, Alecta took Tintin and me out into the street to show us a glimpse through a window into a world of folk tales and magic animals. In silence and darkness, under freezing moonlight, we peered into shadowy racks of antlers. Then Tintin and I made the long journey back to his apartment, he keeping me amused by conjuring fish from cucumbers and showing me our enemies in his scrying mirror; and in the small hours of the morning Cornelius sent word to us.

The next day was Sunday again, but this time it was also Fourier's birthday, a day for peacocks and rummaging, and Cornelius, Alecta, Tintin and I had made a rendezvous at a narrow bridge across a ravine that led straight to the door of a tower that rose above a place of old terrors. We waited for some time beside the bridge to see who else would join us. As I fidgeted and scuffed my boots on the pavement, I happened to look down and see a small white human skull resting between the cobblestones at my feet. I picked it up and found that it was a child's plastic novelty ring, with sharp curving arms that reached round from either side of the skull to embrace the wearer's finger. The others decided that no-one else was coming after all, and I put the skull in my pocket as we set off across the bridge towards that significant door which my companions had tried and failed to open on previous visits without me. This time it opened with only a little sharp pressure, and inside we found strange equipment, empty rooms behind locked glass doors, a reception desk sheltering boxes of snacks and a white wax fish. After a while Cornelius, Alecta and Tintin also found a ladder which pulled down from the ceiling and which they ascended to explore the attic storeroom above; while I stepped through another door and found myself at the head of a winding staircase which led endlessly downwards, past tables and chairs, empty coffee cups and abandoned meals, the carpets growing darker and dirtier as I descended until, afraid of becoming abandoned myself, I hurried back up again to the entrance lobby to find my friends.

But when we came out of the tower we were too late, the city had already changed. It took us a while to realise it, but as we stepped off the bridge and walked back down towards the city, threading our way through the debris of a war between Siva and Ganesh, rummaging through courtyard rubbish and laughing at the comic strips which had been pasted to the lamp-posts, we were already walking in the Underworld. The walls, pavements, windows, doors, lamp-posts, signposts, all were covered with human skulls. Some were grinning and sinister, some were cartoony, some were delicately shaded or anatomically correct, shrunk to the size of a torn fingernail or swollen to the size of a human torso, in the idiom of magic lantern slides or of metal Goth talismans. Skeletons danced, capered or lolled in the streets; bones shattered or burst into flames or reposed at the sign of the Jolly Roger. A tiny silver butterfly lay crushed on an anvil on the roadside where children's hands reached up through the stone from an even deeper level of the Underworld below us. No interpretive delirium

this: we were walking among the dead, and we must be dead ourselves to have made our way to this place so quickly and without any guides.

We were laughing hysterically. The skull in my pocket was coiling and uncoiling its arms in time with my heartbeat. We were dead. We were sailing downhill in a golden ship, with stars and gunpowder our cargo. Tintin was flying above and before us, as fast and beautiful as a landslip, holding a sword in one hand and pointing with the other towards his own mouth from which protruded the dark limbs of hundreds of insects. A six-legged Snowy followed vomiting in our wake. Alone and back in the tower, I smashed through the glass doors of the interior and clambered into a room of tea tables laid with white cloths and crockery, looking out across the city from picture windows. In the corner of the room stood an upright piano, and as I lifted the lid covering the keyboard a frothy liquid like half-beaten egg white began to seep from between the keys and drip down the wooden legs and panels to the floor. Cicadas flew up with a scuttling motion from the holes above the pedals, crackling through the air towards the light. With a great deal of caution I began to lick the piano keys: the texture of their surfaces was granulated, like sugar, but they tasted of stem ginger and tobacco. As I kept licking, the frame of the piano started to shudder and the keyboard rose and fell like a tide. The whole room was inside the bowels of the golden ship and the view from the picture windows flickered monotonously as we rolled along the tracks of the Tunnelbana. Tintin's cloven hoofs clattered across the deck as he stoked the cannon with pearls, ready to blast the hull of the *Demeter* on sight. I know I shouldn't have done what I did next, but it was only meant as an experiment: when he put down his cigar for a moment I stole it and put in its place my left thumb which I had slyly severed with one of the shards of the broken glass doors. He picked it up again without looking, put it into his mouth and, to our mutual surprise, as he swallowed it whole I felt myself being pulled over his teeth and down his throat. An ecstasy of peristalsis … dark sensuality of the submariner … and I became a homunculus writhing inside his soft alembic. I lived in there for several years, or at any rate long enough for me to pupate and to know for sure that he and I were both now illegal life forms. I fed on his ribs, penetrating and entering the outer bone tissue, feeding inside them but leaving the outer layers intact, so that mines and galleries were formed within them. As I grew bolder and hungrier I learned to use my chemoreceptors, assessing the palatability of his internal structure by testing it with series of receptors on different parts of my body. My hind and fore wings on each side developed and began to function as one by means of tiny hooks organised in rows. As for Tintin, with the passing of time his fore wings thickened so that he lost his powers of flight, and he retreated to live in soil and vegetation, learning to breathe by thrusting his spiracles into the air spaces in plant stems and mud. The hairs on his legs became coarser and more plentiful so that he could swim more easily, although underwater his movements were passive and produced by the resistance of the water rather than by his deliberate intention. His penis became long and whip-like, and he began to communicate by frictional mechanisms. The spaces between the cuticles of his flightless wings corresponded to the wavelengths of different colours, by which I mean to say that he was lovely and iridescent as an unkindness of all-seeing ravens.

At last and quite against my own will I achieved oviposition, an ecstasy of peristalsis in reverse. I immersed myself in the wet pulp of his flesh, sought out and oviposited into the writhing spermatozoa, and emerged exhausted and bedraggled to stagger back into Tintin City.

When I came to I was standing on a concrete plaza on Södermalm. Alecta had a dreamy expression and Cornelius was still laughing. It was still the same Sunday. Tintin and I seemed to have resumed humanoid form and were both behaving as if only a few hours had passed since we had first entered the tower. The four of us stood quietly and looked along the plaza towards the moon which was clearly visible beneath the horizon, indicating that we were still in the Underworld. Buildings drew down their shutters at our approach, like lids drawn down over the eyes of the dead. We all took the train back to Tintin's place where we talked and drank wine until long after nightfall, since there was evidently nothing for us to do now but to wait it out. Eventually Cornelius had to leave to catch the last train, and we floated in Alecta's dreams for a while longer until she too decided to take the risk of going home.

Tintin and I were left alone. Outside and far below us, the fields and woodland were dark and quietly breathing. Brightly feathered Venus was no longer visible. Tintin lay asleep with his face in the pillows and the nape of his neck exposed like a fontanelle. If his waters broke and drenched the bed sheets, if his labour pangs gouged the walls of the museum, if he yelled like a crow and put a down of rabbits to flight, he could repopulate the whole of Tintin City, the streets full of corals, the sea full of meteorites, the sky full of fiery angels wielding swords in their left hands. By my reckoning he would be ready to give birth while I was on the plane, but then I knew that my calculations were mainly guesswork and wishful thinking. Sooner murder an infant in its cradle than nurse unacted desires. I fell asleep.

We awoke to find that it had been snowing. Tintin opened all the windows and stood undressed on the balcony, drinking coffee and staring thoughtfully at the copse in the middle distance. Occasional cars and buses glided over the landscape, and the fields were dotted with dogs. Inside the apartment, everything was suspended. The dried fungi on the kitchen windowsill where the plastic skull ring now also lay beside the tiny farm animals and discarded coins; the jam smears on the table top, the coffee cups not washed or put away; the boxes of spells stowed under the bed, the tallboy with its drawers of shining bodies meticulously laid out and labelled; the tiny brown insects living the lives of time travellers, trapped between the double panes of the window; all hovering, shimmering, as if waiting for some gesture, word or cry to set them in motion. To enact the mammalian blood bath, to reignite the revolution. Neither of us could tell for sure whether we were still dead, so I offered to go outside to see. I would meet Tintin to say goodbye a little later.

Back in the centre of Tintin City I found that the city had changed again. Now in the snow everything was pedestrianised, tunnelled through or covered over. Drottninggatan led into Tumba Centrum, Tumba Centrum led into the Tunnelbana at T-Centralen, the Tunnelbana led into the street market outside Whitechapel underground station, the street market led straight back into Drottninggatan again, round and round in an endless loop. As I hurried along one of the many covered walkways on a skateboard I collided with a woman walking towards me and made her drop all of her shopping because I was going much too quickly and could not control my speed. The woman was very angry but I managed to calm her down by apologising profusely and helping her to pick up the shopping and put it back into her bag. She went away pacified, but the collision had shaken me and made me realise that I was really dangerous on the skateboard which I did not know how to ride properly. I kept trying to phone Tintin on my mobile to tell him that I was in the city centre so that I could arrange to meet him, but I couldn't get connected, and after a while I gave up and decided I would have to return to London and call him from there on my landline. Back in my own living room I tried repeatedly to make the call but kept misdialling the number, fumbling the keypad and constantly being distracted by the strange male voice which I could hear in the receiver giving a running commentary as I tried to dial: "Oh you've dialled 35, that means that it's an international number doesn't it, don't forget the plus sign this time though ..." As I became more and more frustrated and exasperated, and seemed less and less able to dial the right number, I began to realise that coming back to London to do this might not have been such a sensible idea after all, that I had left Tintin City prematurely and without knowing when I would be able to return.

I remembered a dream that I had had long before my first ever visit to Tintin City. It was night time in another city which veered between London and some unknown European capital, and I was with Tintin and a young woman who was also a witch. There was a lot of confusion at first about where we were and which way we were going, and I spent a lot of time looking at an A-Z with the young woman and arguing with her over the direction we should take: I was sure I knew the way, and she was equally sure that we should be going in exactly the opposite direction, and so we argued until Tintin intervened and told us that he knew where we should all go and that we should follow him. We found ourselves in an old and rickety underground station, and we had to buy medals to gain admission to the museum that Tintin wanted us to see. I turned to ask him whether he had bought his medal already, but to my alarm he had disappeared, and the young woman and

I had to descend on our own in a narrow lift made of wood, like a little wood cabin, sliding down through the ground while a recorded female voice informed us that when we alighted from the lift at the bottom we would see a lot of night creatures, and that everything would be lit in infra red so that our yellow-vision would be enhanced. The lift stopped and the doors opened onto a corridor that was indeed lit in infra red, and we were both startled to see an emu sitting in a box to our right as we stepped through the lift door, so close that its beak was almost touching my feet. We had to walk through a narrow passageway which was full of coats hanging on wall pegs, and which then dog-legged around past a row of small dingy lavatories, the bowls of which were lit with sinister little red lights. As we were coming out of this area and into the middle of the main corridor, and to my intense relief, we ran into Tintin, who was passing by as part of a group following a tour guide. He was happy and excited, and we joined the group so that we could stay with him. We passed a raven in an alcove under some stairs, then in the next room a group of seals under a table. The animals were all loose, not caged or restrained in any way, and it gave me an uncanny feeling to think that everything was really pitch dark and yet we could see so well thanks to the infrared lighting. Tintin showed me a leaflet he was carrying and pointed back to the part of the guided tour we had missed. The leaflet showed three male faces, like hideous leering vampires, all crowded together, and Tintin was very keen for us to go back and see them for ourselves. He told us we had to see them, they were amazing: but I was afraid, and did not want to go down those dark corridors without him.

London, July 2007

Mattias Forshage

THE HAUNTING

It looks like a smooth surface of sand, but gradually my face is starting to move. Slowly, carefully, disrupting the smoothness, inflating some parts, revealing cracks and pits. The sense of touch is not slowly awakening, since it has been active throughout the long sleep, only on a very different timescale.

There is usually something weird about the outline of such a sand islet. Even though the coastline is shaped by the fairly regular action of water streams and wave impact, the final effect is unpredictable and will often create some bizarre twists. There are spits, bay mouth bars and tombolos, sometimes connecting vague or invisible objects. There may be tracks of stream channels if an old delta is involved, and if it is a postglacial landscape, the ones I know best, many strange lines and shapes might be submerged moraines and eskers, sometimes in complex patterns. And often the whole island is a sort of exception, marking the local spot of sediment accumulation or rudiments with all the surrounding coastline shaped of bedrock and by other processes, other types of lines.

So my face was starting to move and the sounds of the ocean and the birds started making sense. I knew the shape of this islet in great detail.

But it wasn't I. I was not lying there. It was a corpse slowly surfacing by the careful action of a forensic examiner and a small number of technicians. This country was full of them, corpses as well as forensic examiners. I too know how to make an autopsy, I just don't ever have any use for that knowledge. But in North America, forensic examiners are famous, female and beautiful.

I was arriving by conventional means. I had been called down there by a woman I didn't know, to provide company during the last days of this particular forensic examiner, who was called Emma just like one of my very best friends and like several other people whom I associated with death, snow and myself in different proportions. Now this famous Emma had been diagnosed with a terminal cancer, it may have been leukemia or lymphoma or whatever, I probably didn't know the difference at the time anyway, and she was withering away. Her visitor had found my name and contact information on a piece of paper and jumped to the conclusion that I was an old friend who could provide some comfort and brightness for her finale. For some reason I went along without further question, regardless of my doubts as to whom this person Emma was at all. I had a hunch or two, it could perhaps even be called a theory, and it spurred my curiosity.

I arrived at a chaotic moment. All the lights in Emma's house suddenly went on, flooding light over the suburban beach landscape, making it look like a catastrophic scene, weird sounds could be heard, and simultaneously with my arriving in a taxi from one direction (which must have been southwest) another person reached there from the opposite direction (northeast that is); she and I both entered without causing any more commotion, so I wouldn't have to rationalise my entrance, and was immediately thrown into the midst of events.

There were or were not treefrogs and geckos stalking insects at the doorlamp when I arrived. Strangely, I didn't notice at that time.

A bag of human remains that Emma had brought home instead of depositing at the morgue had started moving, simultaneously with several other things throughout the house. The bag had now been opened, and apart from a few fading twitches of the decomposed flesh, the only things moving now were all the insects in the bottom of the bag. A thin background mass of maggots, some flies and beetles, a few ants and small cockroach nymphs. Despite the repellent smell I jumped right into the small circle of people, picking up the insects, identifying them aloud, putting them in vials of ethanol. Selected maggots were collected alive in a jar for hatching. I am not a forensic entomologist, but it occurred to me to be a good idea to pretend I knew what I was doing there.

Nobody knew where the whole crowd of people came from,

and nobody asked at the time; some had been injured by suddenly moving objects or small electric discharges, so we spent several hours calming and bandaging those in need of that, and documenting physical traces of the weird happenings, one after another drifting off, obviously finding somewhere to sleep in the house.

I like ghosts. But it's not a major interest of mine, and what I have to say on the subject may be trivial to the serious student. What I usually refer to by ghosts is memories of subjectively significant people, who have not yet revealed (or at least not yet exhausted) their significance in my interactions with them; past glimpses of the future, interrupted or vaguely imagined relationships, taking on some kind of autonomous existence, acting on the world mostly as coincidental convergences of clues. But I don't know about spirits of dead people. I always suspected that is a mere misunderstanding, sometimes through taking one's own thoughts and actions for exterior (the classic schizophrenic-religious stance), sometimes the other way around of taking more chaotic and diffuse effects for intentional/personalised (the classic paranoid-animistic stance). But I must say I don't know. And it seems obvious that some of these phenomena may be more easily interrogated if conditionally assuming their not only autonomous but personalised aspect. Now in my experience it seems never to have mattered whether those people were dead or just physically absent or whatever. Their voices can be quite compelling anyway.

So there I was, starting a new life with a group of strangers in a rather big modern house in a retirement-style small town on the american east coast, circumstances that I found amusingly absurd. The motley crew gathered in Emma's house was partly a thanatological taskforce and partly a weird household collective. Considering the general intolerance against unconventional families, and in this country in particular, we quickly became rather isolated. Neighbors ceased all casual conversation, even the bored youth gangs driving around pulling pranks and uninspiredly trashing people's stuff were rather quickly scared off. There was a regular exchange of information in the murder cases with the police, but neither side gave the other a full picture. It always creates a weird atmosphere, these occasions where you civilly talk to the police as if they were real, thinking people, which they admittedly can be in a sense, but you must never forget that it is always a matter of negotiations and everything you say can be used against you. But come on, the forensic professionals in our own crew had formal ties with the police too.

The centripetal force keeping us together countering this sinister vortex was the famous forensic examiner's dying. She was perhaps not very beautiful in the conventional sense anymore, increasingly thin, pale and hollow-eyed. The glow of determination and of rich, wordless communication in her eyes was discontinuous. Of course she still had a brilliant intellect and a solid professionalism enough to make her the intellectual center of the group, but certainly not the emotional one. To my surprise I never even dreamed at night of a love affair with her. If she was the person I had suspected when first asked to come here, there was a long and not too nice story behind all this: I was probably the one to have chased her off from home, country and career a decade ago with some thoughtless rumour-spreading. She had a strange disease at that time too, but a quite different one. Perhaps she had written down my name finding I was in the same country, in order to take some revenge? Well, perhaps that was what she was doing just now? We never talked about it and in an almost miraculous way we never ended up in a room just the two of us. Most people don't question the dying. I've been through worse revenges than this.

Mostly, I was sitting on the back porch overlooking the sea, smoking my pipe, taking notes, reading and editing notes. My binoculars were readily at hand, and any odd movements in the corner of my eye got me gazing for whales or rare seabirds or other animals. I am not writing down my stories anymore. They keep on playing regardless, but it's only occasional significant scenes and overall agendas I manage to put to memory. Or, since I don't remember them all I can never be sure that it is actually the significant ones I remember. It could just as well be the opposite. I was just sitting there day after day, most of the others in the group occasionally coming out there to spend some time with me, having coffee, beer or other drinks, discussing forensic or mythological problems or just talking about the weather or whatever came to mind. Strange weather, by the way.

They seemed to be moving around the furniture. That might

have been poltergeist too of course, but there were usually neat arrangements. It could even be suspected that some of us did it to merely add to the confusion.

Often waking up with a short scream, finally reaching the surface, but with some unquestionable presence still in the room, or with the feel of a cold hand between the shoulders or in the neck slowly wearing off. At least twice, probably many more times, I dreamt of being forced to drink poison, thirstily in large gulps from a big bowl, acrid and unusual, a bit like urine, or with a sharp straw penetrating some thin membrane, just like a mosquito. These mosquitoes. Some of these dreams were connected with fits of fever, some not. Usually waking up more tired than before.

The one who seemed to spend most time with me on the back porch was a goth teenager. Her conversation was annoyingly trivial to start with, but usually plunged into wild misunderstandings, rash subjective judgments, demanding personal questions and arbitrary details, in a way which still may be very annoying but also very entertaining and which may constitute elementary warm sociality. I never quite understood what her involvement in the issues at hand was. She said she was investigating some blurry parts of her own past. Perhaps finding out who her parents were. Or who her murderer was, had she been dead. Sometimes she said her parents were dead, sometimes they were rich and uninterested, once she said her mother was a mad young real estate broker, another time that her father was an evil pathologist. Another time she said I was her father. There was nothing else supporting that, but we were able to make up a dramatic and fairly plausible story that would rationalise it. I wouldn't want a goth teenager as a child. But you don't get to choose, that probably being very much the point of it.

The silence of long nights, every now and then interrupted by electrical gadgets turning themselves on, or just electrical crackles or humming. To wake up and have no idea where one is. Sometimes any location will seem equally implausible in this blue light. If some body parts keep hurting, one may conclude one is not in bed, but in some hard place. The bathroom floor, the stairs, the closet under the stairs, if there was a closet under the stairs.

One of the members of this strange group was summoned at almost the same time as I was. It was one of the murder victims, a black woman, local shopkeeper if I understood it correctly. Her accounts would not be juridically valid of course, but she knew where to find good pieces of evidence. She was very frustrated about ending her life early, with a lot left to discover and a lot left to give. I would argue against that, very cautiously though (respect for the dead wasn't only conventional here), that things must always be on their way in different directions and any radical disruption is arbitrary and in a way senseless. Our talks were really interesting. She also showed me how ghosts make love. Nothing strange. If I am deeply engaged in feeling her presence, of course that could also involve local tactile sensations, such that I can interpret them as a human body and the movements and sensations appropriate to it. If she could appear there at all, we could also make love. And we did. Full of pleasure and joy, but whenever it started raising appropriate emotional response as well, this dispersed quite uncompromisingly afterwards leaving mostly a strong sense of nostalgia. All of this was not about love. But why could I be interested if it wasn't?

I remember having read about spectrophilia in a surrealist exhibition catalog long ago, but for very long the only thing I could connect it to in my own experience was the unequivocally caressing quality of warm southeast winds on certain autumn nights, strong and absurdly warm for the season. Winds playing with us just as far as we dare undress for them.

One character whom I took part in summoning myself was a corpse superhero. I had met her before, we had spent quite a memorable weekend in Malmö together. It was obvious we should bring her in, since some of her super powers were about communicating with the dead. Now that is what a lot of these forensic people claim they do too, but usually in a much more banal sense. I was always working hard to relativise the concept of super powers, seriously annoying my acquaintances in the superhero community, arguing that we all have unusual abilities, at least under unusual circumstances and after having cultivated that proverbial disorder of the senses. Worst of all was the mutant superhero community,

rationalising their sect behavior with ignorant genetical storytelling and even claiming to be a subspecies on their own, defying all principles of biological systematics. Many superheroes were quite upset about my campaign, but others found my whining cute. Now the corpse superhero was a major party girl and great fun in a chaotic urban setting. But drugs didn't affect her much. And she had learnt that not having internal body heat production, she had to take a long hot bath before having sex. Unless she found a confessing necrophiliac of course. But necrophily is perhaps more often primarily about common patriarchal notions of sex without objections, without questioning, without scorn, and only secondarily about fetishisation of corpses. However the fetishisation of corpses and even more of artifacts and atmospheres relating to death and horror are far more common and in a sense far more meaningful than actual necrophilia (but also in a sense far less meaningful). With some logic which I accepted but am not able to reconstruct now (probably including speculations about the immune defense system), it seemed appropriate, after initial attraction had surfaced, that she took the position as Emma's lover. As if that was a position. And guarding it jealously.

The waters often seemed so shallow that it would have been impossible to go swimming, having to walk for such a long time before the body could be submerged.

Most people had their own bedroom along the upstairs corridor, which then seemed to have to be a lot longer than would actually fit the exterior measures of the house. But as the doors were all similar anyway, ordinary american doors, whitepainted with brass doorknobs instead of doorhandles, there might be some illusions or very unusual solutions behind this. For my own part, I always wanted to have my bedroom in the closet under the stairs. It is an obvious non-place, and obviously I didn't really want to have a bedroom. Just disappear a little now and then. And if some dancing with the ghosts went along with that, then why not?

Regarding the murder mystery I made efforts now and then in revealing and interpreting evidence, but remarkably little in ringing in the murderer. Of course I wanted him stopped, and of course I hated him for what he had done to my ghost lover and how he kept terrorising the lives of the female population of this town, but I just never managed to get very technically engaged in that part. Someone suggested I even slowed down the investigation by wasting my efforts on recording the weather, lists of bird species and other supposedly peripheral data. Throughout history, many people had always been interpreting occurrences of animals as ghosts, spirits or presages. The birds were among the most significant in this respect. The noises from barn owls in town could have been from any of our demons. The nighthawks. The movements of flocks and individuals of gulls and crows. The silent running back and forth of the sandpipers. The gazes of cormorants and pelicans. And let's not forget the common songbirds with ghostlike ventriloquist skills – of course their warning calls are intended to be difficult to locate, but sometimes they know how to place their voice somewhere completely different. Inside a cabinet, in the corner of the room, inside the corner of the room, the closet under the stairs. Small songbirds watching us, their expressionless peppercorn eyes potentially so much more frightening than the investigative eyes of crows and the stares of gulls or hawks.

Speaking of haunted houses, it seems that approximately every second place where I have lived has been more or less decidedly hostile. There is no need to explain it with spirits of dead people. Some places just encourage bad dreams, uneasiness, poor health and domestic accidents. Some of it is based on the mood and thought modes dominant at the time of moving in, including empathy with previous inhabitants (particularly if imagined suffering), some of it must be the physical circumstances including the local bacterial and fungal flora, but again it is sometimes a lot easier to address it as the spirit of the place. A lot of emotions, thoughts and actions are being directed towards places, making them almost as obvious focal points for heterogenous phenomena as people are. In this perspective, I stubbornly claim that haunted houses are just special cases of geography in general.

On some nights rather grandiose scenes were painted in the sky over the sea, particularly by moonlight and fastmoving clouds. Some were enjoyable as they were, some made me feel some kind of presence of a person I missed, the moon girl, who may have been an acquaintance of mine and the goth teenager both, having run away long ago. It was difficult for me to calculate her present age, but my image of her was paradigmatic for certain people with solidified moonshine for flesh, nocturnal waterfalls of milk, with strangely darkened borders, often painfully incommunicative. I had met several people who were a little like that, and a few times over the years stopped dumbstruck in the street when encountering someone who might have been her (but probably wasn't). Less pleasurable and more frightening were those clouds which sometimes gathered to produce images of thin old women and sometimes even armored skeletons. They wouldn't have had to push it but occasionally they showed unambiguous glimpses of Emma's facial features or even clothes. A huge puppeteer with an ugly grey cardigan of seawrack, of beach pebbles, of skulls, of dismembered human bodies.

Two or three of us were deemed respectable enough to occasionally come along with Emma to the morgue and proper labs. It wasn't only a matter of having looks conventional enough, but also of having an official identity respectable enough whenever we would be subjected to security control. I liked having breakfast with them these days, how they were at once confused and collected as they were preparing themselves for an excursion into an official sphere even more governed by appearances; it was as if the contradictions in their acting was making them even more vulnerable and in a sense thus very attractive. A few times I came along too, not sure whether my credentials were appropriate for security clearance, but miraculously managing to stay out of complications, quite desperately in need of a good microscope as I was.

Recurring stains, cold spots, artifacts not staying in place or continually breaking, why not? Many of these things just don't get their scary atmosphere if the house isn't big, old and dark. And often nowadays, like in Emma's house, the electrical irregularities dominate anyway.

A small seawater aquarium, more like a swimmingpool for children than a real zoological garden exhibit, with the local crabs and molluscs and a few fish, and one night a small group of ducks arriving, common mallards, but one larger duck, an eider, wearing a cape to convince people it's a vampire. I am not going into the subject of vampires here. But those mosquitoes keep recurring, and the disease they are transmitting, saturating the tissues with poison as if it was water, creating a sense of drowning on dry land.

At some point, I had to ask myself what might be haunting me. Conventional answers would suggest bad conscience over some fatal mistakes, some once dear people I had mistreated, or so. But according to the same conventional, psychological economics I would probably have disarmed those simply by openly acknowledging them. I had to conclude this wasn't about me. This was a methodological choice more than anything else, and I might just as well have proceeded along the alternate path. But I wasn't all that interested in me. What I was interested in was this particular epistemological suspension, this indeterminate state, these investigative labors, this productivity of questions.

Another of these weird scenes in the middle of the night when I was watching the ocean alone, the light was so blue and the surface so quiet, resembling a huge blanket under which someone was peacefully sleeping. Discrete chest heavings, some almost imperceptible tremblings. And then suddenly nothing which looked like movement at all. Just a lot of narrow shadows, suggesting the thousands of gravecrosses of some huge war monument. It all looked strangely edible.

I may have been belittling the fact of her dying. Not really knowing her, I found no way of telling where in the process she was. Her fading strength but persistent determination conditioned our work. A lot of those actions can go on autonomously, all of the popular zombie imagery has reminded us how similar to ordinary civilised life things can be by just being dead repetitions of habits and conventions. But sometimes I was overwhelmed with sorrow over all the different possibilities that were already shut down, removed, unreachable from this point. With strong emotions and no adequate channels to act on them, no particular modes of communication opened, and anyway still never seeing her alone, I resorted to praising her before the others. It even got me into difficulties, since the corpse superhero perceived it as romantic competition.

A long time ago I had been involved in — so to speak —

solving a case when a woman was terrorised, the events taking the shape of a real persecution by a particular popular demon. We spent some weird moments there when I envied her the epistemological possibilities in the concreteness of this haunting, and she was scared for her life. Eventually it led to some emergency situations. At that time I came to suspect that the personal aspect of the demon was just her interpretation of common poltergeist phenomena. According to customary interpretations, poltergeist phenomena are usually connected with teenage girls; their frustration and their surplus energy, potency and lack of control. So we took a closer look at the babysitter who was always around, and who really seemed to be the center of weird happenings. She traveled with me back to a larger city, and it turned out she was the cousin of someone I knew, a poet and part-time superhero with whom I wrote a book together before she left, the soft snowfall girl, and they were both somehow related to the one I kept looking for, the lunar woman. Oh yes, writing joint poems about the weather is one of life's pleasures. I tried it with some of the people in the house, but none of them were playful and/or serious enough for it to work.

I don't know about this female puberty poltergeist hypothesis. It seems rather paranoid to blame them. But perhaps boys have relatively more access to socially accepted outlets of frustration and strong but vague desires? Or not. Perhaps boys just have smaller amounts of diffuse energy to spend? Or not. In my own experience, it is actually the case that when electric gadgets have been behaving really weirdly, there have always been energetic female teenagers around, usually having moved away from their parents recently. But such mere anecdotal evidence shouldn't be made the basis of far-reaching conclusions.

The competing hypothesis to explain poltergeist phenomena is that they occur in particular places which are transfer points for spirits leaving earth. Thus their impersonal, senseless, repetitive and violent manifestations distinguishing them from traditional personalised ghosts, would be involuntary byproducts of their quick passing through, without a message or a purpose, in great pain. In that theory poltergeist sites are supposedly all close to cemeteries, accident sites, battlefields and similar. It's obvious that this seems like an explanation at all only if you are also presupposing a large chunk of particular metaphysical beliefs. It seems a bit ridiculous. But I am not going to argue against it. You see, I haven't got an opinion. I never even devised some severe experimental testing. I wasn't too interested in electrical phenomena in and of themselves. But I always found the references to "energies" nastily vague and quasireligious. Electrical fields are measurable. If particular energy fields are subtle but yet able to affect human beings, then human beings are in this connection delicate measuring devices and it should be possible to devise other, equally sensitive measurement apparatuses. But I suspect a lot of the effects are dependent on the human meaning-creating faculties, so that it wouldn't be possible to sort out meaningful patterns from all kinds of noise for those sensitive gadgets. It seems that, in spite of trends, those who try to rationalise their religious leanings by references to physics do a lot worse than those who utilise hermeneutics. The main problem remains faith, which appears as a particularly bad idea in every case. Thus it came to pass that I was busy taking notes for antireligious tracts in the company of ghosts, living corpses, apparitions and occasionally visiting demons.

And of course, one time I needed to go with them into the morgue but overslept. After walking a fairly long distance I actually found a bus that would take me close. Only very old people were on the bus, a lot of garbage, several notable insects buzzing against the windows, and by the exit something that looked like a small elevator. It did not look like it would take someone just down the few steps out, but rather far, far out into the air inside huge barns, or cages for birds of prey, if not just straight to hell. After an additional walk to get there, without seeing a single person, I was not very surprised not to find anyone to let me in to start with. After I had been knocking and yelling for a while a janitor seemed to appear from afar. She claimed for certain that Emma was not there, but agreed to guide me to someone else, someone sitting in a big office, declaring no Emma was working there at all. They soon lost interest in me and I could go on down the hall on my own, not to get to the actual lab area where I know there would be locked doors inbetween, but just to other people to ask. The first one promptly declared she had no information for me at all, the second one said Emma had been away sick for several weeks. If I had been in another mood I might have concluded she was already a ghost and the whole story was a setup. But for what? I was more inclined to regard the conflicting evidence as signs of a bureaucratic coverup. But again, of what, and on whose initiative?

Obviously most ghosts didn't need me to believe in them. Okay, I believed in all my friends there, but I couldn't be sure to what extent or in what sense they were actually real. Not even Emma, she might be just some kind of insidious trap. Long ago, if she was that same person of course, she was shy or aloof, almost unresponsive, and I very strongly disliked her for that. But after a few months I got such a bad conscience for disliking her so much for such insufficient reasons, and started feeling sympathy, pity and a rather perverse fixation. After that nothing was really possible; everything I said or did seemed either desperate or ironic countermeasures to imagined exaggerations. She didn't feel very real at the time, and so it was possible for me to hurt her without feeling bad about it.

I think I was more polite nowadays. Brought together in this strange country we were more in the same boat. It may seem cynical of me to say we were in the same boat when I would likely survive while Emma was dying and others were already dead. Slightly different modes of existence, yes. But still we experienced and reacted to the same rocking of that boat, together and honestly. I wasn't sure of getting out of there anyway. Perhaps the house would claim me in the end. Or the sand dunes. Or these horrifying huge plumed mosquitoes. Or simply my relative lack of the urge toward self-preservation.

The one time I really remembered a nightmare it wasn't a very ghostly one. I dreamt I was a new student at the agricultural university, and there were a lot of students there, we all had breaks at exactly the same time and were supposed to have coffee in the same big room. There was some conversation going on but not much, and whatever tendencies I may originally have felt to take interest in certain other people were quickly muted by their total lack of interest in me. There was no sense of serious reciprocity, no sense of vulnerability, no risks, no efforts; no one regarded it as their task to take just one small step beyond a conventional minimum. This may seem as a kind of a political or moral nightmare, but emotionally it was very simple, just personal despair. Perhaps even more obvious in that country of overflowing conventional sociality. Somewhere in the middle of the dream there was a horror scene which wasn't a climax or anything, just a scene of a little more excitement and human presence; where I was standing in the office of a friend, we were terrified, staring at the ceiling corner, we were holding each other, and I have no idea what we were seeing.

This is all more of a complicated setting than an actual story. I don't write down my stories anymore. It's all just cut out from the perpetual monologue of endless anecdote fragments and critical remarks. Starting from here, quite a lot of different strange turns of events could occur. Or one could decide that some essential element must be sought elsewhere, and leave. So, all just like real life in general.

Mariela Arzadun

MY WIFE WANTS THE KITCHEN PAINTED WHITE

A woman with her dress, a woman with her denominator to indicate a verb. A different drink to remember. From another country. She says: *"come on, it's time to go."* A liquid, a hole in, who repeats exercises. The facts are quite clear. For me. Me. I. Something like I.

Well, I'm angry with you. There has been some confusion of names. You must kill our idol. It's not a way in which a verb conjugates or a form showing numbers. I was born during the irregular second conjugation. I am a point where two things are connected. Your theory is pure conjecture. Do you remember? Now? Do you?

"A particular attitude is appropriate in a particular context": you indicate, as if in a normal everyday conversation. Yes, it's a symbol of fire, a cross full of insects that have to simulate an often boring work. But the creatures are afraid. And you must kill your idol.

A person with a highly developed mental ability speaks in order to initiate a dispute. An interlocutor asks me if you can take part of the story. You can. Men.

She, the woman who read a system of communication inside the house when it started to rain, walks in a small village just outside my area of responsibility. She may do as she wishes over the table. The table is a train where all are writing.

She gives us information about the mechanic. This information will help us build an overall picture of the situation. She's sleeping with an umbrella over her. She is a bridge over the black river. She escapes over the border. She has animals as arms. She's not an hallucination, she's actually present.

Suddenly and with a great force, she increases the metal city daily looking for a mountain. The mountain is a secret idea above a thing done wrongly, a tactical judgment, a serious consequence, a summary of a book.

The hotel where she lives is a limit to reduce the effect of a blow. There the visitors paint a description of the life that they regulate. The gas industry regulator, called Simon, has a popular method to rehabilitate cats. He picks out the cats from a short list of five candidates. He introduces a pipe into their mouths and oxygenates the membranes to cause a mental effort. In order to achieve quick results, he generated a collapse. With this scientific test done carefully to gain new knowledge, he creates a new kind of animal that has the quality of being credible. The researchers are repeating the experiment on birds for some particular purpose. But Simon has many questions and gives them appropriate advice to aid medical diagnosis. He's holding a gun in order to avoid mistakes.

Manifestation of joy. Noise. Sign of air. Infectious disease. She's there now. She arrived at home. She said she declared in that moment: *"We must be free or die, we, I, who speak the tongue. I have been absent in the Spring, when the doctors were visiting there for official inspection. Yet no neurotic birds, nor the ethos, could make me tell any funny stories. The reason was that I was more concerned with the quality of the modeling, the expression of character, and artistic truth, than with the mere rendition of external appearances."*

The agricultural expert, a benefactor under the influence of the Duchess of Alphonsia, suggested: *"We tend to forget, but your formal inventions contain enough general beauty to admit all hypotheses."*

The woman, formed in the sense already discussed, exclaimed: *"I am the Beauty."* And cut as a medium her face, and took out the heart of his body. In an ironic manner with much concentration and drama, she promptly died.

Here we have the story that she wrote when she was absent in Spring. It's a terrifying document for laboratory analysis. These are notes extracted from a tormented mind and damaged by the cultural phenomenon of judgment.

Is this the place where it happened? This would be a good place for a picnic. However. The trees are full of ideas. The ideas are full of people. The people are full of numbers. The numbers are full of doors that have obviously lost their place. A group of buildings

running over the world and saying: *"it's not your place, you have to leave."* A group of houses and flats with the biggest mouths professing obscene words covered with blood, and horses that fight (because some were) to urinate more loudly than the others. And the cars exclaiming with tenor saxophones when the sun is shining and the students pressing keys with fingers that read inside the rooms: *"my wife wants the kitchen painted white."*

A thing made with several parts of the human body put together in a particular way. The real. Illty.

Well, this is my life. My name is Robert. I was born in 1980. My family hated me.

I was a son, a brother, a boyfriend, an assistant who demonstrated the machine in action. I arrived at the hospital at eight o'clock, and all the doctors had the ability to recognize and reproduce any sound because they had large ears. They suspected that I was ignoring everything they were telling me. They always kept their ears to the ground. They were furious with me because I have a slight disorder of the brain that causes difficulty in reading and spelling. They don't understand me and now I'm a large strong bird that hunts and eats small animals. I've a sharp curved beak and very good sight. At the time of darkness, I'm a plant that is much smaller than the normal size but I'm not a creature with magic powers. And it's great for me.

Machines keep running all night and day while my family reads a newspaper. We receive the protection given by the state. We assume the worst for the care of mentally ill people because we don't want to appear deranged. We are clever and quick at seeing how to gain an advantage. We are in the direction of the towers. And I'm spending three days at Oxford University as a tourist.

They paid for my studies. A guttural manner. This. A dark substance in the skin, a hair which causes depression in different cultures when exposed to the sun's light. A parenthesis inside me. I promised to pay them a visit.

I was studying sculpture during a short period of time at an artistic university. Irritated by academic critics who chided me for not finishing my statues, I exclaimed to them that I will never again make anything complete, I said I will make only a design to present abstract ideas that will cause an allergic reaction. With anecdotal interest aside, this story reveals my convictions of the uselessness of completion and of the self-sufficiency of fragments. I often analyzed the depiction of movement, and rather than clinging to a form of realism which might require movement to be expressed by a raised foot, I preferred to suggest potential motion and an imaginary sequence of movements in each part of the body.

I think that to stop or to be destroyed, the body needs more than a direction; the body needs a strong athletic woman sent by sovereign or State to another as permanent representative, or a person out of harmony with period, like me.

When I came back home, my parents declared me invalid. They canceled all liquids circulating in my arteries and veins because I was a large piece of wood or stone for printing, over which voters had an influence commensurate with the number of persons they represented. The same observations could be made for the modernity of my head today. I wrote about my compositions: *"Working directly from life, with mutilated figures, the expressivity of a back, a torso or a hand can be every bit as eloquent as that of a face. All the radiant energy of the soul and its passions, which are normally externalized in the face, are manifested in the way the body thinks, in the commotions which, starting at the centre of the imagination and senses, crash into the space to project a noise into the world's head. It was the same method used to detect the latest batch of extra solar planets. These techniques allow scientists to detect changes in the motion of stars as small as one metre per second. But for me it is a way to find new objects inside my mind."*

Well, it is an exercise for health to be exported to another country. I'm free of sun, free of combustion, free of genitals, free of exotic contents. I'm an operation carried out to test with violent local effect, a literary composition to be eroded. But it's not my fault, it's my responsibility. It's true, I'm destructive.

My father told me when I was six years old that the oviparous origin of humanity was osseous. He said that the orthopedic planets organized a celebration where a pair of lovers, as figures damned like models who posed for a photographer called God, were playing a musical instrument used for preserving flower vibrations that are put into a new form of the world's stomach. I believed everything he told me when I saw it. Because of this, I began by telling you a story. To start to take place.

The reason for my actions remains a puzzle to historians. And I don't understand. Why did they paint the room that putrid color? If you're writing to your mother, don't forget to put a great deal of time and effort into this project. She's very clever, but his manner does tend to put people off. She's an honor to her profession.

I'm happy because I'm away from home now. The bird had to be extricated from the netting. You must have sharp eyes to be able to spot such a tiny detail. To try to win the affections of a woman. Your country is not the same. You have lost the general election.

I'm living now in the most magnificent castle in all the land. A house in the process of construction. Be patient, I'm sure you will be polite in the course of time. A productivity bonus in addition to what is expected.

Robert wants to impress other people and sound important. He's a very attractive person that can hide himself away for months in the mountains or behind the sofa. He doesn't like people because people don't like Robert. How tall are you? The man is a mark showing the highest level reached by the sea or by the flood waters.

In the late afternoon he often describes the distance of something from the ground. You surely remember that he lives in an apartment with a little garden where the books, clocks and animals change when the wind is behind them. The natural environment of Robert is the jungle which causes cerebral hemorrhage. He's a young person. But his age is not important to me.

I watched how he said on Monday: *"Work kills thousand of people every year. The kidnappers who are full of expressions that have been used so often that they have lost their force, have been advertised for the public's attention. The growing number of unemployed don't excite the nervous system as drugs do. Because of this fact, the police have excluded robbery as a motive for the murder and the men have celebrated the exclusion of woman from the temple."*

I will observe how he will say on Friday: *"I'm having a driving lesson this afternoon because sadness is not the same as depression and extra money will be made available for this project. I don't like cars, I don't like a person who practices psychoanalysis, I don't like teaching humor, I don't like the therapeutic properties of food, I don't like the study of the nature of God and the foundations of religious belief, I don't like the simple hunger for affection or pride, I don't like the shoulder where all conventions are consolidated, I don't like control. The people can talk about the different types of cheese and it looks as if they are singular. Adjectives that refer to a group of people of the same type or in the same situation can also be made into nouns of this type. We'll have to find a pretext for not going to the party that human nature promotes."*

Today Robert is waiting for a bus. He looks through the city's eyes to examine various possibilities. He notices that one of the other passengers opens the windows and peers into the dark room. He thinks that Samuel sits in his room gawking at the television all day. If he looks carefully he can just see the church from there. He feels the road above his face, the room towards the sea, the government that reduces the inflation by an extra two percent this year, a child with another heart attack, some old clothes to wear for next autumn, a cat where the soldiers write while the bomb blows up, a sound that crashes with the real and then hunts the wind, animals who know how we die inside the verb. Samuel is a person who describes the tangle of the scene. He's a mathematician who lost a lot of blood in an accident. He describes his attacker to the police. An attacker who marks the prisoners with a bracelet that indicates culpability. An attacker who deserted his wife and children and went abroad. An attacker who says his name is Robert.

"This is the last call for passengers traveling on flight BA 199 to Rome." Where are you going Robert? Do you want to run away from yourself? Are you a ferret? Are you an unsociable person? Do you believe that only matter is real or important? The president made a call for national unity but you are out now. You don't understand what he said. You are a bad person, oh, yes.

Robert watches houses that were built in close proximity to each other, a fox that came slinking through the trees towards the black house, the mayor of the town in his bedroom that writes under a pseudonym, a person who claims to be able to exercise powers outside physical or natural laws, a nerve that has decided to negotiate with the employers about their wage claims, the reports that don't contain any concrete suggestions, the computers that are producing words that have no meaning, an actor that is nominated for the Presidency, people who accept a little unhappiness as a normal part of life, a place where certain other creatures live or produce or change. He wanted to escape from the provincialism of the small town where he had been brought up. Is he ready? You may not get the job, Robert! Your parents aren't here. Would you like to go home? Not all children enjoy television. We plan to meet again in the not too distant future. Because I like most kinds of music and the nucleus is out of me while a considerable number of animals die every day.

Your problems have arisen, Robert. Their philosophy is the greatest happiness for the greatest number of people. The doctor is number one in the oil business. You are a small metal fruit with a cavity in the centre that contains a strong emotion.

You know. A woman who has an excessive desire for sex. A woman with her dress. She wants to help living things grow. I'm absolutely nuts about her but the dog nuzzled up against me on the sofa. In a desert, an area with water and trees, there is a reminder of an offensive word used to express anger. We have a solid thing that can be seen and touched. A distant object. A distant objective to us. An adjective or an obligation. A world without citizenship. The only light came from a tiny oblong pane of glass in the roof. I'm a person who plays a wind instrument. *You are not obligated to answer these questions, but it would help us if you did. Child abuse occurs in all classes of society.* And I'm a specialist in treating eye disorders who is wearing odd socks. You find me very unpleasant but you have to know that the house next door has not been occupied for over a century. The symmetry is not a nice place. But China has unveiled its first national plan for climate change.

Simon is in an unpleasant situation. He was caught in a trap.

He dismisses a lot of modern art as trash. Now he's a bus that makes journeys from place to place. And you say: *"when you walk you travel on foot."* I know. When you travel as a passenger you talk about methods of transport. This expedition took us to places where no-one had trod before. And I treasure your friendship. I'd like to escape from the office treadmill and this is my opportunity. Now I intend to drive a machine.

The machine is a type of movement, a dark liquid produced from sugar with two pairs of sloping legs. You can have the washing-machine for a week to find the best programme. The brutal treatment of political prisoners. You can receive treatment of shock. I still miss you tremendously.

The world is a tribunal for you. It's a group of people who die in a war or work in a musical entitled "You have to win it." You Simon, have to think of a trick to get past the guards or you will finish forming a group of three people singing together. You are a research scientist. Do you remember? Do you? All teachers in school knew about you. The pupils knew about you. And you left the school when you decided to teach yourself. *75 is an excellent score in these conditions*, for adults. They concerned with a particular area of study. But to burn and damage their surface you have to be hot. You have to write.

I'm moving very slowly. I have to touch you if I want to torment you. You are a small electric lamp that runs full of intensity. You are a strong, fast stream. The two wires are touching. And these seats are so high that my feet don't touch the ground. A total eclipse of the sun. Or the moon. You can choose. The violent vehicles are moving along the road.

Robert sees himself as a Romantic poet in the tradition of Wordsworth and Coleridge. He's used for investigating chemical or biological processes. He's accustomed to illustrating a map where all the human components are fighting. He glows when electricity is passed through him.

I will watch how he will probably say on Wednesday: *"This character figures prominently in many of her novels. She's debating around the argument of psychology. Her hero is a woman who kills her mother, kills her sister and then kills herself. All of this makes me feel tired. She bores me. She said to me when I asked her about this question: 'I wasn't born yesterday, you know.' It's not a good answer, you know. It demonstrates unfriendliness. But I don't think about this. Sometimes people collect poems and letters but it doesn't prove anything. People who abuse their parking privileges will have them removed."*

Robert, you are an illegal contortionist. The statement is a highly contorted version of the truth. Can't you guess the meaning of the word from the context? You have to see these changes in context: they're part of a larger plan. Contextual clues can help you to find the meaning. You form part of a large force. Our success is contingent upon your continued help. Please stop your continual questions! Historians see the past, the present and the future as forming some kind of continuum. They were contracted to do this job. Try not to contract your leg muscles. You have to make a legal agreement. It's your responsibility. Do you remember? Do you? The road follows the natural contours of the coastline. The contour of a map. None of the doctors have replied yet. Stop being so noisy! I can't work! The book lay open on the table. You said it's rather depressing. But you had made a promise. You prolong my visit by a few days. You are pressing us to make a quick decision.   How does Simon feel about these changes? Do you know how to shoot a pistol? But Simon said that you were ordered to wound a person but instead you killed him with the gun. This year has been frantically busy for us.

I will watch how he will say on Sunday: *"If I don't send her flowers she says: 'You never send me flowers', and if I do she says: 'What are you feeling guilty about?' Severe brain damage turned her into a vegetable now. Simon noticed that the discussion shifted from religion to politics and thought that it was a dispute between families in which she couldn't do anything.*

"I remember once when I was nine, I got angry with a school friend of mine, Annie I think her name was, but I can't remember what she had done to annoy me. Anyway, I went round to her house one day with another friend and we painted some aggressive drawings to the front door to produce a reaction or response from Annie's parents. Then we rang the doorbell and ran off to hide round the corner. Annie's

mother opened the door, a woman with curly and blonde hair, she was wearing a long dark dress, a white hat and with her right hand she was holding up a chair. Luckily, she didn't know it was I who had done it and therefore she couldn't punish me. But her face was the first art manifestation that I can remember. We knew that the dog had started to bark."

I shouldn't eat so much chocolate but I've had a very interesting morning. Robert, you make me feel rather tired. Are you ready? We've got a long way to go yet. This is a really tricky game and not suitable for young children. It is a counting game starting with one and counting in turn. But you must not say the numbers five and seven. Instead say 'war' for five and 'peace' for seven. So 57 becomes 'warpeace,' and 75 becomes 'peacewar.' Keep track of mistakes - the winner is the one who makes the fewest of them.

Are you ready? Do you remember? You must kill yourself.

Eric W. Bragg

SPIDER

Round and round the magic escalator flew, moving the footprints of keynotes into shuffles pushing the alligator fingers into marred placentas. The escalators would always move, and their simulated piano keys would always make noise. It was no wonder that each of the escalators would ascend into the waving loops of finely burnished wooden housing, or perhaps descend into an inky blackness of couch leather, with a light sprinkling of dust that would periodically fall from the ceiling. In this manner, the escalation of music created the house, and the house in turn created a sense of gravity, where up was up and down was down. The mystery of the house was always there, always reincarnated whether by probing fingers or splinters of kinetic ice. The violence of such spontaneous domestication might have been analogous to a form of mental abuse, but then it also might have been the travel of a mighty train across well-managed tracks leading to the percussion of a radioactive island, on the outskirts of the world of houses.

In one particular instance, the comfortable woodenness of a house might lead to the dirty Mormon secrets that were to be found behind the house, in an oversized lake-like puddle in which a few near-habitable islands were found. One of the islands rose barely above the others, with sandy, industrial-stained mud quickly masking the footprints of recent visitors, as the foul waters lapped the shores while the sun set. The motion of the dark lake water was in stark contrast with the glow of radioactive travesty peeking through the interior dwellings of the island, all nearly shielded by government-issue plastic tarpaulins that were used ever so pathetically in the attempt to contain the radioactivity. In the core of this "island" was actually a grounded barge that had long lost the ability to float. The walls of the vessel had disintegrated, hence necessitating the shielding provided by the tarps. From room to room of this decaying barge were the remains of bookshelves, scientific apparatuses, and cheap furniture, sending out an eerie glow of loneliness onto the flooded beds of surrounding mud and sand with nothing but the stench of partially burned diesel.

The grounded barge was in contradiction with the house, and frequent excursions between house and barge were strikingly similar to the musical escalators that formed the poetic backbone of the house. The journey between these disparate outposts was a long and lonely one despite the insultingly short distance between the two. One was always easily within view of the other, and yet the distance was an infinity of heartbreak.

On one particular evening, after the sonic escalators had finished their rhythmic up and down momenta, the sandy-haired and thoroughly wizened caretaker of the house paused in his rocking-chair and brushed the ceiling dust from his thinning hair. He recalled the safety of the house in which he resided, and then pondered a distant dream of a luscious witch who revealed to him a palm-sized ceramic tile on which the chiseled features of a house were clearly visible in iconic simplicity. The image of this primordial house, in its simple lines and slopes, was enough to impress upon the caretaker that the idea of the future was illusion. Of course, it was to be a happy illusion, but an illusion nonetheless. The day that the witch prophetically held up this curious tile for him to see was not one to be forgotten for many years to come, and so on the day that the old caretaker remembered this dream, it was as if layers of transparent ice were shed and splintered away from a frozen anchor contained within — a special kind of heavy anchor used by seafaring vessels from previous centuries. The archaic but natural curves of the heavy iron belied the outer flakes of icy rust, as if the bloodshot eyes of sleeplessness were wiping away beads of cold sweat from uncomfortable brows that had constantly shifting centers of gravity, remaking the identities of invisible forests. Each forest had one eye at the center, and within many of these invisible forests were leather suitcase factories, where one could find the most important suitcases of all suitcases available: the special kind of suitcase in which one might inside find the velvet hammers of pianos, if the word "piano" was to be used ever so loosely.

The witch never revealed to the caretaker any of this, from her transoceanic visions that she sent to him once every blue moon, but he knew that it was true, and that somehow all of this knowledge came from her, as if she was the mother of his darkness, but also the obsessive swing-set for schoolchildren to whom the witch offered sugary lollypops in order to get to them off-guard, for purposes that she would never willingly reveal.

But the caretaker was not to be deterred, and he knew that he was not very far from being on a plane full of cats when the storm broke loose overhead, sending down a deluge of dirty rainwater over his head. Luckily the house of burnished wood had a tight roof, and so the caretaker remained dry for the evening, not having to worry about the storm of lightning that boomed around the surrounding countrycide in all directions.

Therefore knowledge always had its price. For many years, the caretaker wasn't even sure if the witch existed, as if maybe all of the piano hammers he had installed throughout his house of burnished wood had never even threatened to outwear their felt. He knew that people were not without their weaknesses, including their sometimes filthy predilections for leather suitcases. But whether or not a liking for leather suitcases could really be considered a weakness had yet to be determined. In the meantime, the caretaker got up from his rocker, and stretched his legs and shook dust from his hair. Adorning the hallways within this vast house of burnished wood were the glued strips of piano key hammers, well worn, with the grooves from piano strings worn into the felt, leaving behind the stain of metal and the memories of solid percussion. He was certain that the witch of his dreams might have an eidetic representation of the worn piano-key icon somewhere inscribed on another ceramic tablet, but he was almost afraid to realize the full potential of such an image, as if her hands moving toward the tablet (so as to grasp it within her palm) were nothing but the illusion of timelessness or forgotten manners, plump as a parrot sitting next to a case of tickled ivories on a sinking pirate ship. He could remember what he thought of the wisps of hair that draped over her knowing brow, of the parts of her body that he wanted to smell, and even the sentences that she said to him with her hands, as if his body were words of Braille inscribed onto slate rocks within her unforgiving fortress. Therefore the witch was stronger than a storm, and more molten than the liquid brass wires from a piano, long stricken by lobes of felt, by flattened bulbs of green music that could excite one's senses beyond recall. Upon thinking about the flattened bulbs of music, the caretaker fell asleep and had many troubling dreams.

Within one of the dreams, the crotchety old man saw the witch holding the ceramic tile with the eidetic house on it, and fell into a deep sleep next to the witch. It was a case of dreams within a dream. Horrifying sub-dreams of football stadiums and secret government caves passed through his sub-consciousness. Eventually he saw his dreamwitch again with a lit cigarette in her mouth. She threw the cigarette away and stalked across the floor of the government cave in a pouty sort of way, flinging back her long hair and stomping her high heels on the earth, completely reveling in her indifference to the world. She produced a leather suitcase suddenly, and opened it, revealing a choice piano hammer inside, with well-worn ivory colored felt that covered the wooden hammer bone with a thin strip of colored felt. She was very excited at making this presentation, and yet realized that not a soul knew of her possession, as the dreaming caretaker now became separated from her, dissolving the sense of togetherness into a state of bland anonymity. The separation marred the caretaker's dreamself, and he felt his motion through the universe become jaded, in the way a lofty kite is punctured by hailstones, preventing it from soaring over the next hill. A steady, steep descent to the ground was nothing more than a return to consciousness, and for the caretaker, the result was that he instantaneously woke up from the dream that was within a dream, as well as from the outer dream (that contained the inner dream). Therefore the return to consciousness brought on the strength of the reality principle crashing into his mind, twofold. Or perhaps it was the onslaught of waking reality squared. Either way, it was painful, and a crash of lightning dramatically helped accentuate this unfortunate realization and his return to waking life.

The caretaker rose from the bed and noticed that while he had slept, there had appeared several smashed plastic owls in his bedroom.

The owls were life-sized, and all made out of a brown plastic that had been painted with owlish colors. The main problem was that the owls were hollow and thin, and very easily shattered. How the owls had gotten into his room was unknown, and their appearance was startling. The caretaker collected all of the shattered owls and placed them in a queue on the back porch, so that they could all monitor the grounded barge in the toxic Mormon islands behind the house.

Once inside, the caretaker rubbed his hand across his leathery forehead and sat down in his rocking chair. He turned on the television with the remote control, and began to relax. On TV was a reality show about an assortment of houseflies who were determined to make it to the top of a ceramic Jesus figurine (which from their perspective was as big as a mountain). There were several fly contestants who were all equally determined to reach the top of Jesus' head: Ralph, a rather boring-looking housefly. Nathalie, a metallic blue-colored fly. Sarah, a metallic green. Jennifer, a lovely metallic blue/green shade. Hank, a greenish-gold hue. And finally, Bertha, an ugly grayish color with exceptionally orange-colored eyes.

These six flies were all very eager to win the reality show contest, and they showed it: on the starting line, they were all poised to begin their ascent of the Jesus statue, and demonstrated their zeal by rubbing their forelimbs together in hot anticipation of climbing Our holy savior. After the host of the show swatted at them with a folded newspaper, the flies immediately leapt at their chance of instant fame. And unbeknownst to the flies, a highly viscous, petroleum-based flypaper adhesive had been applied over every crack and surface of the Jesus figurine, causing the greedy insects to remain cemented in the exact same spot where they landed. Upon making contact, the flies realized that there was to be no further travel along the tacky surface of the Jesus statue. It was either an instant-win or instant-lose situation. The biggest loser was Ralph, who landed on Jesus' kneecap. Next came Jennifer, who landed on one of Jesus' buttocks. And then Sarah, who landed on his crotch. Then came Nathalie, who immediately ate the crust out of Jesus' bellybutton (while thinking longingly of the days when she lived in a restaurant). Bertha landed on Jesus' elbow. But Hank was the winner. He landed right on top of Jesus' head, with his bulbous golden body bloating in the sun with the most resplendent glimmer befitting the holiest of flies. Hank certainly was a happy fly that day, although he didn't live long past that momentous occasion to ponder his future. In all truth, these flies would have preferred landing on shit rather than the statue, but apparently the Jesus figurine was the next best thing. After all of them realized their entrapment, they hurled jeers and insults at each other, as if by somehow furthering the verbal competition, they would be able to feel better about themselves and their fragile egos. Regardless of the surly fly-speak, the flies stayed put, cemented in place and doomed for eternity to spend a hollow life with Jesus, since all that remained of them after a few days was some dehydrated exoskeletons. The television show ended cheerfully and was followed by a commercial advertisement for Corporate Control Tubes. The commercial promised to improve the lives of those who owned their own Corporate Control Tube. It was at that point that the caretaker of the burnished house turned the TV off and focused again on the reality that he knew: *the reality that was outside of the television.*

The caretaker hurried to the back of the house, feeling slightly oppressed due to the psychological influences of the reality TV show that he had just watched. He knew that a reckless breath of fresh air would be all that was necessary to recenter himself. Upon stepping out on the back porch, he again regarded the shattered owls who quietly stared out towards the radioactive Mormon barge that had been marooned forever within a dune of diesel-laced mud and sand, amid the stagnant lake. The written secrets within that terrestrial shipwreck could have taken forever to tell, and yet such knowledge was terrifying in its stark malevolence and missionary orientations. The night air fell heavily on the leathery face of the caretaker, as he stretched his aching arms and legs and stared up at the nearly full moon, which had now risen over the dense horizon of trees and bushes submerged in the darkness. The moment of peace was almost blissful as it was disquieting, reminding the caretaker of the moments when cats stalk mice along country fences, searching for new avenues of pursuit rather than the linear methods so well-known to modern vermin.

The clouds in the night sky began to break like a symmetrical

beehive, making a supernova that gave the illusion of great distances. The cockroaches were literally dying to climb the walls, but their legs were useless when the music stopped and they were left to dry out in the hoary night. The caretaker could sense that something was approaching the burnished house, because the musical escalators inside were wound up in anticipation, as if the tension on a base could be manifested by large metal string coils being tightly packed as a pulsating knot that longed to re-extend itself. Usually these musical escalators made such gestures when it became certain that a visitor was approaching. In fact, the approach of visitors in the night was what often made the evenings pregnant for the caretaker as well as for the burnished house. The caretaker began his ritualistic gestures of anticipation, as he moved from room to room, seeking out shadows bearing knives and pulling aside numerous shower curtains which hid not shower stalls or bathtubs, but rather fireplaces and living rooms and tiny coatrooms. There were always these symbolic shower curtains placed strategically throughout the house, allowing the caretaker to move from one moment of privacy to the next, or from one private room to the next. The shower curtains were the glue that held the ancient dwelling together. The musical escalators moved between the shower curtains like centipedes, and their rhythmic motion seemed threatening, but in the most subtle of ways. If a million legs could crawl along the walls and ceilings!

The caretaker knew that the south wind was blowing through the trees, suggesting again that a visitor was approaching, but whether the arrival of the unknown person or entity would happen in twenty minutes versus twenty hours was completely unresolved. He opened a storage closet to find a half dozen guitars covered with many cockroaches. The roaches made no sign of moving, although the sensory hairs on their legs detected the motion towards them. They merely sat on the wooden beams of the instruments that were ever so tactfully burnished, as if each polishing stroke of the guitars' bodies had been orchestrated in the way a conversation might play out between members of parliament or a sports team. The cockroaches merely stood where they were, with their antennae moving to and fro ever so gently yet with an assertiveness that was unmistakable. The caretaker wanted to take one of the guitars into his arms and cradle it like a baby, possibly to pull a few chords from its silent frame, or perhaps just to finger-tap a rhythm next to the strings just for the sake of kinetic gratification. But the desire went unfulfilled. The caretaker simply stared at all of the cockroach-studded guitars, marveling at their silent symphony while the wallpaper on the inside of the guitar closet revealed the passage of unknown shadows in the same way clouds might pass quickly on transparent surfaces overhead. The guitar closet was really a vortex of activity within the burnished wooden house, and the caretaker gently closed the door so as not to disturb the quiet roach music that droned on and on into the early evening. There were still many more hours of the night left for the visitor to arrive, and this perspective was merely reflective of the caretaker's bias in favor of the night.

More roaches were flying around the porch light in back, and their amber bodies were gems that would someday adorn the throat of a tender infant. Crickets chirped in a wave of unison, a droning message of approval, and the houseflies sleepily turned in their hiding places, not having enough energy since the sun had set hours ago. All of these insects were in various states of alertness, regretting that life was not more clearly delineated, as is sometimes the case with colored pathway tape in hospitals doubtlessly used to navigate the unknown corridors. All of the bugs made noise, like a colony of goldfish in a round bowl. The universe was insectoid, since the plants had grown mandibles and even the house was beginning to flex its subterranean muscles. The caretaker was listless and a tiny bit despondent, since he knew that it was more than possible that he wouldn't have what the visitor wanted (or what he thought the visitor wanted, assuming the visitor wanted anything at all).

The head of the caretaker was swimming, and he pushed his hands along the walls of the burnished house in order to reassure it, to convince the house that satanic verses inscribed on the chimney stones were not just for Sunday school purposes, but for amusement on cold winter nights. The passage of time was a quiet agony for the caretaker, until finally he heard the knock on the door. As soon as the door was opened, the caretaker shook hands with the visitor, who turned out to be…. He wasn't sure. All he knew was that after losing consciousness, he actually awoke on the floor, with the feeble houselights causing his eyes to smart and allowing him to hear the receding footsteps of the visitor, whoever he or she was. With his right hand he felt a strange sensation on his forehead, immediately noticing that the aged, leathery skin seemed somehow lighter. While rubbing his hand over his forehead, he noticed there had formed a star-shaped hole that had apparently just begun to open. The normally horizontal laugh-lines across the forehead had instead surrounded the opening star in a concentric fashion, similar in appearance to a spider's web. The wrinkled skin more and more resembled a crooked spider's web, with the opening growing larger, suggesting that the caretaker's head was possibly hollow. At the moment when the light overhead penetrated the empty cranium of the caretaker (who was still very much alive), a spider began to stir and then emerge from the cranial cavern. With eight hairy legs and a bulbous abdomen, the spider most clearly resembled a tarantula. It crawled from the caretaker's head, and then rested on top of the waves of wrinkles created by the unexpected opening on the forehead. The spider knew what it wanted: to seize the hapless insects and then quickly liquefy their inner organs with cytotoxic venom. And finally, to drink their liquefied bodies through the insects' fragile exoskeletons as if sucking soda through a straw. The tarantula, just like its wizened progenitor, was dizzy from the fall, and it trod ever so carefully across the spiderweb made of forehead skin. At the moment a moth bounced off the window on the outside, the spider ran quickly away from the fallen human and bounced up the burnished staircases, possibly disappearing into the attic or one of the unused bedrooms. The caretaker, on the other hand, slowly regained his senses while the gaping wound on his forehead wept a few lymphatic secretions and then closed forever. The wavy, concentric wrinkles on his forehead resumed their original configuration, with no signs of entry or exit of the spider, or any fluid, for that matter. The new difference was that there was no longer any sign of worry or fatigue on the countenance of the old man.

The caretaker felt his weathered fingertips reach out for the piano hammer, one of the key elements of his ancient family's coat of arms. There were of course other elements comprising the family coat of arms, but he could not remember what those were. All that remained was the grimy piano hammer, well weathered along the felt, with a broad furrow etched across the leading edge of the soft striking area. This hammer had struck many a coiled wire, and rather than possessing a typically rotund striking element, the striker more resembled the large head of a disturbed fetus. It was the skull of the fetus, analogically represented in cross-section and made from green and ivory felt, all attached to a grimy wooden shank with a dull patina, which actually struck the piano wire. That there were tiny felt arms and legs loosely hanging from the embryo's skull (the striking element of the piano hammer) was an inconsequential coincidence, as if these limbs had atrophied just as the arms and legs of the Japanese Daruma fetish object had undergone a similar process. Therefore, when the heads hit the wires, music was the theoretical result. Of course, the caretaker never actually saw any babies rubbing or butting their heads against the piano wires, but there was a deepening, symbolic suspicion forming in his mind which tempted him to open up the family piano in order to see what was inside. And at that moment he had completely forgotten about the visitor who had somehow been involved in releasing the tarantula from his forebrain. He stared ahead into the dim living room in an obsessive kind of way, and wiped a few strands of spiderweb away from his thinning hairline.

Meanwhile, the spider quickly explored the house, not finding what it had secretly craved. The arachnid lowered itself from the cracked bull's-eye window and traversed the poisoned sludge of the backyard, the industrial cesspool of diesel and stagnant water mixed with sand and mud. Eventually it found the stranded barge and penetrated its crumbling structures, moving around exasperated bookshelves. The flickering artificial lights were painful to all of the spider's eyes, causing the creature to duck under a stack of grimy boxes precariously leaning to one side. The spider immediately began to create strangely shaped webs that were analogous to impulsive piano chords that were pounded off-key, like when a child bangs on a piano or perhaps when a pianist's fingers are glued together, causing the nimble exploration of notes to become suddenly botched or sabotaged. These webs created a shelter for the spider, amidst the ruins of books and other ancient family effects that had been pushed aside by the caretaker long ago.

In the burnished house, the elderly caretaker immediately became a child after the separated spider had a chance to get settled in the deserted Mormon barge mired in the filthy backyard. The first thing he did was to gingerly lift the lid off the piano keys and have a good go at it with the piano. In fact, he had not banged the piano in ages. The pearly keys responded faithfully to his every strike, every pounding and every penetrative gesture with his fingers. He realized that he had not banged the piano for so long, that he had forgotten how good it felt to bang such an instrument. When he finished with a mind-blowing sonic crescendo, his arms fell limply to his sides, with beads of sweat falling off his matted brow, and he blissfully grinned, realizing that none of this would have been possible without the pianist that was an integrated part of him. How could he have ever forgotten about his inner pianist?

His memories of the visitor returned, as he now realized the degree to which he had mercilessly repressed them. He could remember his woman as she used to look, when she held him by the fire, and how the leader of the pack — some wizened, cranky old man of a beanpole — had attempted to interfere in his destiny, as if six-sided dice were secretly being exchanged for two-sided dice against the caretaker's wishes. The leader of the pack had a strong blade of sarcasm which might have succeeded in making him a terror around those who worshiped him and his money, but it was pale in comparison to the verbal acid of the caretaker, before his tongue had been nearly immobilized with pins and needles and the kind of special felt that is used within musical instruments. This leader fell by the caretaker's words, although now the caretaker could no longer remember what those words were, other than that they silenced the leader quite effectively, instantly dissolving the illusion of fear and certain death that the latter exercised over all who would listen to him. It was after these words had been uttered that some binding spell had been broken, subsequently releasing people from the bricks in the walls in between which they had been embedded for years, possibly even centuries. It was at this precise moment that the caretaker of yesterday met his wife, or girlfriend or whoever she really was. And as soon as she had appeared, she quickly disappeared as the caretaker had encountered the nearest vacuum cleaner store. Why or how exactly the vacuum cleaners might have been responsible for his honey's disappearance still remained a mystery, but somehow the arrival of the faceless visitor from only a few hours before had triggered the reemergence of this archaic memory.

As strange as it might have seemed, the visitor had come and gone. Not one trace of a conversation with any person or entity, but only a strange set of footprints that clearly and smoothly led up to the front door and then away, like the arc of a semicircle. The caretaker couldn't remember any new faces (or any old ones, either) that might have visited him during the night. He was certain that the memories he had revisited were of course only memories, and he did verify that the spider was real, after traipsing over the oily dunes of sand to get to the Mormon barge behind the house. He never spent much time on this grounded ship; all of the books and other antiquities were just too useless to even consider sorting through, and yet he knew that somewhere within these stacks of useless objects there was the spider, possibly building a web, possibly sucking on bulbous insects, or maybe even doing something that only spiders do when they have complete privacy. As if the trail of loose webbing wasn't already a clue, the pile of broken piano hammers, with the felt neatly excised from the wooden bone of the hammer, was a dead giveaway to the whereabouts of the spider. The caretaker found his arachnid cousin chewing on the crumpled bass piano strings in the same way someone might smoke a cigarette after being released from a permanent prison cell. The spider didn't have much to say, although it was by no means unfriendly. The spider tried to tell stories with its spinnerets, moving fresh silk through the morning breeze as if it were smoke, but it was all a language that the caretaker could not understand. He bade the spider a good morning and left the creature in peace, to chew on piano parts in the shade of a crumbling, useless library.

The caretaker, on the other hand, realized that both of his hands were part of a single, resplendent diadem that he might use to crown his lover with, assuming he could make his way back to the vacuum store and then the campfire, the two places where he had last seen her several decades ago. He found a place within the house that had a good amount of magnetic resonance, and he lay down on the floor in that special location and shut his eyes. From there he visited the old factories that DeChirico once knew, paying special attention to the pollution of belching smokestacks and then the dried artichokes that one often found amidst the brambles of wrecked machinery within the industrial hive, with angry cusswords spray-painted in the sinister master control room (with the proverbial master control panel on the wall, with many buttons and knobs) which all now looked not so devious as they once did, decades ago. Atop one of the defrocked control panels was an icon of a throne and an angry feline next to it. The caretaker in his dreamstate at once knew that he had found the right room. Now all he needed was a vacuum cleaner and some pyrotechnic supplies.

When the caretaker woke from his outer dream later in the day, he knew immediately that there was someone else in the house with him, since he could hear the rustling of the burnished escalators overhead, accompanied by nebular birdsong.

Matthew Rounsville

ASHCAN LULLABY

for Ariel Denham

Ariel's voice is orange, striated, the moment of transition between touch and air, an aisle of indentations. Half of her words are nameless, spark like idiophones, retract back into a placenta with one motionless eye stationed at each cardinal direction, and these words lubricate the rest, acting like eggbeaters in the equilibrium, dig sentences that pulse in the prolongation of a scheduled fall that later ignores the increasingly pathetic pleas of gravity. When it ends I stick stripped feathers and upside-down pill bottles in its wake, laughing out of my nose with my tongue folded back. I laugh because I'm lost and her hair is tacked in wedge-shaped patterns on her back, too far away, too frenzied to tow me.

Later I'll say I first met her in a dream at that point where images break down, cataplectic and absorbent, that I first discovered her face in the underside of a breast, in its vein, bruise, scrape, or freckle, the spirals of my fingerprints the first to witness the materialization of her nose, a droplet of my adam's apple's sweat the first impression of her lips — but I met her more in a setting more solitary than a dream, at a dance she took part in, without her meeting me, my eyes darkened in twisted shadows under foreskin eyelids, my left hand luring my lower lip aside while she danced away from the dance and into my head, straight through my teeth. The rest of the audience rattled, a swallowed cough, ears whispering to kiss-close lips, sighs, tear-quickened gulps — and I rattled too, louder, slower — but I felt myself wanting to clothe each sound I made — or pare it into silence — my thoughts and fizzing heart murmur, my feet slipping down the slanted floor with gassy squeaks, the unending roll of my testicles in their sac — I felt myself wanting to disentangle my body's infatuation with itself so I could compress my entire world into taking in the strainless manifold of her clenched neck muscles and the twitching ravines of her deltoids, so I could take her in without the democratic decay of my easily confused eyes. For an hour her anatomy deferred its biology — it became two-dimensional, invisible, decimals of sweatless modules, doubled, refracted, shorn, burnished, forcing my eyes to withdraw, irises and pupils mutually suckling — emaciated, dying, — ecstatic — I watched her eyelessly. When letters began to appear in the grain of my mandible, vesicles of letters piling up, a mass of small hair on one larger, circular hair, the chair factory that everyone sees when trying to find the punctuation for the last sentence before dying, I wanted to mold a scream, something muddy and aromatic, two severed bloody stump eyelashes scotch-taped to an index card, evidence or invitation for my having existed, a curio, an ellipsis spreading from a core of razor fragments to the soft, soothing breath-chaste hell of distant, extemporized space, but there was nothing, and I was the arrow to the nowhere nothing, an ohhhhh-shaped body, naked except for its own swollen tongue.

The dance ended; the world sank, somewhat convex and spotted. If I were a child I would have remained seated with a wet zipper, bending every organ I could to try to escape within myself, to become surfaceless, but I'm older, frightened more easily at more fantastic things, so I adjusted my shirt, stood up with precision, and left, imitating the gait of an amalgamated dictator-trapeze artist, until I was outside, where the gait mutated into the trick walk of a hanging man, my torso completely irrelevant, a cardboard box tethered to an airplane, a limp breath the only tenuous linkage. The bus I planned on boarding, a heavy, asthmatic creature with powerful forelegs, fell dead upon seeing me, its margarine-color eyes embossed with other people, elongated by its sagging lenses. My stomach, erect only with parenthetical columns, eddied, secreting an acrid tea of dried red blood cells, and I bounced along the sidewalk, noticing insects in each crack between the slabs, transfigured muses with wings and rippling eyes, which I would name if they hadn't stared at me, teasing me with their antennae. Under the drooled glow of neon shop lights and the cactic rain of copper streetlights, I tried to find slivers of nonlight through which I could make my way to my apartment. This dedication struck me as absurd, and I soon lost track of what I was doing, no longer pretentious enough to think I could possibly end up in a room, in a bed in a room, or on a road I've been on before. The bulging blue potato of my heart bumbled up and down between my pecs, like a hand squeezing then relaxing a long purple water balloon, completely rebellious to the alien rhythms of my feet. I was marooned, yellowed and marooned. The streets no longer bore titles, shucked their impersonal officiation and scowled, rubbery, stroke-victim intersections. What I knew had died. There was no Edgewood Drive, no decapitated peach tree at the yellow house, no row of citronellas at the corner to douse my hands with in case I had to shake someone's hand, just building after building, teeth stolen from babies and driven into the ground, upside-down, an imported smile offering no lenience. Cars passed and people yelled at me. I went inside a gas station, dizzy, trembling, a fallen leaf kept afloat by being impaled on a nervously twirling stick, needed water, the only medicine the completely ignorant know, let my greasy hands streak the glass door then pulled it open, rush of frost-cracked air. At the counter I dropped all the change I had in my pocket, unable to look the attendant in the eye, afraid that I could be absorbed while in the act of seeing, felt myself turn cross-eyed, fading, and lightheaded as I made my way out, my inner map a greenish gel fondling the undersides of my fingernails. Stumbling in slow motion, with block-long inhalations, I eventually-immediately made it to a dark park, becoming a foetus on a bench, lighting a cigarette that angled straight down. Although I managed to open the water and take a few drinks, I could not figure out how to put the bottle's cap in my pocket. As the water emptied and the bricks of cigarette ash stained my black corduroys, I noticed that I was unconsciously still trying to get the cap inside my pocket. I looked up, and an old woman walking by sneered her eyes at me like I was a junkie, and, seeing her liverspots transposed to my elbowpits above layers of thin, opalescent veins, I trusted her verdict.

Skeptically, I got up with famished arteries and smoke-tarnished eyes, the iron bars of the bench evaporating from my pants. The chain-link fence of a school that appeared buried alive, then disinterred, told me that my apartment was only two blocks away, that I walked by this place every day, that I could do it again, but, when I tried walking past it, it just repeated my name endlessly, like a siren who had gotten bored, apathetically refraining the name of an ex-lover. Redoubling, I hunched and dragged my sandaled feet, scraping toes needlessly on the undulous old cobblestone sidewalk, until my name was out of reach, out of mind. At the next block I could see my apartment, and I began to cramp. A voice from behind me jubilated a hello, and I yelled back, "HI" with a yellow, diagonal tone, feeling that my larynx palpitated with ambient muscle-pains on the contraction. At the intersection, across the street from my apartment, I waited interminably for the traffic to ease, unable to stand or fall because each took too much effort. A happy red light came that I would've kissed laboriously if it bent down far enough, and I scowled victoriously at a man in a grumbling, dirty white pickup truck, careful not to trip on the street's wide white glossy lines. Looking at my stairs, I almost blacked out. It was hard not to hit my knees on the steps. The doorknob was loose, bended away from the key, so I choked it until it relented, jabbed my key in, then came inside, collapsing with skin feeling like a pumpkin, which always feels like dead people to me while still having associations of my mother's wonderfully spiced, best-hot pies.

I sat down on the toilet, naked, smoking cigarettes and putting them out gingerly with a hiss between my legs, wondering if I would ever stand again. The shower lisped and gurgled, steaming and wetting my sweat. When I got up I avoided the mirror's stupid gawking gaze. The shower was cold now, cold heads knocking on my skin, biting aside my hairs to get to my ubiquitously chafed skin. I closed my eyes and saw vague awnings, but I feared going unconscious and losing what I had left of myself, so I unknotted my eyelashes and opened my eyelids. Mostly I just looked at the drain, as if it was a window, as if I was in bed, awake but wanting to go back to sleep, looking for the sunrise that would be a reason to ignore my groggy desire and get on with the day, but suns never rise into shower drains, only grey eyeballs, so I halfheartedly dried myself out and fell into bed, sheets darkened a few shades in an irrational outline of my body.

My damaged thoughts, wet velcro, stuck to the dancer, hating her, loving her, sometimes simultaneously, sometimes not at all, traced erections, lanced amygdala yolks. Wordlessly I searched for the womb of my despair, inconsequentially thinking, "She suicided me," over and over, the inner sound bodied like a neck's 'no'-shake. I had come to the performance knowing its name, expecting a sort of transcendental chokehold, part prostitution, part malaria, something that would antagonize me and maybe leave me catharted and disheveled. It would be, I was told, an expression of death, a necessary counterweight to capitalist this-and-that, life-changing (as all deaths hyperbolically tend to be), heart-breaking, heart-rending, heart-pounding, heart-stopping — and all, and, at first, it was. Captainless fleet of seducing corpses, imploding outlines of a cumulonimbus tiptoeing from one rat trap to another, sedated, then injured, scolding, then autistic, but, eventually, in no apparent pattern, the dancers rolled out of sight, in clusters or alone, groping, wilting, recontracting into pupal form, putrefaction in grey and black, leaving yet-nameless Ariel alone, puddled beside a hard curtain, a glaring paranoiac with inadequate lung functions, barnacled, mouth open in the shape of an indistinct vowel. With terrified calves she got up, gradually slinking or diving from one will-less transformation to the next, ciliate aviaries of ovarian rattles, a mobile in the murk of a sewer, a c-section performed on a padlock, a bat cursed with human eyes, passing through taxonomies, malfunctions, and meals of both. The morbidity that the dance had until then aroused in me had been swallowed, its truths rejected; death — life — meaningless! Meaning: her body had become a white-lipped estuary, not existing or inexisting but *plattering* — her living body, her dead corpse walled her on either side while she impossibly *left*, not in flight but in incompatibility, *plattering*. She occupied a space that was too full for suppositions — her infraspinatus formed a fist and her uvula dangled moldy cherries, a living amalgamation of what lacks in opposing poles.

In bed, sclerotic, scanning the batterlike memory of her performance, sterilized and scentless, I considered that my night's deformity jiggled solely out of the desire *to do that too*, to know what she must know, to catch that drip, because knowing is experiencing and words are the spanish moss that clings to the experience, kept alive by its juices, and surviving it. For hours my dice-shaped brain stuck to that, varnished at times with lust and fear, but — I fell asleep and dreamed.

Driving, driving, little red car with plastic seats, haha eggshell paintjob, mud and butter umbra road, fugitive, bounding curves, sky blind but reflective, granular, I watched the dull red console lights, not meaning anything, tires making the sound of a throaty ohhohhhhh-hhhhh, froggy, vibrating in the diaphragm, no stars because long birds eclipsed them to stay clean. Trees, trees, everywhere evergreens, splattered rusty silhouettes — I spelunked on a plain at sixty-five miles per hour with no rear view mirrors and no world behind me. I was alone in my father's country, indigo, vein-plaque, nonchalantly lost because the lost always converge at a single blue-black point. A drift-confusion came to me — was I going to my parents or leaving them? Glimpses of humps of the countryside arched grey-blue, the stomach of a catfish awaiting the smelly knife after the nail had been administered straight through the skull. I felt a nostalgia for the city like detoxing, the road seemed blurry, underwater windshield, and I noticed that I was becoming uselessly tired. The road narrowed, gravel, clotted, painful, white-in-the-dark gravel, instantly foreboding, clean stench of the cemetery. Crowning this menace, an arching sign over the road, like a campground's but with a sort of cuneiform engraved script, welcomed me into skid row, where corrugated, prefab, matte tin warehouses, barrel fires, flat men in burlap coats woven from the finest shadows, dogs chasing their tails, and swirls of smoke reinforced my fear. I let my foot off the accelerator, not wanting the engine to draw undue attention to me, turned off the headlights, slouched down, not wanting to be shot while deliriously sleepy. *Don't disturb the natives they bite*, I thought. I stared at the shadow men, who had no features, no eyes, but were still watching me, measuring me, waiting for the moment to converge upon me, to feast upon my wealth of features. My eyes turned away from them, focused on the road, and I noticed an electronics company up ahead with a couple streetlights and a clean parking lot occupied by two cars, and I wondered if anyone was inside. It seemed so close that I could jump out of my window and be there, yet it took my car agonizingly long to reach it, to the point where I doubted its existence, or mine, or the ability to traverse short distances,

but, finally, I made it, paved street, well-lit, serenity of folded-back nature, but the street ended, not far ahead, in the brutal sketchy teeth of a forest. I pulled over and parked the car, hoping that the lights warded off the men but expecting that they'd slowly overtake me. I was too tired to go on, too afraid to turn around and pass the shadow men again, so I resigned myself to waiting for fate or dawn, whichever comes first, trapped in the open in a sulfurous red box.

At the climax of my fear, one of the shadow figures came for me. Fear bubbled my nape, and curiosity bulged my eyes. Only a few feet away — I could feel saliva slip down my throat in regular drips, landing on the spanish-tiled roof of my heart. It was a woman, blonde with clusters of coagulated hair, reeking clothes, looking at me silently, expression somewhere between an orphan and a cannibal. Expecting that she wanted something for drug money, I got out of the car, popped open the hood, and looked at the cerebro-mechanical engine so I would look busy and uninterested, only to glance back at her waiting, mud-flecked eyes.

"I'll feel you up." Her voice, square-shaped, seemed to emanate from the splotches on her face, was direct, even brutish, though vulnerable, in an unscrupulous way.

"No thanks." I looked away stoically, eyes drawn peripherally to the engine, and I asked myself why she said 'feel you up' instead of something cruder.

"You know you want something." Insistent but apathetic.

"No, I don't." I imagined what her dirty cheeks would feel like against my inner thighs, if her tongue, too, was dirty.

"Well I want to get out of here." Impatient, nagging.

I tried to ignore her and look at the engine, which, I thought, by now, was broken, but, again, I had to look back at her. She had changed. Her face captivated me, blemishless, smooth, intense, despotic, with a hint of midnight blood underneath. Her slender body lent credence to a pink-faded-grey dress that must've been elegant, at one point. The mixture of body and head, while either in isolation would've been merely *attractive*, created something alluring — the head of an idol, sneeringly omniscient, and a girlish body, mutual foils sutured at the suitably elongated neck.

"I want to go, too." As I spoke I looked at how she listens: although she had been looking at me, her eyes became more direct upon hearing allied words.

"So let's leave."

We got into the car. I tried to turn on the headlights, but I couldn't find them. My hands rambled everywhere, no luck, and I began to feel frantic, almost impotent, across from her nonchalant glance. A heavy group of the shadow men were coming for us. In a frenzy I tried to find the headlights, becoming more and more violent, less and less successful. My mouth opened, functionless, and I started the car in the dark, sliding it into reverse — I realized, this moment, that I had been in the backseat this whole time, and I climbed into the front, car still grinding backwards.

"What were you doing?" Her voice was incredulous, cynical, but amused.

"I was trying to find the headlights." I was embarrassed.

She laughed. "You'd be trying forever, back there." This signified that I could do it now, so I reached out and turned on the headlights, which, instead of turning on the headlights, actually turned on the dawn.

A sense of fragile ease came over me. I drove away from the warehouses, feeling as if I was driving away from a hospital after a long, death-close illness. Although I didn't know the layout exactly, I knew we were in the outskirts of Dallas, in the painfully decaff morning traffic. I found myself glancing over at her, nervous, hopeful — attracted — taking in the humid silence of our breaths. Glance readjusted to the road, I realized that I was driving horribly, swerving recklessly, controllessly, and I remembered that I was tired, so tired the road seemed to be a malevolent garden of dangerously dense metals, that my fatigue had now spiked up to the point that I had trouble seeing and staying conscious, the terror of crashing the only stimulant to keep me awake. It was obvious that I had to get onto I-45, and just then I drove up its onramp, bouncing on and off the concrete barriers, fearfully looking over, only to see her, impeccably calm.

"Where do you want to go?" I tried to sound like a moviestar.

"The Museum." Downtown, softly.

I lost sight of the road in hearing her voice and seeing her face. Instead I saw my parents' old home. I wanted to take this woman there, to sit down at the kitchen table beside the tall, screen-shaded windows, to sip on a glass of orange juice and read the morning paper, occasionally nibbling on a butterlogged piece of rye toast, sometimes glancing at her with clenched eyes and a loving half-smirk, for our mantra to be a half-interested "oh yeah?"

This in mind, I asked her if she wanted to get some coffee, even though I hate coffee. Maybe the cafe would have some tea or raspberry smoothies.

"I guess so, sure." Her indifferent voice fell into her cleavage where it fused to her skin, ecstatic.

Something seemed to tell me that I should watch the road. Jerking in fear, I swerved from one near-collision to the next, a moth with torches for wings amidst a complex of bayonet-lights. I thought, "I'm going to be dead before coffee. I'll never make it downtown." Then I asked myself where the highway went, missing my turn and almost wrecking — the car in all its weaving felt like a wave-fucked boat in winter.

"It's okay. Take the next fork." She looked at me, reassuring me, but I took the left side of the fork, which was elevated, bridge-like, culminating at a wooden road block, then nothing.

"I'm too tired to drive. Can you drive the rest?" I stopped the car.

She said 'yes' with a padded voice, erotically, unclogging my anxieties, ruffling my intestines. "I was going to ask, but it's *your* car."

"Thanks." I said it impossibly meaningfully, then got out to stretch and walk around. She slid over to driver's seat, where she crossed her legs, overtly displaying the extravagant crack of a soft, pressed-up gastrocnemius under a sensual but unexcited posture, inviting without containing, so we started to talk.

The words were irrelevant, if they existed. We seemed not to focus on what we were saying, completely dissolved into the intercausal dynamic of our pitches, rhythms, tempi, and shapes. I tried to keep slow and measured, a little distanced in an attempt to filter myself into a form that she could withstand, when I really wanted to lose myself in a multifaceted, uncontrollable current of pure positive charge. It felt as if we were kissing, my lips both coarse and slick with fluid molecules, my tongue a child in a husky breeze of salt rain wheezing down a gutter through soft leaves and warm buttons.

A white van, much like my father's when I was a kid, pulled up, old and dirty but amiable, like an old man who has worked all his life and, when his last tooth left, decided not to stop working, and to smile more. It parked, and a man, barely shorter than me and with a mediterranean tan, wavy hair, and a long, thin nose got out.

I greeted him with a caustic hello, angry that my word-kiss had been interrupted.

He smiled at me knowingly, then nodded to the woman, tipping his cheap, mesh-sided baseball cap. "Nice day." His voice was overly friendly, pet-like.

"Yeah..." I scanned him — dirty pants, greasy shirt, a mechanic.

Begrudgingly, I made small talk with him, while she quietly showed her boredom in the driver's seat, wiggling her legs. I was troubled by the man because I disliked him for no reason of his own doing — in fact, he was incredibly nice and good-spirited, which, in my lust for the woman, seemed malicious, more so for the unending flow of words issuing from his general area, which I avoided looking at. Still talking, he walked around to the back of his van, opened its doors, and turned on a television. A soap opera quietly droned in the background. Deciding to leave my grudge behind, I became more friendly, and we walked out to the edge of the road, looking down from its unfinished bridge into wetlands, which gave me a satisfaction upon seeing their molten, fragmented forms.

Chummy, we walked back towards the van, and I found a grating on the road, some sort of cover for a drain. I bent down to see what was inside, my left hand's fingers between the grates. He had been looking off into the distance, admiring the morning, and he accidentally stepped on the grating, nearly severing my left hand's index finger. A weak tape of skin kept my fingertip from completely falling off, but I was startled to notice that the finger had no bone or nail, was almost penis-like. It didn't hurt, but I felt disembodied at seeing part of the inner workings of my body, the tree-ring-like circles of muscles, the unspilling blood caught in place, casually making its rounds, not curious enough to peek out.

Balancing the fingertip back on my finger, I walked over to the woman, almost proud to show it to her. She was reading a magazine and had a large bowl of chow mein in her lap. I held my finger close to her face. For a moment she looked at me. The look had a forceful directness, the bluntness of hard intimacy, repetitive spirals violently drawn on an increasingly fragile page. She pulled off my fingertip and threw it into her bowl, not angrily but incitatively.

I looked back at the man to see his reaction, but he was getting into his van.

She resumed eating. I threw my hands into the bowl while she kept on eating, now savoring each bite. My left hand's index finger seemed to lead my search, its stump over-sensualized, burning in her food. I pulled out chunks of beef, each one resembling my fingertip, which, by now, I knew she had eaten. Her lips, rapt in their chewing, smiled, and our eyes locked, lustful, violent.

Months after waking up aroused and frightened, drooling somewhat on a gold satin pillow I took from a lover years ago, I met Ariel and spoke with her frequently, never in the same manner, always with a mixture of fear, desire, admiration, intimacy, and distinctness — speaking to her is like constructing a rope bridge, throwing a knot as far as I can, only to have it swallowed by a chasm, which, in the end, is the best place for bridges, since their leaves are always fuller in the darkness. The first time I spoke to her on the phone she answered my virginal, questioning hello with what must have been two minutes of continuous laughter while lying in an ashen park, the victim of a freak razing fire; at that precise moment someone had told her to get off the phone, even though she hadn't been on it, so my call was like punctuation to a missing sentence — the laugh wounded me, made me recoil, seemed as if, instead of calling a human, I had been connected to the disembodied fumes of a fired Erinys — sharp, pleated, umbilical laughs, round organs swelling as they retreated into silence, each one identical, piling in my throat. While I recovered from her laugh —

from her scouring of my scraped knee — she said 'hi' five times — in my confusion, seemingly to anything but me, a whole salmon in a meat market, a stray cat with shaved legs, an airplane banner, a blind man's walking stick, a blue-blotted cotton swab. I tried to sip some tea to compose myself but burned my tongue — maybe it's that I hardly talked, but the burned tongue seemed to affect her speech more than mine; the conversation, based on my perhaps inaccurate perceptions of what she said, took the form of a fencing duel, where my mannered parries were rendered useless by the bluntness of her expert baguette skills, which I, in turn, took to be a much needed starching of my shirt.

During our talk I plucked the strings of an ancient, out of tune autoharp, washes of a magenta wave bleeding, delicately whiplashed from behind her aorta-studded voice. A fan blowing in the background made it seem as if she talked from atop her roof, a talking mast. I gave up the pretense of knowing everything she said. Settling into a sort of comfort, back against my bedroom's closed door, her descriptions felt like a symphony of fireflies, severed wings still flapping in the air, more iridescent for their sufferings, a bath lit by horizontal lightning. Instead of catching onto entire sentences, phrases, words, my attention seemed to react to her phonemes, vowels formed in the smooth edges of lip-slowed inhalations, MRI cross-sections of her words — though resisting the temptation to become meat, tumors, bone, and fat. I found myself growing increasingly distracted, faced with the duality of wanting to explore a person while still happily listening — I wanted to understand her anatomy, which books, with thick hazard-trumpet lines, have forced truancies, forgeries, lies, laws that inevitably slip between her organs, failing to catch in her ubiquitous fornix. I asked her what she experienced when she danced, what happened that bare moment between dance and afterwards, how there could be terrestrial life when she seemed transferred to an everywhere elsewhere, if she ever found it funny. Her answers sounded like, "Yes." Yes, plainly, hard, pole-like, imploringly. As the talk went on her words solidified, and I no longer found myself crippled in their wake — the prejudiced fear that I had found at the dance, in the dream, had been licked away and there seemed — a mutual glance at the forever teeming undersurface, a breakneck highway view of an irreplicable, unpackageable swamp from different cars at different speeds, driven with no conscious control, an honesty bounded by nervousness and ambient room noise, unbounded by the desire to come in contact with — and remain in — the generative fountain of our lives, untainted by diurnal delusions.

We finished our words for the night arbitrarily, without a cadence, and, alone, I hummed myself a wordless microtonal lullaby. Ariel stored my number on her phone, later telling me that, as an avatar beside my name, she chose a baby with three hairs sprouting from the top of its head, something she had never used before. When I was fourteen in Louisiana, happy to have what seemed to me to be facial hair, not wanting to shave away my most distinguished proof of manhood, I bragged to my father about the dark hyphens coming out of my face. My father laughed at me and said, "What's that, a three-hair goatee?"

Ariel described to me her dance in the park's ash, how her body seethed and burned afterwards, but how she was hesitant to clean herself, and, after telling her to stay 'filthy,' I mentioned to her that I often used ash in drawings, that it's a 'between material' to me, born of transformations, and that I tended to get as much on my face as on the paper, without knowing it, and people were always pointing out that my face was smudged, wiping me and pointing at me. She told me that she wanted to give me some, in a coffee can. Images instantly fluttered in the juicy cores of my eyes, and I imagined an urn resembling Jindrich Styrsky's fishtank, in which all of his favorite items swam and intermingled, an urn of still warm ash, sprouting wild fragments of flowers, boar tusks, pristine tongues, locust-shells in the shape of clouds, a portrait of the composer Alexei Stanchinsky, the fingers of gloves, lovers' expressions the moment their glances disentangle, the bit plastic tips to shoelaces, star-shaped pills half-dissolved on scraps of construction paper, and Ariel herself, the stamen from which everything seemed irradiated and certified, dancing away from the dance.

Daniel Boyer

WITHOUT MEMORY

The keythong took a header off the boulevard fastened by the tuning-pegs of violas, misspelled for the benefit of a heckuva potboiler which triumphed in Fantasyland, Sinatra's last stand at the kafuffle instigated by the ice-hockey player in the teakettle which was beginning to rumble in the vague way popularised by *West Side Story*. Faust, the producer of the entire disreputable production, had begun such with a diorama constructed by poodles who had received diplomas (presented by the benign gondolas) in jumprope, poodles who had volunteered to be keyed by sinister hoodlums wearing kicky leather boots as they sat in the parking lots overgrown with snodgrass with its milky green sickly strands and vibrant shining gold flowers shuffling their pollen on its cracked and sullen surface, on which the mystery glove had been laid in the era before the policemen danced the polka which had familiarised them with the agony of algae at that precise moment when their blue green forms were swallowed by the sperm whale. (This was a distinction that was beginning to be made that made him feel uncomfortable.) His road had diverged far inland from the crackling waves that made a sound like bacon frying, even farther inland than a Connecticut where his rotting carcass, torn in two by the same ravages of time that had eaten into her prom dress like a muffin, sat in the calm of the day to be dodged by pickup trucks and laughed at by college students hanging partway out the back, slamming back wine coolers, by vagabonds and bottle-collectors to whom the entire world was green, seen through the same beer-goggle glasses that had resulted in the birth of a firstborn son who would be kidnapped by the dwarf whose skin was green, even. Further inland, even, than the bloom of the red algae off the forgotten cape where he

158

had kissed at her neck so white and pink and her shoulders, at the worn existence of which he thought he would pass out those years before the revolver put an end to both their lives, and the life of his sister.

Another sister had had auburn hair and harboured vague ambitions of becoming a nun before the nunnery was destroyed March 12 by an iridescent tornado that turned back as it bellowed like a train over a field of summer squash, turned back after waiting for a moment, and with a scowling ice pulverised the seat of her hopes into shards which still bore the form and memory of their destruction. (From that ice she could construct half the back of Superman, but the rest had been lost to unnamed villains.) Later, even before her death at the hands of the elusive diamond spider, her auburn hair had begun to mummify, and the irreplaceable stench was like a pike thrust into the heart of her lover, the pioneer, who heard voices after the aubergine took up his career of singing in vaudeville, strumming a ukulele and wearing a funny little hat.

He obeyed everything the aubergine and his sidekicks the reptiles said. They muttered in the low whine of criminals about analog computers and the mysteries of New Mexico among its low hills of turquoise, light sandstone (was it really sandstone?) and lapis lazuli atop which invalids performed their vague ceremonies and beyond which the aliens had landed in their gleaming crafts constructed of egg white and creosote. They had had to navigate through the aquamarine trees which were so short they were more like scrub-brush, like very small hands twisted with arthritis struggling against the sky, and when they came closer still in their machines which glided noiselessly (except for their chirping language so annoying to the Air-Force sergeants from the Middle Ages over the sonar) over the sierra the sand took on the colour described in some book of paint samples that I forget. There was no one to meet the visitors except for the bodies of some cows who had frozen to death during one of Gadsdena's frequent snowstorms, on some of which someone had laid fedoras as a sign of respect; not even the abandoned gas stations you would figure that had been run by the tumbleweed and his sister back in the 1950s, their tanks rusting in the flaking air with its silvery, even metallic taste that was practically beginning to bleed, saw their arrival, because everyone had been forbidden by the Grand Duke to see the nakedness of the trees the grey figures who had begun to look like priests in the cycling light had come to plant.

The trees were just dandy in every way except that they liked to eat human flesh. In their tender branches they contained several small cocoons that silverfish, scattered by the light the arrival of which had been retarded by jet lag, reunited, on which to feast, before they remembered that it was summer, and returned to Harvard's murrey halls to yawn and bask in the mirror's reflection. These cocoons would never hatch, because the gerbils who had been given the task of supervising that fell asleep again after a soporific lecture on Algebra II, and the coat of snowfall that would crust with the temperature shift in the mid-morning would provide their blanket for the deliciousness of sleep along those trails unknown to John Wayne. (It had been thought that knight would arrive at the airport, but the huge black meteors of Wednesday had dropped like eggs to shatter every airport, but every airport alone, making his arrival as impossible as that of the Japanese at Raratonga.) Meanwhile, the duped enemy in his Zeppelin, wearing leggings of yarn and cunning, had been constructing a monument to sleep in the midst of Monaco-Ville, using slingshots and stumbling slot machines, mummified by the latest sounds of the Moors' retreat, as his tools. At height, he had remarked how the face resembled the last lemur that had been seen in Nova Scotia, an odd handkerchief-hoarder distressed by the rumble of particular subways that spoke in low tones, stubbing out his figure-eight on the rumba of the assembled widows. Some liked to describe him as a "kook," but he didn't care — he knew that lawn tennis in the presence of the wayward towers aligned with the third coast and its rocks jutting from white surf pounded with eye-blue water along which supermodels frolicked in thankfully skimpy swimsuits could bring on a course of leprosy. The salt bit at his eyes and insinuated itself into his fur and ate away at his drowsy sinuses before he wondered if he, the counterfeiter, had enough of the gold coins for a seafood lunch. He had eaten it with the girl on whose nose, the most beautiful nose in the world, the most beautiful freckles in the world appeared, eaten prawns and appetizers and geckoes, and then he had eaten her, but a miracle of digestion transferred her into his soggy pocket as he staggered down to the disinfected beach wearing a dark hat, batting the dilapidated sunlight away from his dazzling eyes as he ducked piers with splintering rotten wood crowned with lobster-shacks several sizes too small, the wooden beach with its wooden ponies and the coffins of artists that had watched up on the shore. The smell of coffee had brought with it jaundiced jellyfish arrayed in necklaces as if for war, the partly burned eggs of the dodo he had for lunch, and beach grass growing like alfalfa on the beach that the "magic hour's" sun had now turned some beautiful shade from the paint chips (like "Tucson Sunset") he absent-mindedly popped into his mouth, guided perhaps by a very faint notion that they were the only things the dog, a beautiful Irish setter who had contemplated letting his fur grow into dredlocks, would eat. A small sandcastle with a long breaker he used as a retaining wall (after the requirements of the retaining order with which the beautiful girl with the breasts had papered her eyes) would protect him against the bloated corpses of the analysts, who bobbed in the surf and made eyes at the vanilla woodpecked who, very far away, was turning into copper because the hobo's calypso had put him in awe of the ragamuffin who was wearing a wig that had not yet been disinfected by the sort of lice who wear capes to hoodwink necromancers. The smell had brought with it twitching forms of creatures he speculated were from the Mindanao Deep, and they had bitten her foot that flat and barefoot was the most beautiful thing on Earth and he had covered her foot with kisses that day her skirt had whipped in the salt air. Their trace had run twelve miles and into the mid-afternoon of the movie theatre with the feature about the woman who had carelessly slept with two men only to be followed by two demons who had driven a Volvo. Then night played upon her insecurities, and as the stunned patrons left the theatre a misting rain like listless obsidian followed them as they filed silently to their cars, which were black as well except for the grey exhaust which deigned to turn, into the air lit with small lights softened by tears, like very small corkscrews, and they drove along the elevated artery that was littered with bodies and dominos and the very sharp yet barely perceptible odour of burning cheese. He pitied those who had to live in its shadow, which was like a bear shifting its form,

consumed by football watched through their faces of cracked cement embellished by the four coats-of-arms the consumers had crudely painted on the windows of the supermarket, somewhat to his regret, because earlier there had been distended spiral creatures of glowing presence whose walk had been like a walk of coils before they were scraped away like something on his shoe.

Like a sleepwalker he went down to the lace edge of the distant ocean marred by two large stones that erupted from the surf, but that was otherwise characterised by a glass nothingness, and the line reminded him of the caked salt designs of extinct sweat in his t-shirts. He was comforted by being caked in filth, a filth which was home to various kinds of minute insects, and he stretched out his arm to move the spray (with its definite smell) like King Canute. A crab shuffled by on his way to the stock exchange, because morning was dawning, but only in a tiny croissant the chess-rooks had put up on a string over the island with its superficial gallows. He yearned to chew on a piece of licorice but he remembered the legislation decreed by the king who had again allowed coffee to contain the dried excrement of leopards — no one who wears a newspaper skirt can eat licorice.

He sighed the kind of sigh that is only permitted in winter, or certain kind of cockpits lit up so as to look miraculous, cities of jewels lying in the black capes of vampires. Before, the bombing had taken his entire family, and his attempt to put together the four limbs of the high-school had been put on hiatus after the spring schedule was announced, and he had been left kicking around the schoolyard where four humble umbrella plants had begun their ministry to the insane.

The kingpin had been an old Malaysian whose yellow beard was haunted with wingnuts, and who, despite a certain arthritis he only experienced in the presence of cucumbers when he worked at the tannery, gave him an extreme pleasure certain members of the clergy said was improper. In place of two ears he had small spiderwebs, but they allowed him to record every move of the United States Navy on miniaturized compact discs of leopard skin he passed out to kingfishers after his revolutionising the swim team when he served as vice principal of the high-school for men who would grow up to have ties which were too wide. Soviet sub hunters were aware of his activities, and they circled like brown sharks in the wake of caterpillars in the ocean that had now been placed where imaginary Idaho had been, utterly destroyed after it refused to marry him — he realised this had been a fit of immaturity, but it was too late now. Maybe he had tried to glue Idaho's two wings back on, as if he were a sort of midget potato, but that had just been a stab of guilt, and after all...

He went back to his wife and the pineapple plants that grew through the crackling concert in the yard, and the children who played on the swingset and each of his children had two heads. Every book in his library had fish gills, and heels as well, and he thumbed through them absently, because none of them were in colour, and this was all he was interested in when it came to books. He had tried to hammer this home over the cell phone at the brewery, but the cell phone with its shimmering blue eye shut him up with a long and very boring story about the adultery of the cello. He suddenly felt about a million years old and the grass cover of the billiards table with its four pinko bouncers that shone like rubies through the fields of pasta beginning to encroach on the necessary pockets that left her screaming with pleasure, and then with an angry, frosty remonstrance, left him cold, and he shattered the cue over his own ribcake, feeling a prickle of joy at the unexpectedly smoky taste this left in his mouth. He longed to kiss her eyelashes and feel the tiny, tickly feeling they made on his lips, to kiss her teeth and keep kissing her lips and her ear, but that feeling had passed after about 1870, when the boar drove one tusk into his lower thigh and he stopped remembering what letter came before O and Q, only to be resurrected by the cameo of the red rocks that led a pattern along the edge of the stream where his hunting dog would become lost twenty-seven years later after forgetting (stupid dog!) to unlock the yarn made from ravens from the veneer with which he had capped his incisors, so they were forced to go over to the turreted farmhouse and meet the farmer's daughter only to be separated in a fog that the setup for a lame joke said was like the lace in Belgium.

Entire cities had been destroyed in the night those four years he spent at Yale, lost in twenty-nine cups of coffee and, perhaps, several more cigarettes as his professors kept murmuring about the crucifixion. Entire villages had been pulverised by lemonade, churches smashed by creeping crud, granaries bulldozed by almonds whose creepy little eyes wrenched him out of bed in the preying night to barf up everything. He had been abandoned by everyone except a lonely buffalo who wandered outside the window that had been overtaken by tinfoil and crabgrass towards which telephone wires tangled in a menacing (but not, really, technically, legally threatening) way, attempting to force him to do the foxtrot. A completely superfluous membrane was all that was left to keep him and his dogs safe from the portfolio brandished by the three dancing skeletons, but really all they wanted to do was whisk them away, though it discomfitted him that one of them was going to have to wear high heels.

He remembered them being slick and folding dollar bills like a small tent. They had passed truck-stop prostitutes wearing short denim skirts, ATMs lit up with an internal glow of green in the middle of blocks, and squares with muffled cries that were difficult to interpret, as they seemed to come from narrow fissures of sand and docks which had become separated from the piers and passed discussions to set up tontines and were swatted at by treasonous polar bears. It seemed like one of those movies where there's a love triangle, but one of the lovers had a hair on her head that reminded him of an electric substation, and the other was noted for her practice of wearing a paper kimono. He had begun to determine that the one was pretentious and the other was a violinist whose hair and the side of whose arm were constructed of a shivering alabaster, and she was all he dreamt about every night, though his roommate had told him to shut up because he kept talking in his sleep before the intruder had come in and murdered them both.

A man whose shoulders and black clothing and breath crackled with electricity should have been an obvious threat, but he and his girlfriend were as oblivious as a toothbrush those days. The supermarket had shone with a blue and green light and they had gone shopping for melons and her eyes were darkly lit and they were lit with sparks and the lambent necklace illuminated her laughing eyes and teeth before it was ripped off her neck with the moles in just the right place by an unemployed orangutan.

The ape had been a lumberjack, but the job was shut down to protect the spotted owl. Various village personages, whose heads were filled with sawdust, organised a protest along the street which ran by the side of the brick mill whose wheel was so lazy it refused to turn, unless it was another time, when it turned backwards. Football players, some from the 1970s, some from the 1960s and some from the 1800s, assembled later that week to fight the longshoremen, and in the first pitched battle of glowing steel figures, lugubrious dumbbells who were perched on pierced octagons of separated pavement battled to a standstill under the watchful eye of the local luggage supervisor who had surveyed them skeptically from a wooden porch decorated with hunting trophies — heads cut off burlap creatures they had severed in a display of "sportsmanship." After the warning lights were given by his buddies the two volcanos, with whom he had gone drinking many moaning nights after his divorce, they decided against an impromptu killing spree and opted for a relaxing night of building an igloo in the July heat.

With the exception of one red-haired truck driver who suffocated, it all went really well after they managed to demolish the local junior high-school (it had been built by some numbskulls out of daffodils), which was standing in the way. The inevitable nostalgia for those years they made love in the pole-vault pit and pounded in the footsteps of Lord Coe along the courtyards of some Cambridge college had not been a particular obstacle after an obliging doctor had performed an emergency lobotomy, though it had left them unsure as to how perform certain pieces from the oboe repertoire. Their overdone jokiness, their sedulous labour on the pimple plantation, their abortive plan to scrape a peephole into the girls' locker room, all seemed very far away anyhow now that they were men of savoir-faire with mutual funds and wives who wore diamond breastplates and tiaras they had bought at auction from the estate of Josephine Baker; they listened to Learn Japanese in 30 Days in their headphones on the airplane and stretched out their leather shoes, unruffled by that, after certain discreet assassinations and stripping of pension plans, they were the masters of the world. They no longer bothered to think about the night the bodies of their fathers and the jobbers with their brown bowlers rained down from the sky after the carriage bombs carved a hole into the exchange bordered with savage diamond that would later be painted by a 19th century master who saw five green dots in the sky over the sharp, chalkly, unsentimental Mediterranean coast unsupervised by nodding, senile forms, forms of no-nonsense secretaries in lip-licking boots, lovers in a sentimental mood at the trattoria, barrel-chested noblemen. Even their parrots did not dare to repeat the truth they learned from the winking phonograph records that no longer bore even the memory of being carried with their portable stereo from the raucous prep-school days they bounced on their beds covered with cobwebs and sliced the mud with its delectable smell from their cleats and pores after the struggles of rugby and cross-country's lonely, wintry pilgrimage. Around these icy edges there emerged a flory or perhaps a trefly pattern like the increasingly elaborate bordures etched on the shields of knights who waited, with lances bristling, to have at the infidels on the other side of the copse from which men in rough brown wool gathered faggots and switches of birch pink as your buttocks into which the black triangles of stylisation cut; the sergeants had discussed burning this possible hideout, an exclave in this stinking swamp of blood into which they had been plunged. The horses who had been bred for pounds turned up the earth in thick clumps that had the refreshing smell of mud where later the XC runners would thunder under the overpass on which the girls in their wool skirts watched, clutching books to their breasts, one of them wearing the beret she had purchased in Paris after MacMahon had leveled the city into an indifferent expanse of dusty white, with nothing left, not the welcome respite of bakers and not the sweet curlicues of jazz slipping into the air of a night air weighed down with possibilities and kisses and closet suicides who had meant to weigh their pockets down with stones but had actually just placed in their black coats they had started wearing after listening to The Cure very hard, white peeled potatoes, so that he floated in the dark Seine cut with zebra stripes of green and did not sink and slip as might be sung about on those glistening records on which his black reflection spun and bobbed, his edges framed by the pink diamonds of the groove and the white diamonds the spinning of those LPs of gothic music made with their impenetrable darkness.

Since his black hat had been lost after he was hanged his twin had removed from the red box (as if it were for the Queen) the key (made of the bones of a small Chihuahua and the pearl teeth of his smile) that would lead him to everything he needed to know to kill the president. They had met in hotel lobbies and they drank iced mochas as they sat in whinnying chairs in which they slumped back with a delicious slumping as they saw the women pass by wearing nylons and the trained chimpanzees pass by wearing hats made of unicorn fur and all the while they were oblivious to the knives being sharpened for them. The muffler collector, who was missing one of his lower front teeth and had not washed his hair in 3.5 days and wore a flannel shirt of the tartan of a Scottish clan that never existed over his wife-beater, had planned to murder them as soon as they got to the radiator like an asthmatic dog who hissed and sighed (small figures of magnetic filings did not, however, dance in his enigmatic shadow). In the garage which had now been painted with delicate watercolours on Ecuadorean swimsuits and in which he was carefully reassembling the body of Cab Calloway's taxicab, the garage that had now found its way into armory and the garage with its walls lined with pinup girls, he had had to care for the giraffe fetus, which was particularly difficult to do now that some heroic terrorists had taken out the power with the aid of a rocket launcher they had purchased directly from Mt. Zion. The giraffe fetus, covered in part with a thick dark horsehair, lay sessile on the cement floor, several millimetres from death, and he could not help but think that if the Pope had not smoked dope, none of this would have happened. He waited to hear any muffled sound, as muffled sounds were invariably accompanied by the scent of vanilla, but the geothuk and the geoduck were of no assistance; they were playing with a rope in which they had tied some very beautiful knots and were accompanying themselves with a bawdy song they were playing (along with the lasso) on the virginal. The tour for which they were practicing would eventually be held in front of all the crowned heads of Europe; they had seen Limberger, with its delicious smell, and Kafka, whose horse galloped across the dark form of metaphor. They had been caught by the Red Army as they attempted to cross the frontier smuggling seven red eggs; while in prison, they attempted to build a bicycle pronto out of vinegar that would have all the characteristics of Pegasus, but they didn't know what a pegasus was and had to look it

up in a dictionary. Every day's passage was marked on the walls made
of duct tape, along with the various things they had to do in person
that day: do the laundry for a number of silhouettes, conduct a career
of rack and ruin at midnight, make lemonade for the privateer. (The
privateer was cut of rock crystal and had a particular enthusiasm for
hamburgers.) Every day the guard, who had to smoke cigarettes as he
had short, red hair and could bench-press 220 pounds, would knock
out of few more of their teeth and chat with them about the Danish
philosophers (he had even met some as he wandered down the beach
in cutoffs and flip-flops, accompanied by this ancient jaguar). The bars
were made of string beans but they didn't dare to budge from the perch
they had, in a moment of paranoia, constructed out of sasparilla: the
whistling sound that assaulted their dears all day and all night appeared
to be an emanation of the echo Cahill had left after he stamped on the
wall with mysterious socks an emblem of blood. Down the hall there
were hillocks of salt through which they would have to zip-zip-zip like
pinballs if they were to escape, wearing white Panama hats invented
by Bon Jovi and drove driven cars made out of pink lemonade like
those driven by Miami-Vice detectives. The girls who cooed to them
out of the distant shade and the verandas constructed on the side of
the volcanos, the palms that waved out of the unread breeze like some
sort of prefiguration of a second coming, they would shrug off like her
ill-conceived hairstyle inspired by the last days of disco. They stubbed
out their cigarettes in Art Deco ashtrays and forgot about socks for a
while and screwed up their faces as they thinly sucked in pot out in the
parking lot with squinty eyes and joked about what a crock the lectures
of the economics teacher were, and their pride in coming from Stanton
Township led them to make jackets with designs burned out by lasers
they had borrowed from the Pink Floyd show. They skipped class and
went to buy records at the store with the clerk with the red hair and
bee-stung lips, their hair filled with dust and shards of skeet, out of
which (the hair) they brushed it with strong and beautiful hands. They
laughed at their political hair as they shuffled along with drugged eyes
and thought about Naomi Watts if her hair had been very, very straight,
like a pin, and seen through a keyhole in the door to a cabin in a yacht
at sea, ploughing and foraging in waves of tan. These musings had

not yet been set aside by the bookbinder Amanda, who imagined that morels grew from his eyelids and precepts. (The sun of the desert, ungloved, had caked her lips and her two secret fingers for seven days after her entry into French West Africa, followed as she had been by concerned cattle.)

Pansies bloomed impromptu, formed by the closing of her eyes. Her nightgown took up a rampant position. It was followed down the hall by the sodden footsteps of the National Socialists. Small forests, a miniature world in which they could do studies, sprang up in each of these shameful wetlands, that nevertheless were followed by shameless and adoring sympathisers wearing the medals they had been awarded eighty-five years ago. One of these medals was a mischievous butterfly whose pranks at the Milwaukee Institute of Trucking against the pariahs were the stuff of legend. He had had two cuckoos guard his nest in which he had posters put up on the walls, an elaborate stereo system, and even his own television on which he watched the "cop dramas with the innovative camera angles." He opened up his television to do some work, attempting to make his black-and-white set into a pink-and-white, as he had begun to take a more cosmopolitan view of the angels holding their demonstration across from the central bank, with placards written in Magyar, though the letters had been decorated with superfluous hairs in some places (palaces). He turned the knob off, followed by a satisfying sizzle and zap — he had imagined that one of these days he would organise the multidinous varities of these in a catalogue, though they would have suffered if he had done so, pasted to the page like beetles pinned to a board, Paul and Ringo struggling to escape, waving arms and drumsticks though after all they never made people able to grasp the beautiful world of entomology. Brighter than any armor arrayed for kings the breastcoat of the stags and dung-beetles glistened as they began their crusades of sidewalks as grey as her hair, and he would still bend down, before the pinpricks of snow drifted down caught in the flood of light, dancing on the air with its fall cool, to hear the quiet scritch-scritch of their progress, rolling the sun along the sulking sky.

March 21-22, 2007
Dodgeville, Michigan USA

Ribitch

MORSELS

"The Moon"

The years of pantomime, a mask or a judge, a whisper of a night that smells like lizard. A room filled with glass, the moon, the frozen stooped shoulders of a claw in an evening gown designing flesh. I disrobe the mantle over a precipice of impossible disfiguration and the laughter that moves about the room is clasping hands. The light, the moon, the womb, the period of darkness beneath the storm. Hair, bandoliers of breath, fingers twitching where the mountains crust scab splits, spilling a black blood across the sky's swollen chest. The years of porcelain, swelling in an immense throat, where voices tremble in a blade of monkey blood. Nothing quivers like the quiet solution. The earth barks back. The moon, the womb, an egg filled with grasshoppers ready to explode in a crystal shroud of forbidden whispers. The moon, the womb, and a face that lingers with the deep breathing wells that haunts with the night's skin.

The room stumbles. The shank of my leg detaches itself from my body and promenades before me, hung in a handkerchief. I look at the woman, who looks into a dark mirror. Her feet are caught up in thorns. A wasp is hung on her thighs. Her thighs that are wooden ships with sails of powder moth wings and perfume. A midget clings to her legs, grotesque and twisted; he is an image wearing a black robe that smells like cat. He looks like a cat, the soft fur running off his face, the slight tilt of his pointed ears. "Uranus, your moons." She said. "My clitoris is hanging from the stars. The blood is my lips separated with the horizon's soft pink legs. Uranus, savory juice of love! Uranus, the moons of your folded smile elude toward the rivers of infancy. My lips hunt the fox. My vagina is grass and the seed of the sun. The stars exclude the horizon that bleeds in my palms. Morning moistens its thighs on my eyes of locust and my tongue of burning oil."

My heart moved in a circle. The twitch of a song split through the night with its warnings of herons. The woman stepped within a circle, dragging the midget, who opened his wings. The night was full of blues and the sweet weeping alabaster of arms. The night of contagion in my legs stretched into glass harps. I found it hard to speak, but finally my vocal chords released themselves. "I came here because I heard you were a teller of fortunes," I said.

"The future is like the ringing of silent bells," she cried. "A heart in the sky, the moon, the moon. A feather floats as time. You came not for the fortuneteller's wheel, but for all time's sunsets. The past with the dead knocking for entrance into the present, the present is like a fool on the border of sanity and the future is an automobile run out of gas. Nothing shall return, but the alchemist glass and with it the letters of science shall be broken. You came not for the future, but for the moon."

"The moon?" I asked.

"The womb," she replied.

"The womb?" I asked.

"The frozen specters on this desert," she replied.

The midget looked up at me with his eyes a cold white. Hunger lingered within the shadows of his face. A carousel horse danced across his lips. He spoke! "Are you afraid of the night?"

Everything puzzled me. I looked around for something familiar. I spied an old hat and placed it on my head weeping. The woman lit a candle and formed a circle around it. "The moon," she said. "And the mirror reflecting Uranus, the gowns shadow and the mist. Swallow the night, swallow the night. We first walk through the doorways of a darkened tent. Pass through the dream, the tent waits."

"The Tent"

I entered the tent, which smelled of bread and sandalwood. The tent was entirely black except for silver patches cut into various positions of the moon. The tent was entirely devoid of furniture and objects, except for a red cape which was illuminated by the moon patches. Through curiosity or intuition, I was led to sit beside the red cape. There was a bowl of red fluid sitting upon the red cape, into which I gazed. The fluid shimmered as if it were crystal, as if it were a voice of fishes, as if the morning were samples and the light were seas of flesh.

I sat for what must have been several hours, the dark silence a gloved hand over the tent's mouth. My body felt heavy, as if it had been sprouted from enormous wings. My breathing was a rhythmic force of songs like frogs, like coyotes, like spiders, like all the creatures that speak with the moon. The silence was soft, but had sharp edges. Something stirred in the air like a brush with the breeze or the smoke of sensation. It felt like a salamander's storm or a winter full of smelts. The grey dawn with its arms dressed in lace; a face dressed in dreams; I heard a voice as sweet as salt. "Enter the moon of the first part, the golden diatessaron and the carousel of sleep." I fell into a deep slumber and dreamed.

"The Dream"

A wombat fell out of space, caressing in its arms a fog that was not truly clear and seemed to bleed across the floor. The eye glass, a hole in the center of the earth; from it rose a smoke as sweet as the rushes. The seams split open throwing forth great spasms of shrill smoke. A white light was in the passage of the second darkness, the second swallow and the second hunger. The passage into the smoke smelled of fish with their arms wound around a secret voice, the voice of dry cracked leaves. I lead three faceless horses toward a pond of silver. Stalks of grain rise out in a display of wreaths. The tips of each bleed translucent ruby red. If the faceless horses separate, stairways are revealed. Stairways to where? The horses run past splintering the air, but they are devoid of the light of space. Awakened from sleep, I wander amongst the debris of snails, wandering where the first step takes the second going. I desire the length of a wall or beyond the mixture of advantageous delusion.

"The Stairway"

The stairway did not go down nor up, but at a horizontal illusion. That is to say perpendicular to the wind. I know that my legs are thrown back. Time does not exist in the parallel, only strange whistles and faint figures that parade through the misty hallways of ambiguities' smile. The ambiguous stairway and the forgotten object are like an ostrich in the act of disappearance. The perspective of a well in mutation is far too deep. The stairway is like a voice caught in a tunnel, translucent and invisible, a raging forest of sensuous arms. Frogs cough bitterness in the roots of playful laughter. I enter the stairway entering me, following the dawn's hermaphrodite through the stairwells of hallucination, through my eyes of moon thighs.

My lungs though collapsed were birds. My lungs though collapsed were monuments of feathers. The voices wind a heavy preponderance of holography. Sensation is alive with a woman's waist. An umbrella of eyes winks beneath the faucets, letting dreams dribble along the slender waist, along the swollen thigh, along the forest of night where lips wait for the dawn to drive them from decay. The swallows in the walls are hermetic whispers and pearl inset within the eye's pupil to create a voice of clouds. Stairways like the voices that penetrate my belly. A hole in the hole where shadows linger possess their shadow's finger. A night of crows and there are no hand rails, only smoke to cling to.

The soft pillow of dawn possesses me like a clinging knife in the cupboards of sweet whispers. It is the moon's relaxation that eclipses the sun's overbearing hunger. I count hundreds of intentions with their wavering glass blades that lick to and fro like a pendulum. Across the eyelids a fish swims with arms whose fleshy milkyness is a parade of hallucinated dreams of wet fire. Ice crystals and domes of vision are scarcely out of the passage of view when they intertwine in a dance of moths. Their feelers wield their gowns of translucent whispers. Interiors are far beyond the spectral of light, far beyond the measure of silence and far beyond the dark underbelly of the centipede's silver circle. The interior's warm and at the end of that is a Mozambique canvas and a pearl casket. The sharp remark is from silence's quivering pale

monolog. Time is incandescent and it is also a spiral watch. To descend or to ascend the stairway's darkness is a parade of costly tongues.

"The Plain"

"Enter the moon of the second part," a voice suddenly burst like fire. "The moon of the second part, Osiris is searching for his bodily remains amongst the reeds and the desert sands." I smell the smell of hay burning upon my eyelids. I look and see a man dressed in brown pajamas coming my way. I await his arrival, counting the burns in the sky.

"Ho," I call out to him. "Where are you going and why the unusual dress?" He passed me by saying nothing, but dragging his entrails behind him. He was the dreamy pestilence of fish. The fog of thick walls surrounds the medieval dance and I am alone skirting the sands' sweet song. The dry mouth searches the sky for a moist tongue. Where birds hide, fountains express their desire. Boxes of burning secrets are those desires. The sun is forgotten in its linen of crossed legs. A mass of thighs have crossed an ill forgotten dream on a sea of fish that are frozen voices and a magic of sumptuous time. I cry out like the night's robe. Grains of whispered salt are the arms that swim and the plaster face explodes where birds migrate. The straight jackets of magician otters entreat a pleasure for a parade. The forgotten paradises of pleasures sit in the elevator of eyes sinking deep into a moist mouth.

I felt that I must follow the man dragging his entrails, but something gripped my heart. As he disappeared, I saw a faint outline of a paint brush in the sky. I sat and watched as the clouds unfolded their arms and the brush moved in a slow dance.

"The Painting"

A bird's beak could not pluck from the sky a more delicate wish. The fleeting moment of silent whispers is a stroke of green on Seurat's flesh. I have listened to the gentle flow of water passing over my chest in a guarded fashion. Silence awakened the stars' ears. Some mysterious hand has reached up and struck a torch to the sky, setting the clouds aflame and letting loose a thunder of voices that ask for directions to the fallen mill. What could have been taken for nuns, were actually penguins huddled near the railway station. They were waiting for their hunger to be brought down with the shades. Darkness and a painting of the moon beside the moon, it was a picture of a woman's lips hidden in the crevasse of my own lips like a foaming tongue of the ocean. A picture of a word making love to the swollen rubber in unseen places under the breast where the moon only goes out at night.

The seductive clouds that hang in the air resemble a bandage over an immense wound. My eyes have lifted themselves from my face and stand with the birds on the horizon. A picture of an old man is weeping into a cave. There are little stones arranged in the form of symbols at his feet. The picture has some words written across the sky, "Les Temps du Poisson." The whole painting can be misconstrued as a fable, a mythical applause, and a magical dance of squares or a motion of movement sounding out unheard whistles. Hyenas howl in the distance. By the sound of their voices I know that their shadows resemble roosters. Wolves awaken in the briars beneath my pillow that I carry in my arm.

The seasons, the stars and the breathing sky are a moment all pressed in the quarter of the hand that is as small as a bird's wing. A voice from out of the depths is cold as the abyss of shadowed whispers. I parade them amongst the foil's reflection. The soft whisper of a stone floor angles out in a direction that only droplets of blood can follow. The myth can not be complete without aura of Eros and the dance of a thousand moons faces the hovering bed of iron. Fortune cast its left eye into a black hole and rabbits speak loudly about the horned frost. The moon, the black moon never is silver under a night of blood. Its brilliance only comes after the sacrifice and then only with leather shoes.

MOSTIANBO

After an uneventful train ride, I was nearing my destination.
Scientific study or pleasure, I was about to embark upon a most
remarkable journey. I was to be met at the station by Dr. Louis DuVille,
the esteemed professor of cultural anthropology, who would then guide
me to my final destination, the island of Mostianbo. This island up
till now was unknown to the outside world. It had been only recently
discovered hidden within a blanket of thick unmoving mist off the
coast of Northern California. This event had caused quite a stir in the
media, for this body of land had eluded even the most sophisticated
satellite observations. Now I was to be amongst the first of a team of
observers to record conditions on this remarkable island.

Dr. Louis DuVille was waiting on the platform and after
vigorous hand shakes and greetings he ushered to me to a waiting car.
"We must hurry," he exclaimed to me. "The window of opportunity is
indeed very short. Approach to the island can only be taken at certain
hours and under very rare conditions. The tides are right this very night
and we must make haste. I have a boat waiting for us, fully rigged with
all the recording equipment that you may need. I will explain further
in the car."

The excitement in Dr. DuVille's eyes as he spoke was very
contagious. "The island, only discovered a few days ago is full of
unusual anomalies, curious plant life and its inhabitants are truly
amazing," he explained. I could hardly contain my own excitement
as he tried to describe what he had only heard by word of mouth. The
only abatement to my delirious excitement would come with first-
hand observation of this marvelous island called Mostianbo.

The Island loomed before us, hidden by a shroud of mist so
thick that it only appeared after we were almost upon its shores. A
sonorous music could be heard, that seemed to float across the waves

as if to greet us strangers in a strange land. It was soft and melodic, almost as if it were produced by electronic and synthetic instruments. I looked quizzically at Dr. DuVille, who in turn looked as equally baffled by this musical phenomenon. Our boat was anchored just off shore and we took a skiff to the beach. At first glance there was nothing unusual about the beach, just long stretches of sand, jutting rock and the interior cutoff from view by a wall of foliage and trees. But then something caught my eye, there was a slight shimmering hue about the sand, a slight glow that was almost undetectable to the eye. I reached down and picked up a handful of sand and let it sift through my fingers. The sand floated rather then fell, in a luminous cascade that resembled stars or bits of light. It took a full minute for the last luminescent grain to settle back upon the beach. I placed a small sample into a vial, for further analysis and placed the vial into my back pack.

The music seemed to be coming from just beyond the trees so we continued forward to discover its source. At the edge of the forest we stopped to examine the plant life that grew at the edge of the sand. The first plants we came upon were small, gelatinous succulents of about 6 inches in height that were festooned with small berry-like fruits. The young unripe fruits were hard, yellow, about the size of a pea, while the ripe fruits were the size of my thumb and bright blood red in color. I picked one and held it to my nose; it had a sweet rosy smell with a hint of cinnamon. I bit into it and my mouth was instantly filled with a sensuous array of flavors, like none I have tasted before. I almost felt drunk with the richness of the flavor. The texture of the fruit was chewy like gum but then completely dissolved after about four minutes of chewing. The next plant was a flowering bush, whose blossoms were the shape of small birds hanging by their beaks. I examined these briefly, promising myself to make sketches of them later in my note book. The music was louder now and its source could now clearly be seen. The trees at the edge of the beach towered above us nearly 50 feet, their trunks were about ten inches in diameter and were covered with small holes of varying sizes. As the wind blew from offshore it passed over the holes in the trees like air through a flute. The tones played off each other, the rising and falling of the gusts would change the level of the tones in the air. Quite remarkable:

music created from the natural environment.

As we moved further into the interior our eyes were met by more wondrous sights. Just beyond the stand of musical trees we came across what appeared to be the first signs of intelligent life. We came into a clearing of about 30 feet in diameter, clearly cut from the trees in a perfect circle. In the middle of the clearing there stood a totem. The totem circumference at the base was 3 ½ feet; its height must have been 75 feet or more. It was made of polished, smooth black stone. It was very intricately carved with the shapes of some anterior life forms. These figures seemed to be laid out in a biogenesis of a species. They wound around each other in an erotic dance that seemed to be a continuous flow of sexual communication. The creatures seemed to be of a polymorphic nature as they blended and molded into the next. I walked the circumference of the totem, trying to follow some logic as to how the figures were laid out. When I reached the point of view in which I had started, my senses felt a sudden shock. The figure on which I had begun my visual inspection had changed, or so it seemed. The change was subtle, as if it had moved. To confirm this phenomenon, I retrieved my digital camera from my pack and took a picture of the figure and the surrounding figures. I then marked a spot in the sand and walked slowly around the totem. Again the figure had changed. It was swallowed by and was swallowing the surrounding figures. I set up my tripod and took several pictures in a time-lapse mode to inspect this change. I called Dr. DuVille over to confirm my observations. The figures were indeed changing. They were metamorphosing one into the next in an exquisitely slow dance. I put my hand very lightly on to the surface of the totem. I expected the surface of the stone to be hard and cold, but instead it was warm, almost velvety in texture, and it moved! I could feel it pulse and shift. A living totem, pulsing out its own biogenesis, it was creating its own history in this moving stone flesh.

My heart was beating rapidly from the excitement of this incredible discovery. So lost was I in the meditation of the totem's movement that I began to feel a dislocation of my consciousness. It was as if I were being pulled into the biogenetic thread of this life form. I began to hear a voice that was not my own, but it was in my head as if it were my own thoughts. "We are phantoms," it spoke. "We are the empty spaces that fill themselves with the marvelous. We are the loose threads that begin to unravel on the fabric of your reality." I opened my eyes and looked at my hand resting on the totem. The totem had wrapped several small tentacles around my fingers. "You are looking into the heart of me, of us, of yourself. You are surprised. You seem to have been expecting something else; something flesh and blood." The tentacle was now wound up to my elbow. "We are the stuff of your dreams, your wildest imaginings and your deepest desires."

"Why are you here?" I asked.

"Why are you?" questioned the totem.

"Because a new land was discovered, where none had been seen before," I replied. "Because the world had been thought to have been charted and that there was nothing left to discover. I find myself caught in the dilemma of the curious."

The totem seemed to convey a sense comfort in our ability to find a bond of communication between us. "You speak as if discovery has become a rare commodity. Discovery is! It is the very fabric of my species. Today we are, tomorrow we will be… and in between is the discovery of becoming." The end of the tentacle touched my face and explored my features. "Your face is rigid. The change that takes place is only subtle. The face of your birth is not too distant from the face you will wear at death. We are polymorphic. Yesterday my haunches rode high and I was a male, today I am female and my vaginal cavity secretes another species, which will in turn swallow me in its passing. I am a river of water that flows over ever changing stones. I am and we are… just wisps of shadow that shift from one surface to another."

"How is it you exist?" I asked. "What is your sustenance? Do you eat food, drink water? What is it you dream?"

"Sustenance is what you term as poetry; it is the law of entropy released from an envelope. You have taste buds, we have buds of taste. This totem is a complete biosphere in of itself. Existence is what we dream and dreaming is the breath of the biosphere."

"Are there any more of you on this island?" I asked.

"There are many such biospheres," the totem replied. "The dance of dreaming is not a solitary act. Our consciousness is separate but our dreams are hyper connected by a system of lobes far beneath the surface of the island. This is the way we communicate amongst ourselves. This is the way we sing the song of our genetic histories. If you sit with me for long enough I will tell you stories with as many endings as there are beginnings and endless possibilities of twists in plot. If you approach another such as myself, the tale will lead to a different conclusion altogether or may have a slight deviation in the structure of language. The linguistics may vary from one to another with fine threads that will weave a tapestry of the possibility of a multilevel sense of reality. Reality changes as often as the surface of our skin and the polymorphic structure of our form. The time of migration nears, we will be in movement soon."

The tentacle receded and again became part of the flow. Dr. DuVille touched my shoulder and I felt no more connection with the totem. "What is it?" he asked. "You seemed too caught up in a trance."

"It spoke to me," I said as I turned to him. "You did not hear it? It's alive! This is truly amazing; we have met with the indigenous life of this island. There is so much to learn here. I'm trembling, look at my hand." Indeed my hands were shaking. The song of the trees began to rise in pitch and tempo. The winds from off shore had picked up and were creating a crescendo of sound that was becoming unbearable.

"We must get back to the boat," shouted Dr. DuVille. "I don't think I can bear much more of this sound. My ears are beginning to hurt." We picked up our things and proceeded back toward the beach. Before leaving the clearing I turned back toward the totem. It began to quiver all over, and then it began to twist and contort. Pulling itself from the ground it then simply floated away, dividing and separating as it disappeared into the interior.

POLITICIANS OF THE DEPRAVED

Motion sickness is necessitated by the flow of hair that is the under balance of clouds. Too many voices call out in the rain to be constituted as a replenishing of dead saints. Who stands at the apex of the day wearing the clothing of the dead, who in their despair depart on woeful wooden boats to seek the silent rose petals of the silent? So silent is their breath that they may be mistaken for the dead. So loud are their tremors of doubt that their ears are pinned to the floor. Here in the stale mists of ammonia a woman whose hair is lit on fire by frail exasperated monks takes repose in the heat of the day by examining her own forehead with forceps made of glass. She opens a small cavity in the flesh revealing a colony of spiders that eat at her brain causing a frontal lobotomy that leaves her transfixed in a state of agitation. It is in this state of agitation that she speaks in mumbled tones and caustic automatic phrases. "The somnambulant fish, the veiled interruption of shadows follows me to the edge of the well." She grins at the walls with no response. She pulls at her eyelids, lifting them to release a flock of birds. "Too many," she responds with a despondent glance. "There are far too many to hold on my tongue." She turns toward the door as if to leave, but her skirt is caught by the light, preventing her from any kind of movement.

Outside on the pavement a crowd gathers to elicit the crowning of the weather. Storms gather around their feet in small eddies. These pools of climatic conditions whirl about like crows. The disturbance discolors all the chaotic visitations of meteorological transmutations. The crowd shouts wordless obscenities that are frozen to their palates like thin wafers of dead skin. Policemen gather around them and peer into blocks of distortion glass that reflect the seasons of their latent brutality. It is under the guise of this reflection that they began to dislocate the tiny nerve endings of their cranial cortex.

The woman stares out her window at the crowd gathered below. A deep sorrow overtakes her and throws her into a deeper melancholia than she had ever experienced. She began to cry, but the tears were hard droplets of glass that fell to the floor shattering, leaving tiny shards of pointed glass that gathered at her bare feet. As she paced back and forth by the window the glass cut into her flesh leaving behind a trail of blood. Her nervous condition prevented her from feeling the small cuts left by the glass and only agitated her sense of despair. "If I cry out," she thought, "they will discover that I exist and they will come for me and if they come for me they might uncover my chaste and lonely solitude." She placed her hands against the panes of glass wishing she could push away the intrusion. "If my solitary self-imposed imprisonment is discovered then they may seek to liberate me from my exile and seek to force me to reenter the world of their prying eyes. My shame would be extracted by a flock of birds and dropped like seeds into soil that is moribund and evil; the result would be the growth of weeds that would engulf the earth with the despair that is my own."

The crowd began to grow; filling the street with upturned faces, salient whispers, shouts and cries. Their faces revealed a certain degree of futility and anxiety that exposed the temperament of mob madness. They began to stomp their feet in a cadence that suggested the heated insanity that was about to lose control. The air was thick with fear and the heat of fury; all sanity was lost as they rocked back and forth, from one foot to the other. The sky began to crack, opening up a gap in the clouds that resembled a wound. The crowd cried out as the wound began to bleed and the blood flowed down into the streets. At the height of the frenzy something dreadful began to take place, thousands of dead birds fell from the sky, finches, larks, doves and ravens, birds of every description and size. The panic that ensued fell across the crowd like a tsunami of menace and malice.

The woman in the window collapsed to her knees, weeping, her body convulsing with fever chills that swept over her, possessing her every fiber. "I am discovered, I am doomed, and the whole world is as if it were my flesh, cancerous and filthy. I have been daunted by the very life that has cursed me from birth. I should have passed into death from the womb, still born and lifeless like dust." She dug her fingernails into her palms, drawing blood. She licked her hands, the acidic salt taste consuming her in delirium and loathing. "If I must, I'll remove my face and implant it with another. I'll rip my soul from this dried shell of a body and fling it to the stars where it may be consumed by a black hole or left to wander as an aimless comet without

a tail."

     She rose to her feet and peered out the window at the crowd assembled outside. The crowd had amassed into a sea of alarm. They moved about as if blinded, aimless and without meaning. Their cries reached a vociferous pitch of ear-splitting decibels such that the very air began to tremble. From a low rumbling opprobrious call that opens oceans of monolithic dinosaur jawbones to the shrill high pitched soprano reverberations of mucus beetles, the nervous twitch of the air created a habitual catatonic excitation. Maldororian ossification of the senses took every ounce of strength the woman possessed. It was by sheer will alone that she stood before the window with her forehead resting on the pane, her fingers splayed on the glass like spiders, her eyes filled with the fog of a distant sorrow. "Has there ever been a time," she cried out, "that I have not been the focus for such suffering." Her head taped the window glass. Tap, tap, tap, and tap in a rhythmic pulse, tap, tap, and tap. "If there were a God, would he have condemned me to this wretched soulless imitation of life? If so, then his is a miserable humor. The joke of it all lacks all amusement and taste." Tap. Tap, tap and tap. Her head bounced off the window glass. The glass began to shatter as her head reverberated off the thin pane.

     The glass gave way with an explosion, raining shards of razor sharp glass onto the crowd below. The glass fell; cutting through flesh, tendon and bone. Their cries were cut off as the cries escaped their mouths, falling to the ground like a cold whimper. The woman above waved her arms in the air as the crowd fell to their knees. She howled out in the blood stained night, "EVIL, reverse the letters and it is live. To live is to be drowned in the excesses of evil." She looked down on the carnage below and shouted, "All of you, the dead who think you live, you are the face of evil, the mirror of darkness and the skin of the earth. Your souls are eaten by demons that resemble yourselves. Do you recognize them? Do they greet you in the morning when you shave or brush your teeth? This bastard universe that spawned the vile stench of murderers, rapists and child molesters, you are all politicians of the depraved."

Philip Kane

MY GRANDFATHER, THE CARTOGRAPHER

When I was five, I realised that I had the ability to lift myself from the ground and float away like a helium balloon. My mother, after two rather alarming occasions outdoors, when I nearly drifted beyond her reach before she could grab hold of my foot, began to tie a long piece of string to my ankle whenever we left the house. She was a cautious woman, but all the same it was probably a sensible precaution in the early days, until I'd learned to control my flight and to come down as well as go up. At home, though, I was allowed to fly without restrictions.

I took to reading near the ceiling, rolling over onto my back and placing my feet onto the ceiling itself to steady my position, as I had quickly discovered that even a slight breeze through an open window could cause me to bob about uncontrollably like a buoy in choppy waters. I read *Alice in Wonderland* that way; it seemed to make more sense than it would have done if read on firm ground.

My parents, obviously, watched my adaptation with growing concern. Grandfather, on the other hand, began to absorb my levitation into his own games. He would, for instance, fling apple cores at me as I read beneath the ceiling, but never maliciously. Each direct hit would rock me a little, as if I'd met a slight patch of turbulence in the flights of my imagination. He was, in his usual way with the unexpected, fascinated rather than repelled by this strange condition of mine.

It was at about this time that grandfather began to develop new interests in the study of static electricity, map surveying, and the properties of broad beans. He would come to his researches, suddenly and unexpectedly, for various but always eccentric reasons. His fascination with the broad bean, for example, was born from his reading about the fall of the Roman Empire, and from his resulting hypothesis that the Empire's decline was due, at least in part, to the effects of a flawed vegetable diet. Fortunately such obsessions tended to be short-lived, although still, writing down these memories of him, I find that the sour-sweet taste of broad beans, experimentally eaten raw, lingers upon my palate.

Grandfather's interest in maps and cartographic art, however, had a greater energy behind it. He would spend long hours poring silently over any map that he could lay his hands upon. He began to gather together quite a collection. Street plans, navigational charts, old atlases with broken bindings, maps of territories known and un-known...The dusty stacks of them began to grow on every bookshelf, a few of them filed more neatly in the old bureau with the rest of his more valued paperwork. Sometimes he would sit in his chair, idly turning a small globe that he had bought for the purpose, his eyes soft with tears.

It was inevitable that, sooner or later, the desire to survey and create his own, original, maps would emerge from his cartographic passions. For a time, a year perhaps, he walked the streets near home, pacing out each one, making obscure notes, reproducing their regularities on a large sheet of paper that he preferred to keep a secret from the rest of the family.

Except from me. I think that he recognised in me a fellow-spirit, another imaginal nomad. If we were alone together in the house, Grandfather would frequently unroll his evolving chart across the living-room carpet, weighing it down at each corner with hagstones; and I would make my way to my favoured reading-place beneath the ceiling, with a feeling almost of reverence, to gaze down at it. There was a detached sensation in these moments, as if I had become separated from my own world and was looking back at it from a considerable distance. As if I was a ghost, my substance becoming gradually thinner.

Soon enough, Grandfather tired of his immediate subject. The neighbourhood, even the town itself, had exhausted itself for him. His attention turned to mapping the past.

As always at such times, his memories turned back to the village of Bungay, in Suffolk, where he had lived and adventured through the war years. The earliest maps that he attempted in this state of nostalgic reverie were necessarily vague, made up of his recollections and story-weaving. It was very quickly obvious that he was dissatisfied with the results.

As was usual — or perhaps simply because I had already become his co-conspirator in the enterprise at hand — Grandfather took me into his confidence, musing aloud on the problem while I listened sympathetically.

"I am trying," he said, "to map memories rather than land-scapes. The problem is not one of geography as such, but of man-ipulating geography to reflect memory."

At other times Grandfather would say nothing at all on the matter, but would sit gazing through the window, towards the big rhubarb leaves at the far end of the garden, silently turning his own questions over and over in his daydreams.

Then, one morning, he suddenly looked up at me from his thoughts. "It's impossible to properly survey any map from ground-level," he said.

While my mother was occupied in the kitchen preparing fish and thus somewhat distracted from her usually disciplined mood, he first broached the subject with her.

"No," she said, "and no again." I could not see, as I was reading in the adjacent room, but I distinctly heard a wet fish being slapped forcefully down onto the kitchen table. "I will not allow you to take him off on some fool's errand all the way to Bungay. He's too vulnerable, and he's still too young for it."

Grandfather spent several hours pleading and cajoling, determined to change her mind, but it was all to no avail. Once my mother's mind was made up, that was that. Another plan was required. Grandfather settled back into his armchair once more.

A week later, he spoke again. "Memory is not fixed absolutely to one location. If I go into a butcher's shop here, it reminds me of a butcher's shop I knew in my boyhood. They are not the same shop, in fact they are very different, but like distant cousins who have never met they are still related to one another." I could tell that he was warming to his theme. "If I see a blackbird flying overhead, it reminds me of the taste of crow pie." Grandfather began to pace the room, animated by excitement at his discovery. "If I walk through the woods at Cobham, I remember walking through the woods at Bungay. I can look at the River Medway and my imagination finds itself looking instead, or simultaneously, at the Waveney."

"Here's the solution to it all," he exclaimed, as he took to writing hurried notes. There was a renewed frenzy to Grandfather's activity, which soon translated into long walks by the river, or through the woods. He would often take me with him on these perambulations. He was a fast walker, and took long strides, so that I inevitably struggled to keep up with his pace. When I began to fall too far behind, still panting with effort and the muscles in my legs aching with strain, he would turn and come back for me, sweeping me up and onto his shoulders. That way we would continue, like a single creature with two heads and four arms, stalking determinedly along country footpaths or the length of the old seawall by the estuary.

I think it was this, mingling with his continuing thoughts on the art and science of cartography, which gave Grandfather his next major breakthrough.

I always believed Grandfather's pockets to be vast capacious vaults filled with obscure treasures. If I plunged in a deft hand, and he either deigned or feigned not to notice it, I might pull out a fistful of hard-boiled sweets, a conker already boiled in vinegar and strung ready for combat, possibly even a shining thrupenny-bit. So I was not at all surprised when, one bright Sunday morning as we were making our way along the seawall again, he produced a ball of strong green twine. He bent down and tied the end of it carefully — tightly, but without discomfort — around my left ankle.

"Now," he said, handing me a pencil and a small notepad, "I want you to go up and start drawing the things you can see. The curves of the river, the shapes of the woods, the way that the road snakes. Then we can draw them all into our own map of Bungay."

"Alright," I said, "but can I have some sweets for doing it?"

"I think you probably can."

Grandfather grinned and delved once more into his pocket. When he opened his hand, three barleysugars lay in his palm, glowing orange as alluringly as a sunset. I nodded vigorously. The prize seemed worthwhile.

"You won't tell, will you?"

"No," Grandfather promised, crossing his heart to prove that he meant it, "I won't tell anybody."

I allowed myself to drift upward, with Grandfather holding tight to the ball of twine and letting it unreel as necessary while I slowly gained altitude. I had never, before this, been higher than the space below the ceiling, but a degree of natural trepidation was soon overcome by the fascination of the adventure. Grandfather, who had always appeared as a long-legged giant, dwindled. I could imagine keeping him in a matchbox, like the peabugs that I sometimes collected. Fields and a string of nearby houses shrank down to the scale of models. The river, normally so broad and grey, was a ribbon sewn with sequins. How far could I go? I began to wonder about the existence of cloud castles, and glanced up to see if there were any passing overhead.

At that moment, the wind began to gust more strongly. I felt myself shoved forcefully sideward, inland. It was as though the river had raised one gigantic hand and was pushing me away. Where my attention had been momentarily fixed upon the clouds, the first sudden buffet caught me by surprise, and I began to swing uncontrollably. As the next gusts drove me further and further from the river's airspace, so my increasingly frantic attempts to stabilise myself actually had the opposite effect. I think I even began to flap my arms, vainly, like some ungainly bird.

It was quite obvious that the force of the wind was overcoming Grandfather's ability to reel the twine back in, and that the distance between us was increasing steadily if slowly. I tried deliberately losing altitude, but again the wind simply drove me back upwards again, and in effect it was all I could do to maintain a degree of equilibrium in my flight.

The land began to rise. I continued to drift inland. I was also being driven a little further upriver, so that my flight path actually took me on a somewhat diagonal route away from the seawall and into town. Beneath me Grandfather, still holding on doggedly to the other end of the twine, scurried anxiously on his long legs. We passed through the grounds of a factory, across the main road, past the *Ship* and the *Cricketer's Arms* where Grandfather barely had time to acknowledge his friends with a perfunctory nod of his head before I dragged him further on.

By the time I found myself crossing over the broad expanse of the cemetery my vain struggles had quietened and I was feeling in quite a serene mood. Grandfather, however, had to weave a path through the disorderly tombstones while still keeping his eyes on me. I think that he bruised both his knees against the stones on several occasions, because I noticed that he had earned a distinct limp.

"Grab hold of the trees," I heard him shout. Sure enough, up ahead was a line of mature beech trees. For a moment, his suggestion didn't make sense to me. There were so many trees, how could I grab hold of them? But then I realised that he meant for me to catch onto a branch as I passed by, in order to stop my own movement.

It was already too late. Serenity had merely allowed me to gain even more altitude, so that the trees were far below me when I reached them. Grandfather was clinging desperately to the final twelve inches of twine.

A sudden swirling of the wind spun me and I ended up facing backwards, back out over the breadth of the valley and the river's long tail curving through its landscape. I thought of all the stories that must be stored in such a place; and stored in the cemetery, too, underground with the people buried there, the stories they had all heard and told and lived. Stories forgotten but gradually dissolving into the soil and the water and the air, to be recycled. With a kind of bright clarity, in that moment, I knew that I did not want my story to be forgotten.

With my attention elsewhere, and looking the wrong way in any case, I didn't notice the approach of the church until my back bumped against stonework. At last there was an end to my uncontrolled drifting, as the wind pressed me against the stone of the church tower and the tower refused to yield. Yet my situation remained precarious. I found myself at the very top, not of the tower's main structure itself, but of a slender turret that had been attached to one corner of it. The turret was topped with a small conical roof and a black weathervane, and the wind threatened still to push me around this point and into open space once more.

The weathervane appeared to be the most secure anchor I could find, until the wind dropped at last and allowed me to sink safely back to earth. I somehow clawed and crawled my way up the remaining few inches of the conical roof, and clung to the cold metalwork of the weathervane like a limpet clinging to a rock in a storm.

When I dared to look down, I noticed that a small crowd had gathered at the foot of the tower. Grandfather's friends from the *Cricketer's Arms* had quickly downed their pints and, their curiosity roused, had followed our progress en masse. Their numbers were gradually being swollen by passers-by whose attention was being drawn towards the growing commotion. The vicar had also appeared, and was standing in front of Grandfather, with whom he was deep in a heated discussion of some kind. I thought I heard, "Too damage. Who'll pay weathervane?" The words curled up through the air like smoke, and gently dispersed.

I was becoming self-conscious. My strange ability had been a matter for family circles only, but was apparently about to be made common knowledge. Having recently started school, I was already aware how quickly the other children could register and punish any sign of difference. I was also beginning to slip down the shaft of the weathervane, where it was difficult to retain my grip there.

Fortunately the wind, although strong, was a steady north-easterly and the long arms of the vane were staying relatively still.

So I clenched my fists tightly around them and hoped that the wind would not veer away, spinning the arms of the vane, and drag me from my place of temporary safety. The world seemed very far off, a place that had slipped just beyond my reach.

There was more activity below. I glanced down again. Grandfather's friends were busily removing jackets and rolling up shirtsleeves. The vicar had disappeared once more. I was wondering where he might have gone, when there were hurried footsteps nearby, then a loud rattling, and the wooden door that led out onto the top of the church tower creaked painfully open.

The vicar was red-faced from the exertion of the long climb. There was a long coil of rope in his hands. For a few moments he stood there blinking, as if he had seen something unexpected. Then he shook his head, pushed a few strands of damp hair across his forehead away from his eyes, and said, "Nothing to worry about, young man, we'll soon have you down from there."

He was a tall vicar and could reach up as far as the conical turret roof that I was perched upon. In one end of the rope he tied a large knot in order to weight it; and swung it, quite gently, in a wide arc out from the tower. Several times the heavy knot struck stone a little below me, bouncing away to be hauled in again. On the fourth or fifth attempt, however, the vicar had the precise distance and the rope slipped through the narrow gap between my leg and the shaft of the weathervane.

The knot tumbled down into the vicar's hands as he paid out a little more of the rope. He bent over it, working dexterously to loop the rope with a slipknot. Carefully he pulled the noose tight around my ankle.

"There we are," he said, "Now we're ready." And threw the rope over the edge of the tower, into the crowd below.

Grandfather's friends had lined themselves up with the far end of the rope, as if preparing for a tug-of-war. I heard Grandfather's voice, loud above the general hubbub.

"Heave," he called.

They heaved. The rope tautened. But I was still anxiously clutching the two black metal arms that had anchored me in my strange little world among the clouds.

"Let go of the weathervane," shouted Grandfather, "It's alright, we've got you."

"Yes, let go, let go," called the chorus.

Nervously, I released my grip. The wind instantly plucked me from the roof and dragged me away from the tower's solid presence.

"Heave," Grandfather commanded. I felt myself tugged along several yards against the current, but seemed no closer to the ground.

"No, no," I heard Grandfather say in an exasperated tone, "Not like that. Hand over hand, like *this*...Now. Heave."

I went downwards at last, and surprisingly fast. Grandfather's friends were strong, and they were in a competitive mood. Within five minutes there were big hands holding onto me and pulling me the last couple of yards onto firm ground.

There was clamour and fuss all around me. A cup of hot tea appeared magically, as they tend to do at such moments. Grandfather was holding me tightly and when I opened my eyes we were inside the church. Grandfather was already telling the story.

People were laughing, the way they do when they are as relieved as they are happy. "Don't worry, Wilf," one of them said, "We won't talk. But it'll cost you, down the pub." There was more laughter.

Grandfather winked in my direction, and reached out. The three barleysugars were in his hand. He was true to his word, as ever. He didn't tell.

I had learned a lesson about my ability to float into the air at will, or rather about the limitations of that ability. I didn't try again in public, fearing that a clever wind could sweep me away, beyond any hope of return. In any case, that strange talent of mine faded slowly as I grew a little older, along with Grandfather's passion for cartography as he discovered newer and more pressing concerns. When, at the age of seven, I changed schools and entered a world that increasingly consisted of examinations and preparations for my future adult life, the ability deserted me altogether. Often, and especially on days when I gaze up at the sky and consider the existence of cloud castles, I miss it still.

THE GIFT

The hotel had drifted into a deep slumber, and Charles could hear the slight sibilant whisper of its dreaming, when he decided he had to visit the bathroom. It was a little way along the hall; he padded along the thin carpet on soft feet. He didn't take long.

When he came back down the corridor, he found that the door into his room had been covered completely with gift paper, the kind that he might have chosen to conceal a birthday present for his daughter. It was red, and in the shallow cast of the hallway lights it had about it the dull glimmer of fish scales. The door knob poked through, where the paper had been roughly cut around it. Warily, he turned it and pushed the door slowly open.

A dozen or so candles now half-lit the room. He moved to step through the doorway, but hesitated on the threshold, unsure whether or not he should shut himself in. There was a large but vague shape on the bed, also covered with wrapping paper — this time bearing a pattern of stylised pink hearts — and tied around with at least a yard of red ribbon.

Charles closed the door. It clicked tight behind him. Five paces took him to the side of the bed. He took hold of one loose end of the ribbon, and gently pulled. The paper fell open like petals unfolding.

What was revealed was a woman, a woman who sat motionless in the middle of his hotel bed with her knees raised, arms folded across the top of them, and her head lowered to rest in turn upon her forearms. She was naked. Absurdly, the sight of her sitting there amid the opened leaves of the gift paper reminded him of the illustrations that had often accompanied his daughter's favourite fairy stories.

Still, the woman did not move. He bent slightly towards her, closer to her left ear. "Are you alright?" he whispered. Then, when there was no sign of a response, he said it again, rather more loudly this time, "Are you alright?"

There was still no reaction. He realised that her skin was cold to the touch, that her body was quite rigid, as if she had been dead for some time. He began to wonder how he might explain away the presence of a dead, naked, woman on his hotel bed. He had the sense of being trapped in some terrible, vindictive, practical joke.

Sitting down in the shabby armchair by the bed, he tried to consider his options as calmly as he could. Phone the police? Or call the hotel staff? Dispose of the corpse himself? But the situation didn't feel real enough for him to act on any of them. Surely he would wake up soon.

He gazed at the dead woman again, feeling curiously detached from the urgency of his own plight. It was then that he noticed the small white tag, clearly attached to a short cord, which was just visible where the long blonde hair had parted around it. Cautiously, he peered closer. There was writing on the tag. Small, neat handwriting.

"Pull me," he read.

Gingerly, he did as he was told.

The dead woman said, "Oh."

Charles fell back into the armchair, eyes widening with a new emotion that was somewhere between relief and terror as he watched the woman slowly unfolding herself from her clenched posture. She stretched herself out full length on his bed, releasing cramped muscles, seeming completely unselfconscious in her nakedness. He noticed that she was lithe, catlike in her movements. She sat up abruptly, and looked at him, cocking her head slightly to one side as she regarded him.

"Good evening, Charles," she said.

"Um, yes, evening," Charles responded, groping for the familiar patterns of politeness. He realised that his dressing gown had fallen slightly open as he had hastily sat back down, and his hands fumbled as he tried to conceal himself properly.

"Do not be shy," the woman said. The warmth in her voice, and the light smile that she gave him, were beginning to melt Charles' distrust.

"Who are you? How did you get into my room?" The words rushed out of him.

Her soft laughter washed over him like summer rain, and she gestured lightly towards the discarded petals of the wrapping paper. "I am a gift. And you will need to give me a name. If you want to."

Charles was quite lost for words. The woman stood up from the bed, moving sinuously towards him until she was very close. Her body was certainly warm now, he thought. She drew the folds of his dressing gown aside. Embarrassed by his own arousal, Charles was about to stammer an apology when she lightly placed a finger on his lips to hush him. Then she straddled his lap.

Charles awoke slowly, the aftertaste of the night's peculiar dream still lingering. Peculiar, but enjoyable. Still dozing, eyes closed against the light filtering through the thin curtains, he smiled to himself. He rarely had erotic dreams. And real sex had never been that good, not even in the first days of his marriage. How long since the divorce? Seven years, maybe. He missed his daughter. How old must she be now? Twelve? No, thirteen.

Drowsily, he stretched his right arm across the pillows. His hand brushed against something soft, soft and warm and alluring, and Charles sat bolt upright in the bed, all the last traces of sleep shed in that instant.

She was still there, the strange blonde woman, sleeping peacefully in the hotel bed beside him, as if the borders of reality had been breached and his dreams had come flooding through. He was afraid. Who was she? What did she want?

She turned, languorously, opening her eyes and gazing up at his face. "You are awake, Charles, did you sleep well?"

"I did. Yes. Thank you." He was conscious that, beneath the sheets, her hand had found him, and that she had begun to stroke him gently.

"Do you want me again, Charles?"

He did. There was no denying it, not even to himself, surely not to her. This time he let the lust carry him along, taking her vigorously, enjoying the sense of power it gave him.

Afterwards, he went to the bathroom down the hall. Coming back into his room, he found her lying stiffly on her back in the bed, arms straight at her sides above the sheets. She was staring up at the ceiling.

"What's your name?" he tried again.

"Charles, you have not given me a name yet." She sounded a little reproachful.

Momentarily, dizzyingly, he felt he was embroiled in somebody else's fantasy, with no knowledge of any of the rules or boundaries.

"Alright, alright," he said, giving in to her, "How about Christina? That's what I'll call you, Christina."

"Christina," she said, as if contemplating the name with a slightly detached interest, "I like Christina."

He laughed. "Well then, Christina, I'm hungry. Where are your clothes?"

"I have none."

"Now you're playing. You must have been wearing something when you came here. Have you hidden them away somewhere?"

"I have none," she repeated, flatly.

Charles thought, briefly. He'd go along with it. Maybe she was angling for a new outfit. It would be a fair enough return for the night, and for the morning, he supposed.

He dressed quickly. "I'll go and buy you something to wear," he said, "You just wait here and I'll be back soon."

"Yes, Charles," she said, "I will wait here."

He bought some underwear that he guessed she might consider sexy — at least, he did — and a black dress that didn't look as if it was too cheap, then returned to the room. It was only when Christina had dressed in them, without comment, that he realised he had forgotten to bring her any shoes. She stood in front of him, barefoot. He assumed that she was hoping for a compliment.

"It looks good. You look beautiful," he said.

Hotel slippers. They had come with the room. He vaguely recalled tucking them under the bed. Finding them, he waved them at Christina. "Here, put these on," he suggested, and she did, apparently content with this solution to her shoeless state.

"Fine, shall we go down to breakfast?" he said, indicating the door.

"We shall go down to breakfast," she agreed, walking ahead of him into the hallway.

Charles observed her carefully as they left the room. She

had an immediate sensuality, pantherish even while wearing the ludicrous slippers. It gave her an air of danger that only made her more attractive; a predator, Charles thought, and felt quietly thrilled. There was something about her that tugged insistently at his memory, though, as if he had seen or even met her before, but the actual circumstance eluded him.

They came down the stairs into the hotel restaurant — truthfully, more of a cafeteria — and he saw heads turn to watch them enter. He suddenly flushed with pride. They sat at a table and Charles studied the breakfast menu.

"What would you like?" he asked Christina.

"What would I like?" she responded, sounding genuinely puzzled.

"To eat," he said, "What would you like to eat?"

"Why do I need to eat?"

Charles felt confused. "Are you on a diet?"

"No."

"Then you should at least have a cup of coffee. Or tea, or an orange juice," he suggested.

"Why?"

"Because," Charles started to say, with a rising sense of desperation beginning to sound in his voice, and then let the sentence die. There probably wasn't much point, he reflected. Maybe she was just fussy about eating. He shrugged. "Do you mind if I eat in front of you, then?"

"I do not mind."

Charles strolled over to the counter. He helped himself to four croissants, butter, jam, several rashers of bacon, a couple of sausages, four slices of bread. He was feeling oddly lethargic, not tired, but a lack of energy that was almost as difficult as a shortage of breath, so that everything he did was an effort. He hoped that a big breakfast would improve things. And he needed a coffee, badly.

He cast around for the coffee pot. As he did so, he caught sight of Christina sitting at their table, waiting patiently for him. Her posture was rigid, her lower arms were rested stiff and still on the plastic tabletop, her hands open yet unmoving. She was staring straight ahead, blankly, at a fixed point on the far wall.

There was that tingle of memory, again. This time he could place it. The last time he had seen his daughter had been on her sixth birthday. He had given her a present, a doll, and she had clung tightly to it all day. The next morning, she and her mother had both gone.

He found Christina, when she was not in movement, strangely doll like. There was an unexpected lurch of fear in his stomach. He still didn't know her. Who was she? What did she want?

Charles went back towards the table. Christina remained absolutely still, unblinking. He noticed that, under the harsh restaurant lights, her skin had the same faintly reflective surface as the tabletop.

He stood in front of her. "Who exactly are you, Christina? What is it that you want from me?"

She looked up at him with big blue eyes. "Daddy," she said.